A CARTOON NETWORK ORIGINAL

ADVENTURE TIME COMICS™

VOLUME
⑤

ADVENTURE TIME COMICS Volume Five, July 2018. Published by KaBOOM!, a division of Boom Entertainment, Inc. ADVENTURE TIME, CARTOON NETWORK, the logos, and all related characters and elements are trademarks of and © Cartoon Network. (S18) Originally published in single magazine form as ADVENTURE TIME COMICS No.17-20. © Cartoon Network. (S17) All rights reserved. KaBOOM!™ and the KaBOOM! logo are trademarks of Boom Entertainment, Inc., registered in various countries and categories. All characters, events, and institutions depicted herein are fictional. Any similarity between any of the names, characters, persons, events, and/or institutions in this publication to actual names, characters, and persons, whether living or dead, events, and/or institutions is unintended and purely coincidental. KaBOOM! does not read or accept unsolicited submissions of ideas, stories, or artwork.

For information regarding the CPSIA on this printed material, call: (203) 595-3636 and provide reference #RICH – 782181.

BOOM! Studios, 5670 Wilshire Boulevard, Suite 400, Los Angeles, CA 90036-5679. Printed in USA. First Printing.

ISBN: 978-1-68415-190-5 , eISBN: 978-1-64144-005-9

JUL 3 0 2018

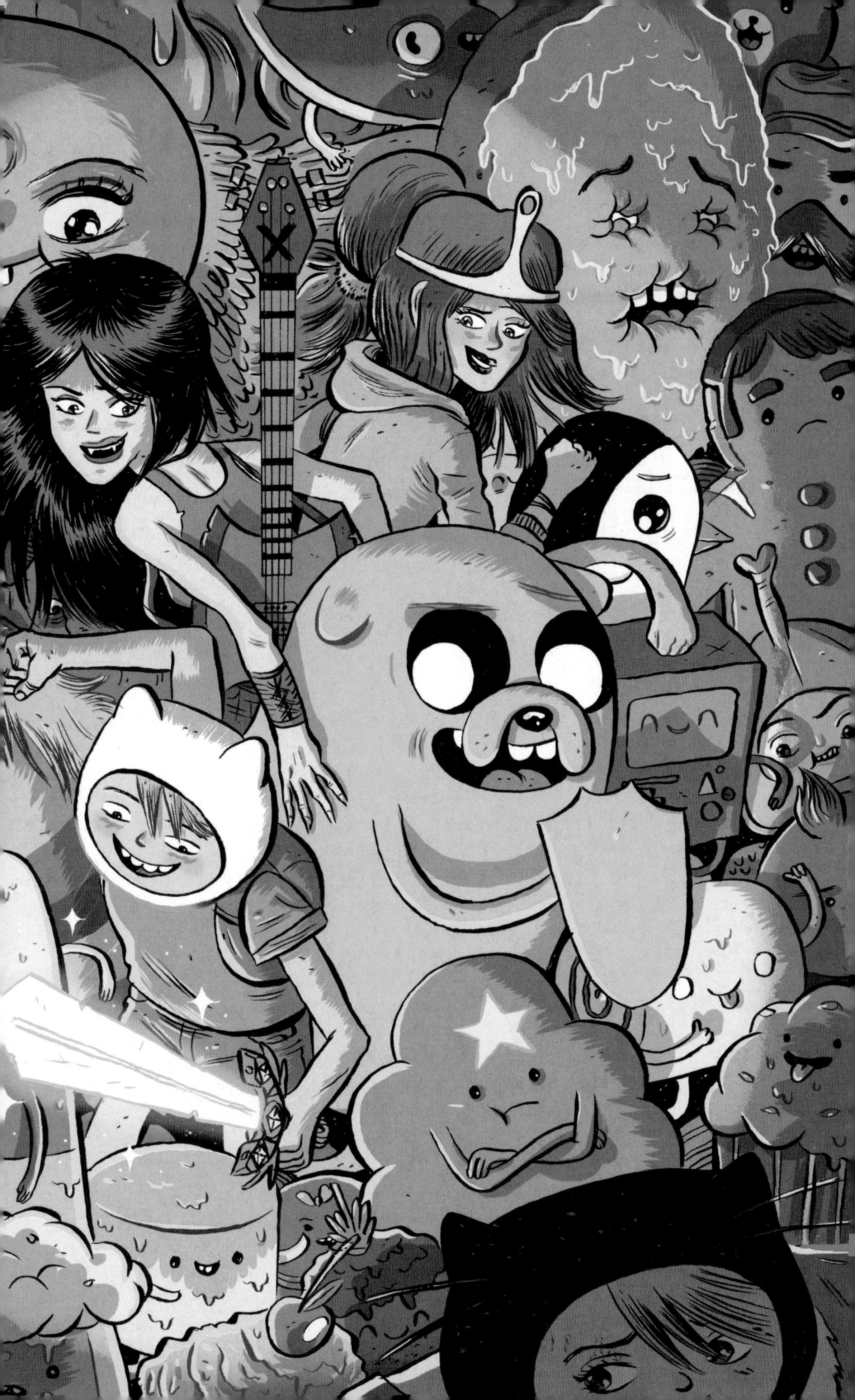

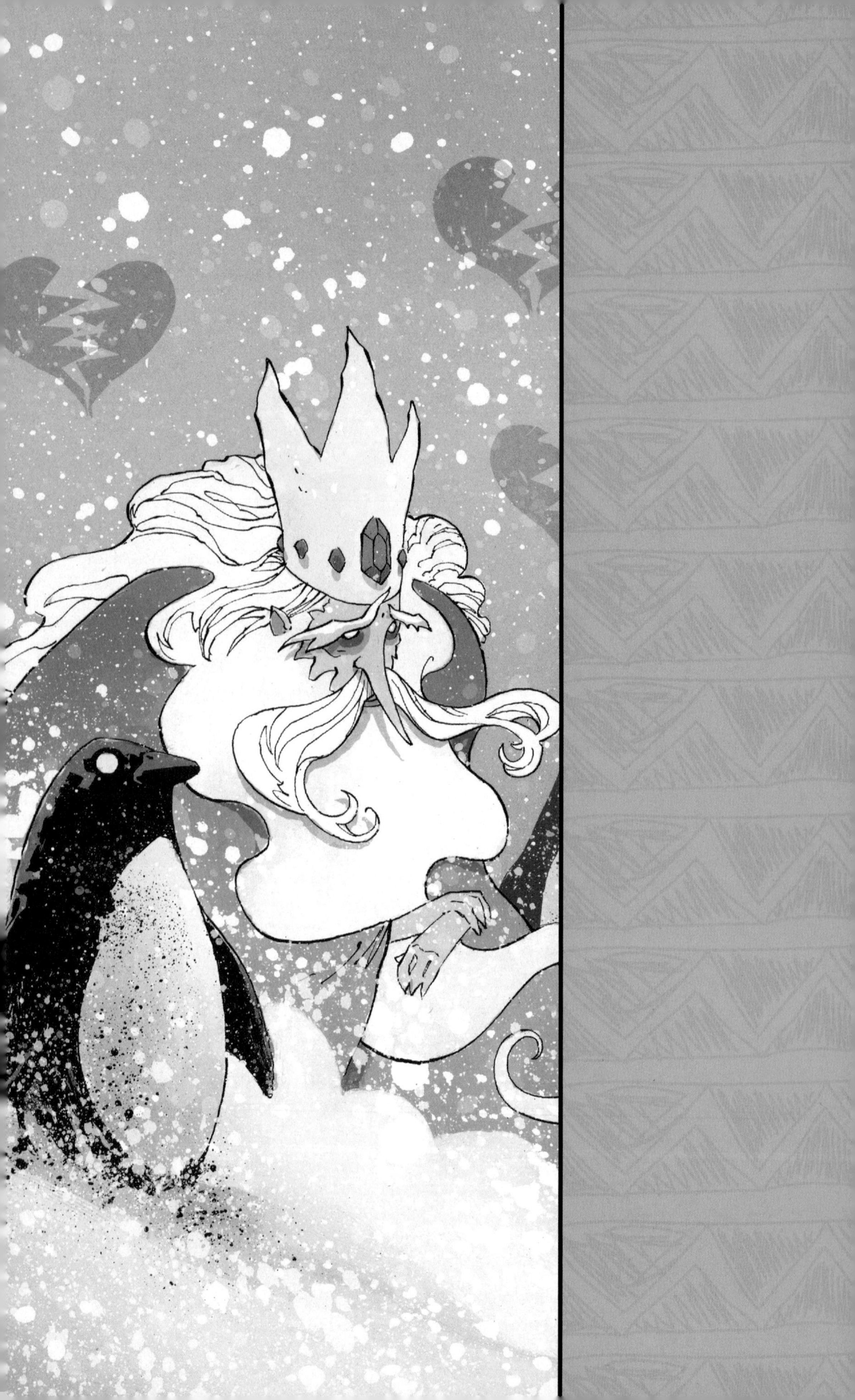

ADVENTURE TIME™
Created by **PENDLETON WARD**

"HAPPY BIRTHDAY IN OOO!"
Written by
MICHAEL MORECI
Illustrated by
CHRISTOPHER MITTEN
Colors by
ELEONORA BRUNI
Letters by
WARREN MONTGOMERY

"MARCELINE'S LUMPY
SPACE PARTY"
Written by
PAT SHAND
Illustrated by
SPENCER AMUNDSON
Colors by
JOANA LAFUENTE
Letters by
JIM CAMPBELL

"ESCAPE ROOM"
Written & Illustrated by
DEREK LAUFMAN

"FINN'S SANDWICH"
Written & Illustrated by
JEFFREY BROWN

"MAGIC PENCIL"
Written by
SCOTT NICKEL
Illustrated by
WALTER PAX
Colors by
JOANA LAFUENTE
Letters by
JIM CAMPBELL

"VISIONS OF PATERNITY"
Written by
RYAN CADY
Illustrated by
JORGE MONLONGO

"DREAM A LITTLE
DREAM OF OOO"
Written by
STEVE FOXE
Illustrated by
MEG OMAC

"VAMPYRE TIDE"
Written & Illustrated by
DANIELA VICOSO

"THE IMPOSTERS"
Written & Illustrated by
PATRICK MCEOWN
Inks by
RAPHAELE BARD
Colors & Letters by
MARIE ENGER

"A DAY WITH ICE FINN"
Written & Illustrated by
MARUMIYA

"BANANA MAN'S RACE
AGAINST DEATH"
Written by
NICK CRON-DEVICO
Illustrated by
ALEXANDRA BEGUEZ
Colors by
VLADIMIR POPOV

"MARCELINE THE
DERBY QUEEN"
Written by
CHELSEA VAN WEERDHUIZEN
Illustrated by
REIMENA YEE

"EPIC YARD SALE"
Written by
JAMES ASMUS
Illustrated by
CRISTINA ROSE CHUA
Letters by
MIKE FIORENTINO

"CAVITIES"
Written by
JASON COOPER
Illustrated by
JENNA AYOUB
Letters by
MIKE FIORENTINO

"PRINCESS BUBBLEGUM"
Written & Illustrated by
EMEI BURELL

Cover by
JORGE MONLONGO

Designers
CHELSEA ROBERTS
JILLIAN CRAB

Assistant Editors
KATALINA HOLLAND
MICHAEL MOCCIO

Editor
WHITNEY LEOPARD

With Special Thanks to Marisa Marionakis, Janet No, Curtis Lelash,
Conrad Montgomery, Kelly Crews, Scott Malchus, Adam Muto
and the wonderful folks at Cartoon Network.

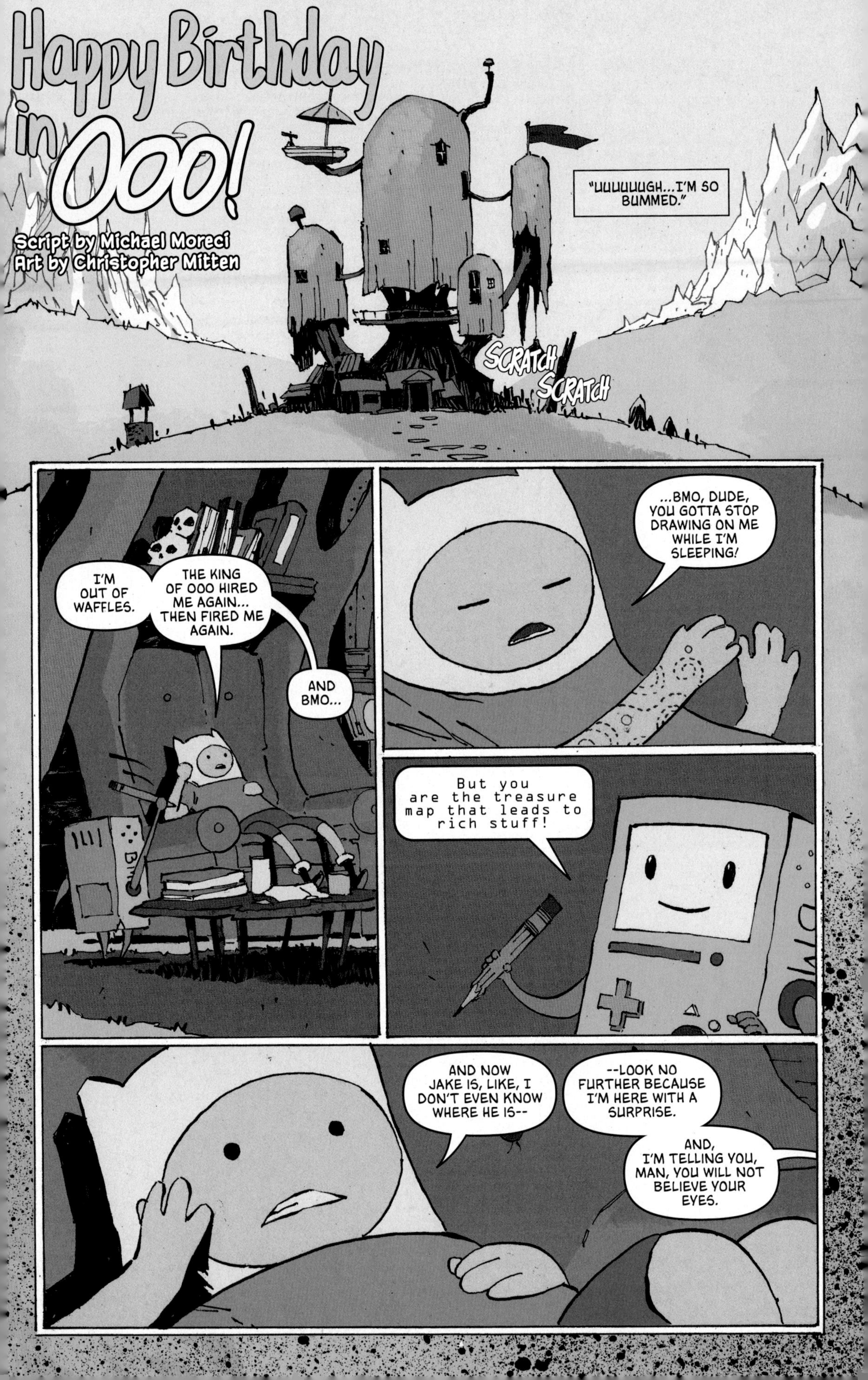
Happy Birthday in Ooo!
Script by Michael Moreci
Art by Christopher Mitten
"UUUUUUGH...I'M SO BUMMED."
SCRATCH
SCRATCH
I'M OUT OF WAFFLES.
THE KING OF OOO HIRED ME AGAIN... THEN FIRED ME AGAIN.
AND BMO...
...BMO, DUDE, YOU GOTTA STOP DRAWING ON ME WHILE I'M SLEEPING!
But you are the treasure map that leads to rich stuff!
AND NOW JAKE IS, LIKE, I DON'T EVEN KNOW WHERE HE IS--
--LOOK NO FURTHER BECAUSE I'M HERE WITH A SURPRISE.
AND, I'M TELLING YOU, MAN, YOU WILL NOT BELIEVE YOUR EYES.

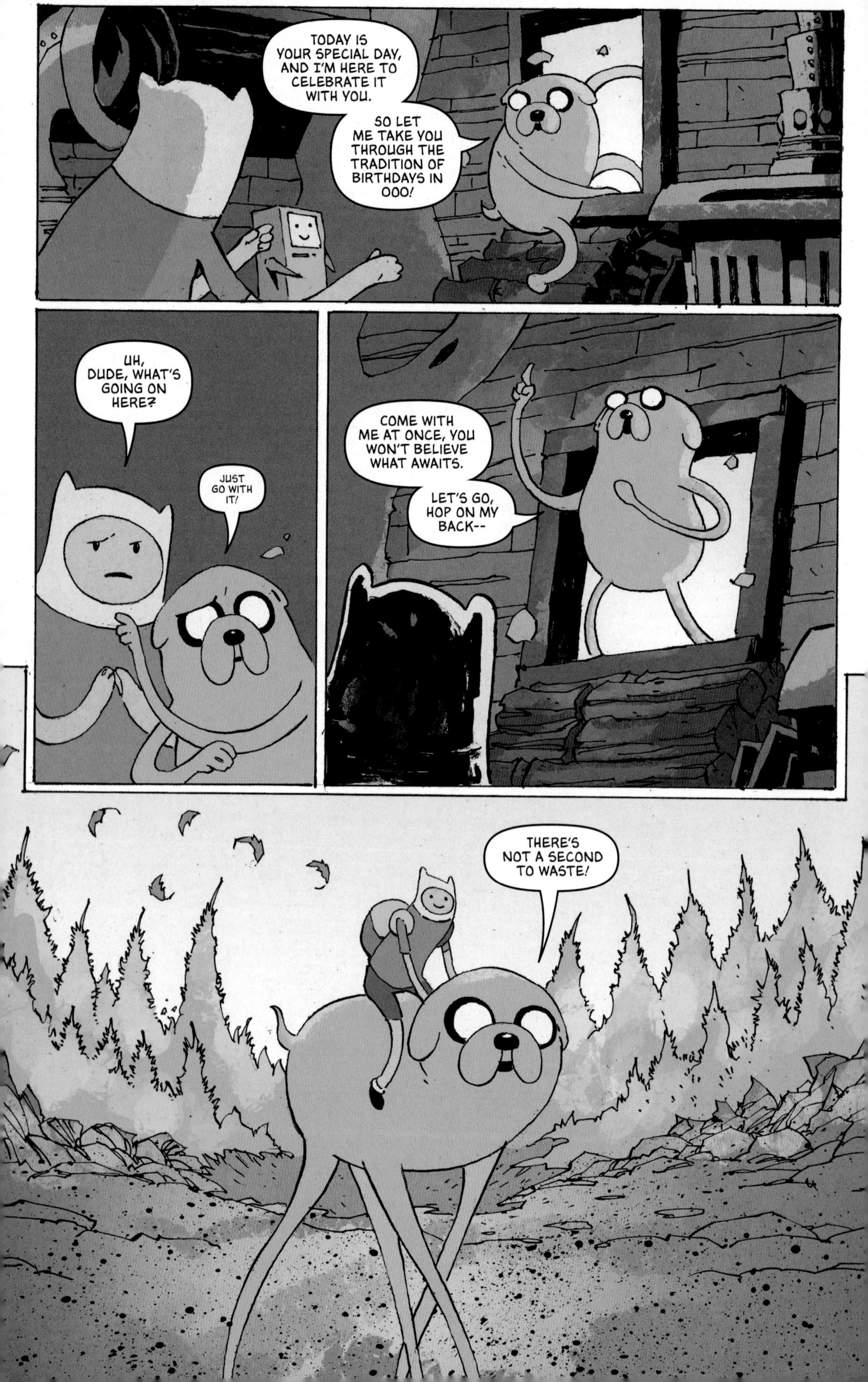
TODAY IS YOUR SPECIAL DAY, AND I'M HERE TO CELEBRATE IT WITH YOU.
SO LET ME TAKE YOU THROUGH THE TRADITION OF BIRTHDAYS IN OOO!
UH, DUDE, WHAT'S GOING ON HERE?
JUST GO WITH IT!
COME WITH ME AT ONCE, YOU WON'T BELIEVE WHAT AWAITS.
LET'S GO, HOP ON MY BACK--
THERE'S NOT A SECOND TO WASTE!

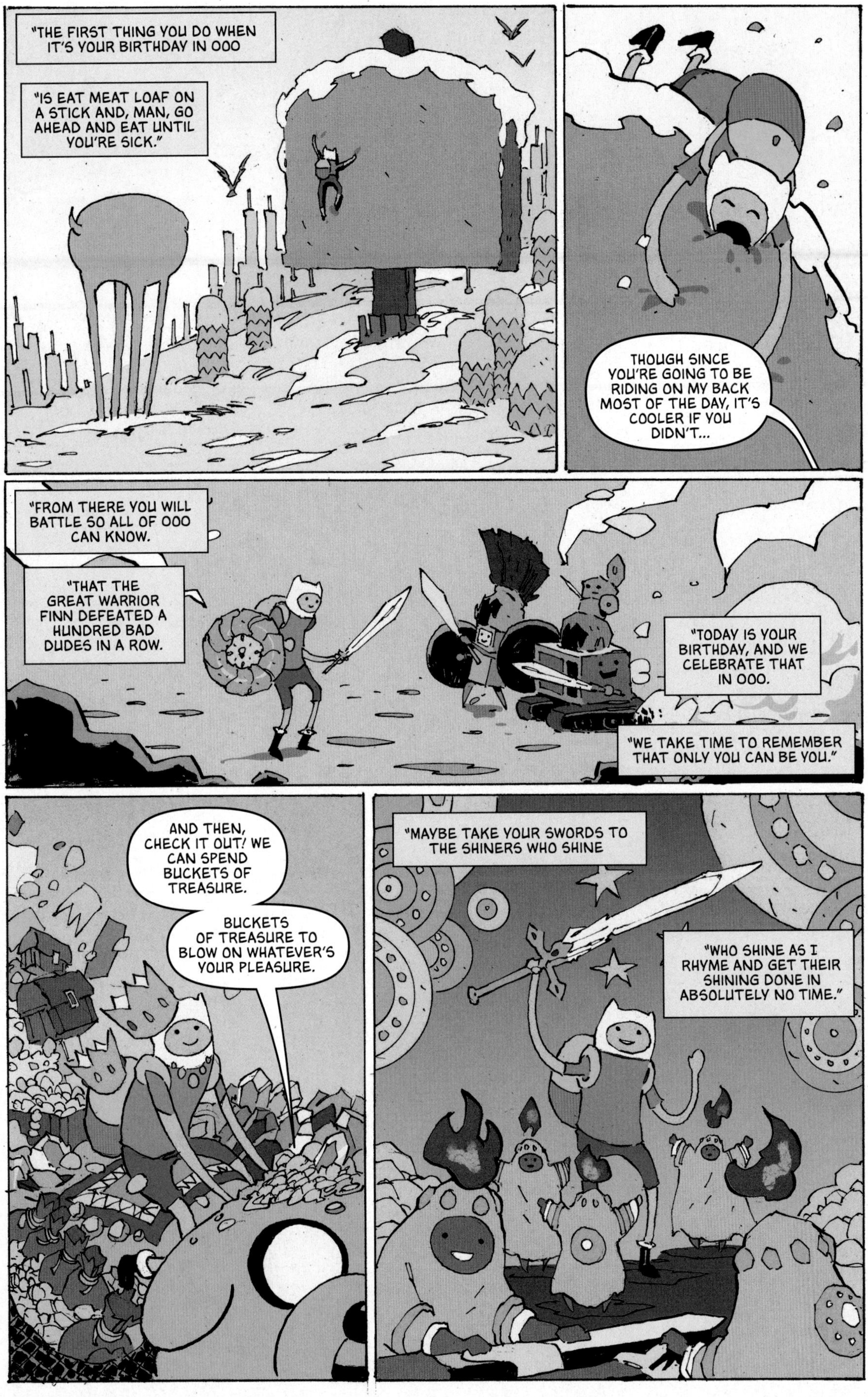
"THE FIRST THING YOU DO WHEN IT'S YOUR BIRTHDAY IN OOO
"IS EAT MEAT LOAF ON A STICK AND, MAN, GO AHEAD AND EAT UNTIL YOU'RE SICK."
THOUGH SINCE YOU'RE GOING TO BE RIDING ON MY BACK MOST OF THE DAY, IT'S COOLER IF YOU DIDN'T...
"FROM THERE YOU WILL BATTLE SO ALL OF OOO CAN KNOW.
"THAT THE GREAT WARRIOR FINN DEFEATED A HUNDRED BAD DUDES IN A ROW.
"TODAY IS YOUR BIRTHDAY, AND WE CELEBRATE THAT IN OOO.
"WE TAKE TIME TO REMEMBER THAT ONLY YOU CAN BE YOU."
AND THEN, CHECK IT OUT! WE CAN SPEND BUCKETS OF TREASURE.
BUCKETS OF TREASURE TO BLOW ON WHATEVER'S YOUR PLEASURE.
"MAYBE TAKE YOUR SWORDS TO THE SHINERS WHO SHINE
"WHO SHINE AS I RHYME AND GET THEIR SHINING DONE IN ABSOLUTELY NO TIME."

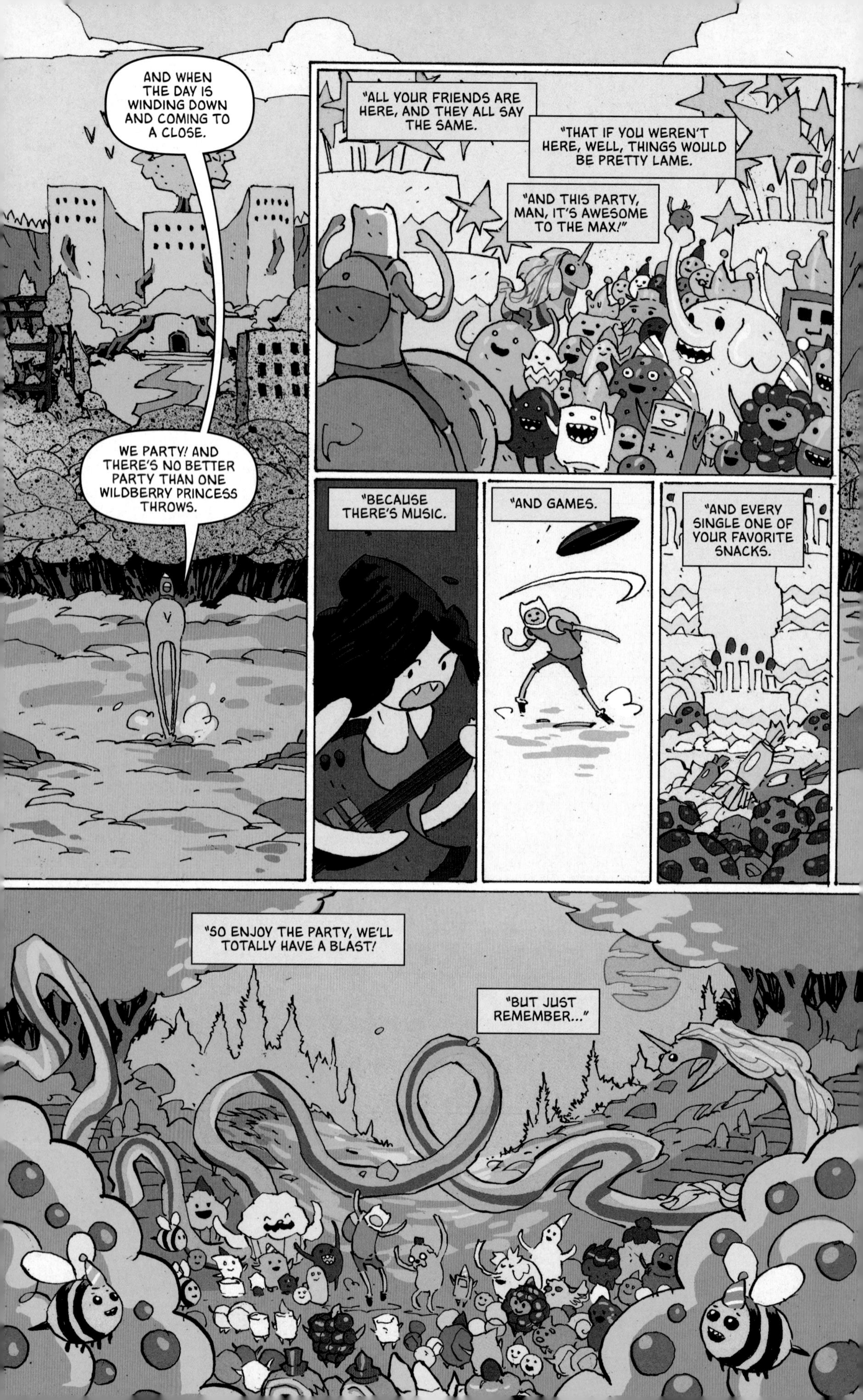
AND WHEN THE DAY IS WINDING DOWN AND COMING TO A CLOSE.
WE PARTY! AND THERE'S NO BETTER PARTY THAN ONE WILDBERRY PRINCESS THROWS.
"ALL YOUR FRIENDS ARE HERE, AND THEY ALL SAY THE SAME.
"THAT IF YOU WEREN'T HERE, WELL, THINGS WOULD BE PRETTY LAME.
"AND THIS PARTY, MAN, IT'S AWESOME TO THE MAX!"
"BECAUSE THERE'S MUSIC.
"AND GAMES.
"AND EVERY SINGLE ONE OF YOUR FAVORITE SNACKS.
"SO ENJOY THE PARTY, WE'LL TOTALLY HAVE A BLAST!
"BUT JUST REMEMBER..."

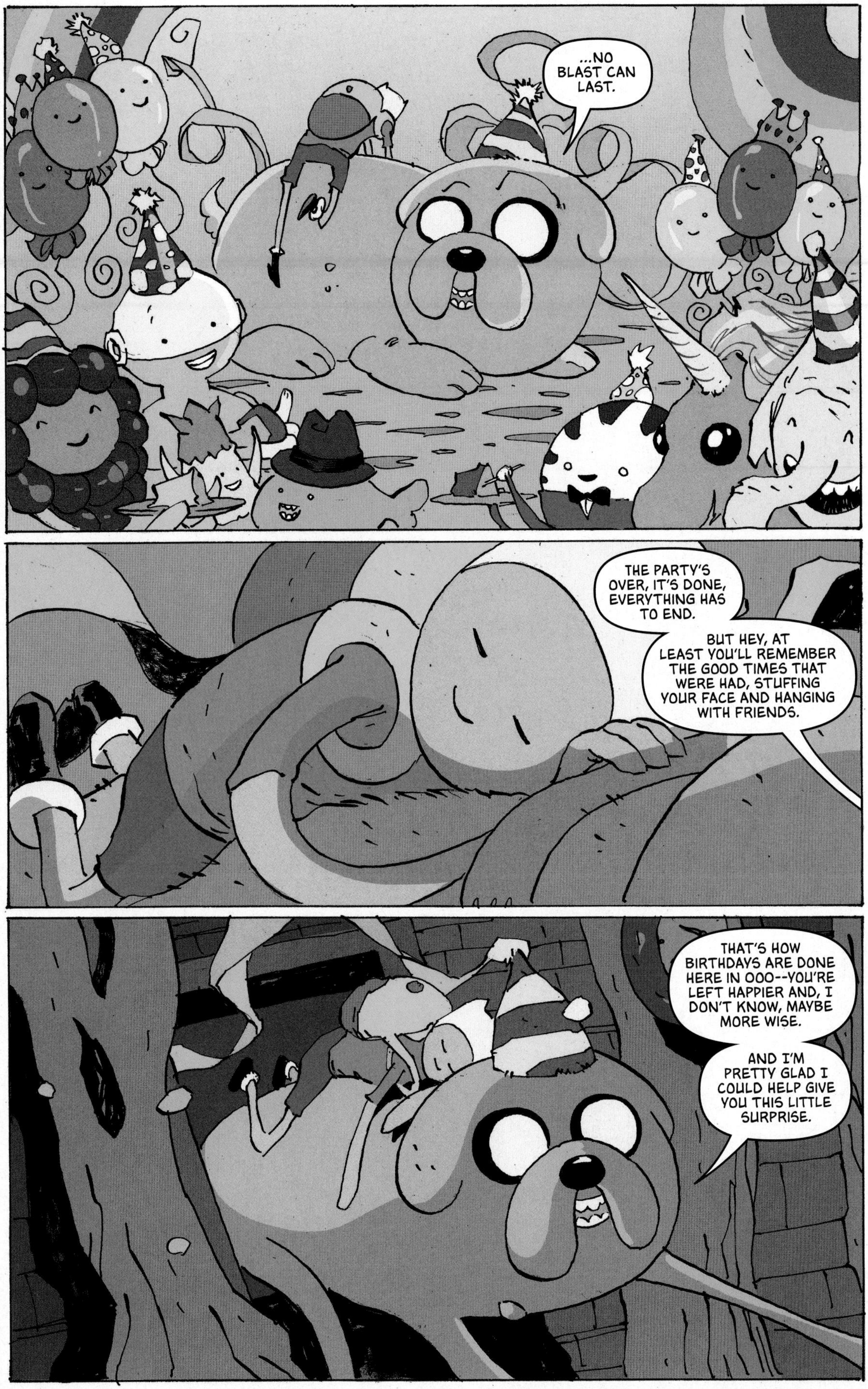
...NO BLAST CAN LAST.
THE PARTY'S OVER, IT'S DONE, EVERYTHING HAS TO END.
BUT HEY, AT LEAST YOU'LL REMEMBER THE GOOD TIMES THAT WERE HAD, STUFFING YOUR FACE AND HANGING WITH FRIENDS.
THAT'S HOW BIRTHDAYS ARE DONE HERE IN OOO--YOU'RE LEFT HAPPIER AND, I DON'T KNOW, MAYBE MORE WISE.
AND I'M PRETTY GLAD I COULD HELP GIVE YOU THIS LITTLE SURPRISE.

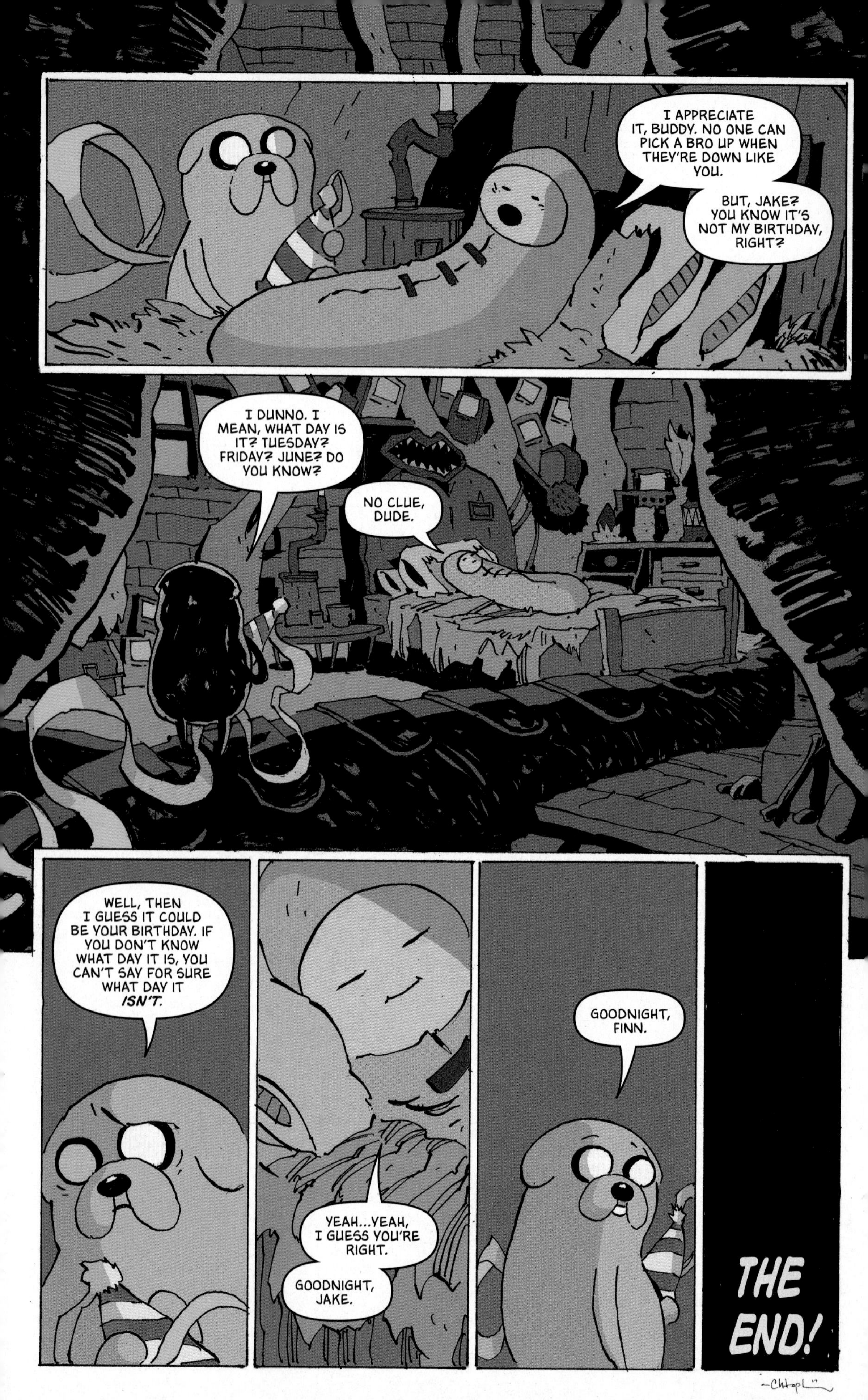
I APPRECIATE IT, BUDDY. NO ONE CAN PICK A BRO UP WHEN THEY'RE DOWN LIKE YOU.
BUT, JAKE? YOU KNOW IT'S NOT MY BIRTHDAY, RIGHT?
I DUNNO. I MEAN, WHAT DAY IS IT? TUESDAY? FRIDAY? JUNE? DO YOU KNOW?
NO CLUE, DUDE.
WELL, THEN I GUESS IT COULD BE YOUR BIRTHDAY. IF YOU DON'T KNOW WHAT DAY IT IS, YOU CAN'T SAY FOR SURE WHAT DAY IT *ISN'T*.
YEAH...YEAH, I GUESS YOU'RE RIGHT.
GOODNIGHT, JAKE.
GOODNIGHT, FINN.
THE END!

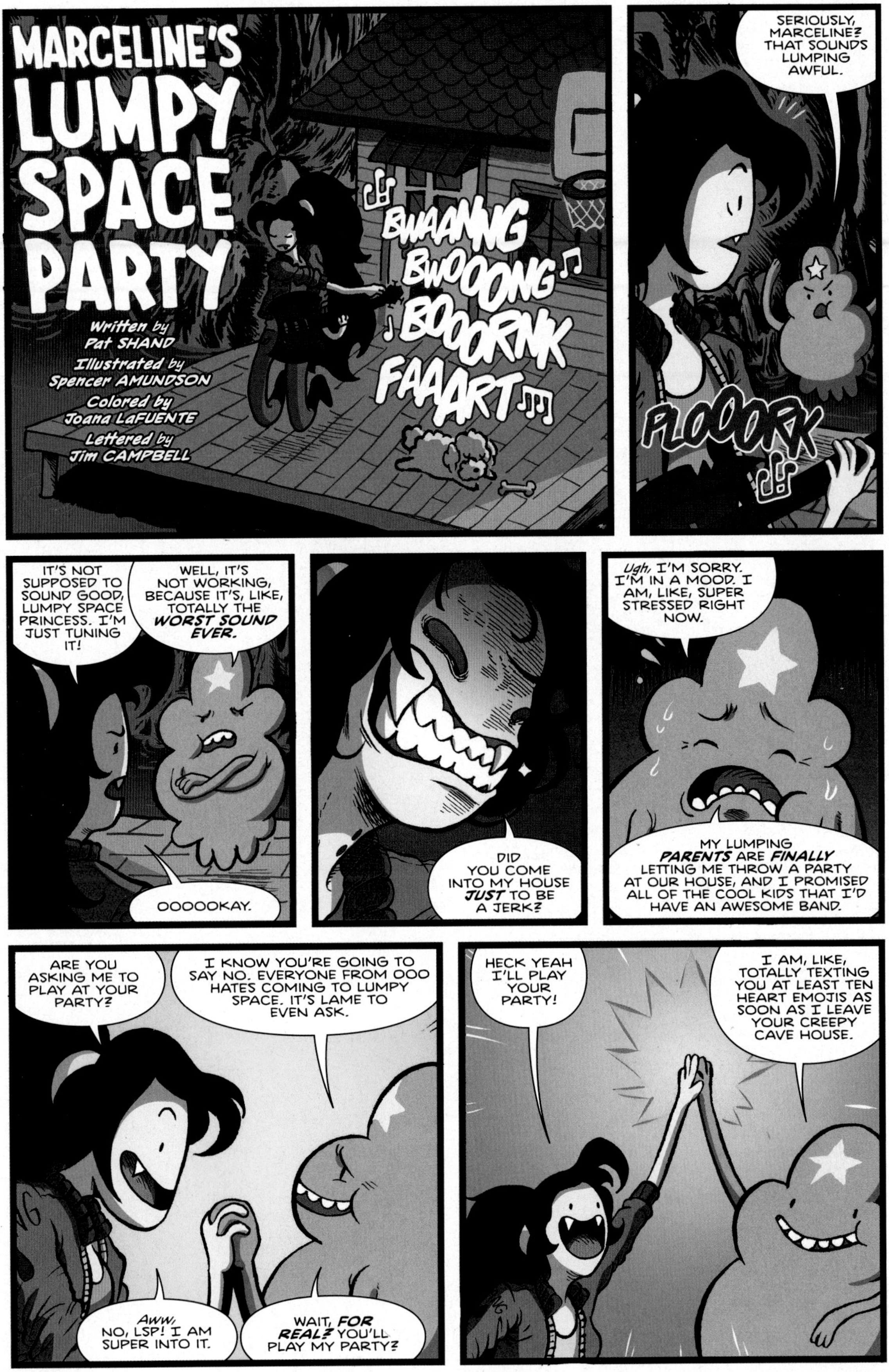

MARCELINE'S LUMPY SPACE PARTY
Written by Pat SHAND
Illustrated by Spencer AMUNDSON
Colored by Joana LaFUENTE
Lettered by Jim CAMPBELL
BWAANNG BWOOONG BOOORNK FAAART
SERIOUSLY, MARCELINE? THAT SOUNDS LUMPING AWFUL.
PLOOORK
IT'S NOT SUPPOSED TO SOUND GOOD, LUMPY SPACE PRINCESS. I'M JUST TUNING IT!
WELL, IT'S NOT WORKING, BECAUSE IT'S, LIKE, TOTALLY THE WORST SOUND EVER.
OOOOOKAY.
DID YOU COME INTO MY HOUSE JUST TO BE A JERK?
Ugh, I'M SORRY. I'M IN A MOOD. I AM, LIKE, SUPER STRESSED RIGHT NOW.
MY LUMPING PARENTS ARE FINALLY LETTING ME THROW A PARTY AT OUR HOUSE, AND I PROMISED ALL OF THE COOL KIDS THAT I'D HAVE AN AWESOME BAND.
ARE YOU ASKING ME TO PLAY AT YOUR PARTY?
I KNOW YOU'RE GOING TO SAY NO. EVERYONE FROM OOO HATES COMING TO LUMPY SPACE. IT'S LAME TO EVEN ASK.
Aww, NO, LSP! I AM SUPER INTO IT.
WAIT, FOR REAL? YOU'LL PLAY MY PARTY?
HECK YEAH I'LL PLAY YOUR PARTY!
I AM, LIKE, TOTALLY TEXTING YOU AT LEAST TEN HEART EMOJIS AS SOON AS I LEAVE YOUR CREEPY CAVE HOUSE.

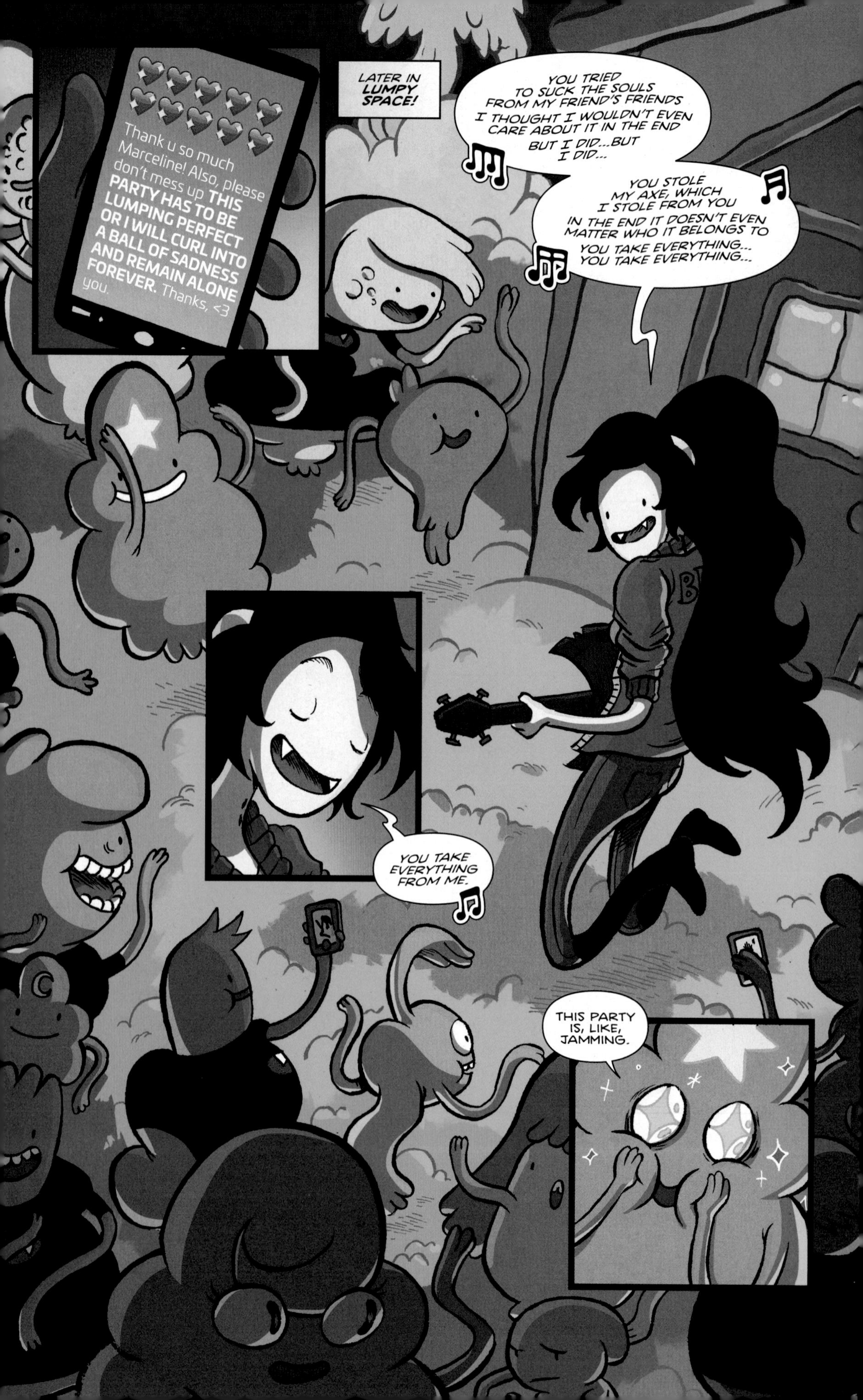
Thank u so much Marceline! Also, please don't mess up THIS PARTY HAS TO BE LUMPING PERFECT OR I WILL CURL INTO A BALL OF SADNESS AND REMAIN ALONE FOREVER. Thanks, <3 you.
LATER IN LUMPY SPACE!
YOU TRIED TO SUCK THE SOULS FROM MY FRIEND'S FRIENDS I THOUGHT I WOULDN'T EVEN CARE ABOUT IT IN THE END BUT I DID...BUT I DID...
YOU STOLE MY AXE, WHICH I STOLE FROM YOU IN THE END IT DOESN'T EVEN MATTER WHO IT BELONGS TO YOU TAKE EVERYTHING... YOU TAKE EVERYTHING...
YOU TAKE EVERYTHING FROM ME.
THIS PARTY IS, LIKE, JAMMING.

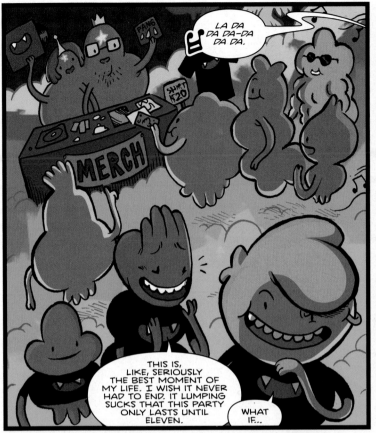

LA DA DA DA-DA DA DA.

THIS IS, LIKE, SERIOUSLY THE BEST MOMENT OF MY LIFE. I WISH IT NEVER HAD TO END. IT LUMPING SUCKS THAT THIS PARTY ONLY LASTS UNTIL ELEVEN.

WHAT IF...

...IT NEVER *DID* HAVE TO END?

WHAT DO YOU MEAN, CHARLTON?

BECKY, SHUT YOUR MOUTH BEFORE SOMEONE, LIKE, OVERHEARS YOU, OKAY? I HAVE THE LUMPING BEST IDEA EVER, YOU GUYS.

IF WE BITE MARCELINE AND INFECT HER WITH THE LUMPS, SHE WILL HAVE TO STAY IN LUMPY SPACE, LIKE... *FOREVER.*

SHE'LL BE OUR BEST FRIEND AND PLAY AWESOME MUSIC WHENEVER WE WANT.

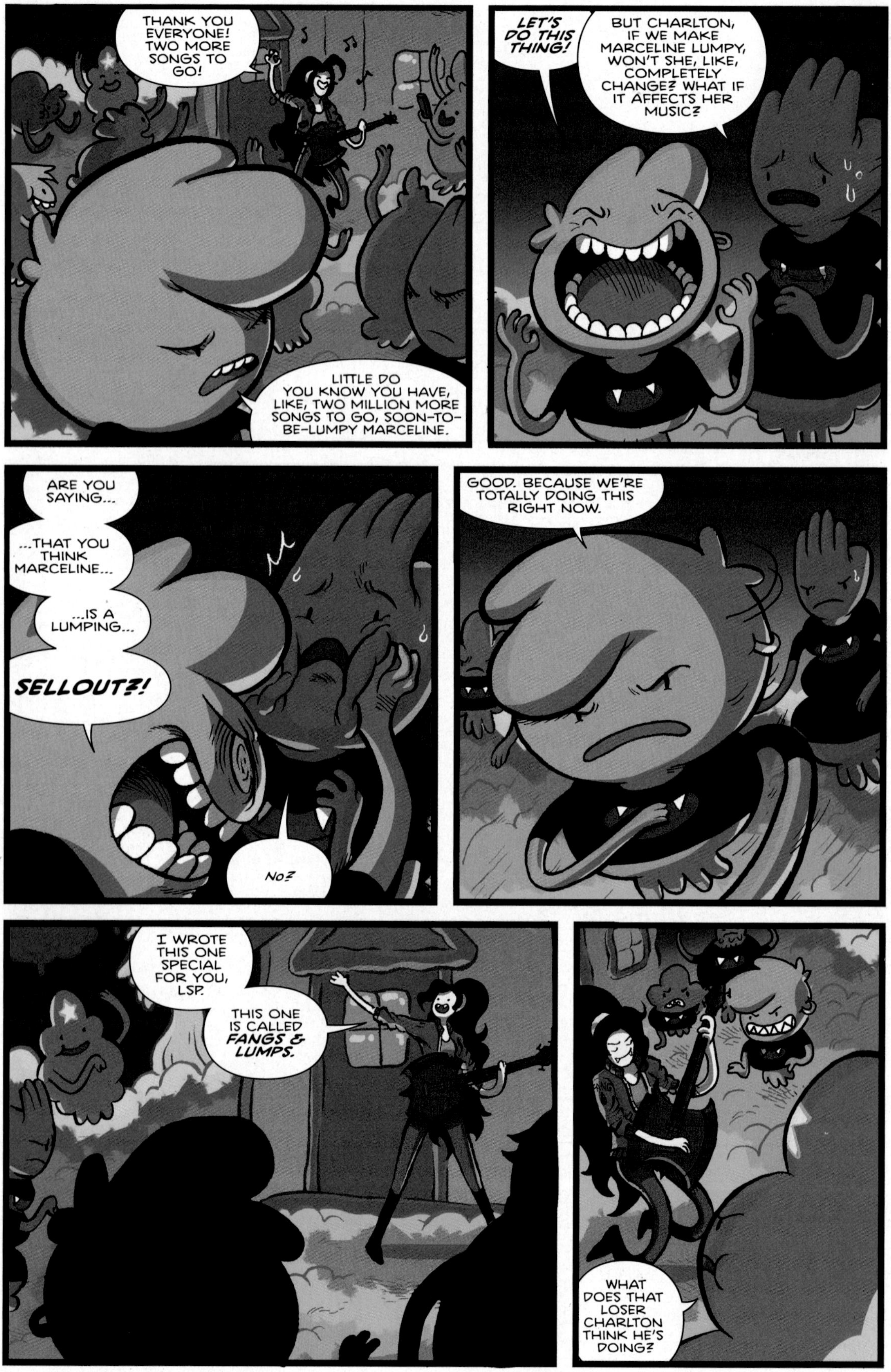
THANK YOU EVERYONE! TWO MORE SONGS TO GO!
LITTLE DO YOU KNOW YOU HAVE, LIKE, TWO MILLION MORE SONGS TO GO, SOON-TO-BE-LUMPY MARCELINE.
LET'S DO THIS THING!
BUT CHARLTON, IF WE MAKE MARCELINE LUMPY, WON'T SHE, LIKE, COMPLETELY CHANGE? WHAT IF IT AFFECTS HER MUSIC?
ARE YOU SAYING...
...THAT YOU THINK MARCELINE...
...IS A LUMPING...
SELLOUT?!
NO?
GOOD. BECAUSE WE'RE TOTALLY DOING THIS RIGHT NOW.
I WROTE THIS ONE SPECIAL FOR YOU, LSP.
THIS ONE IS CALLED FANGS & LUMPS.
WHAT DOES THAT LOSER CHARLTON THINK HE'S DOING?

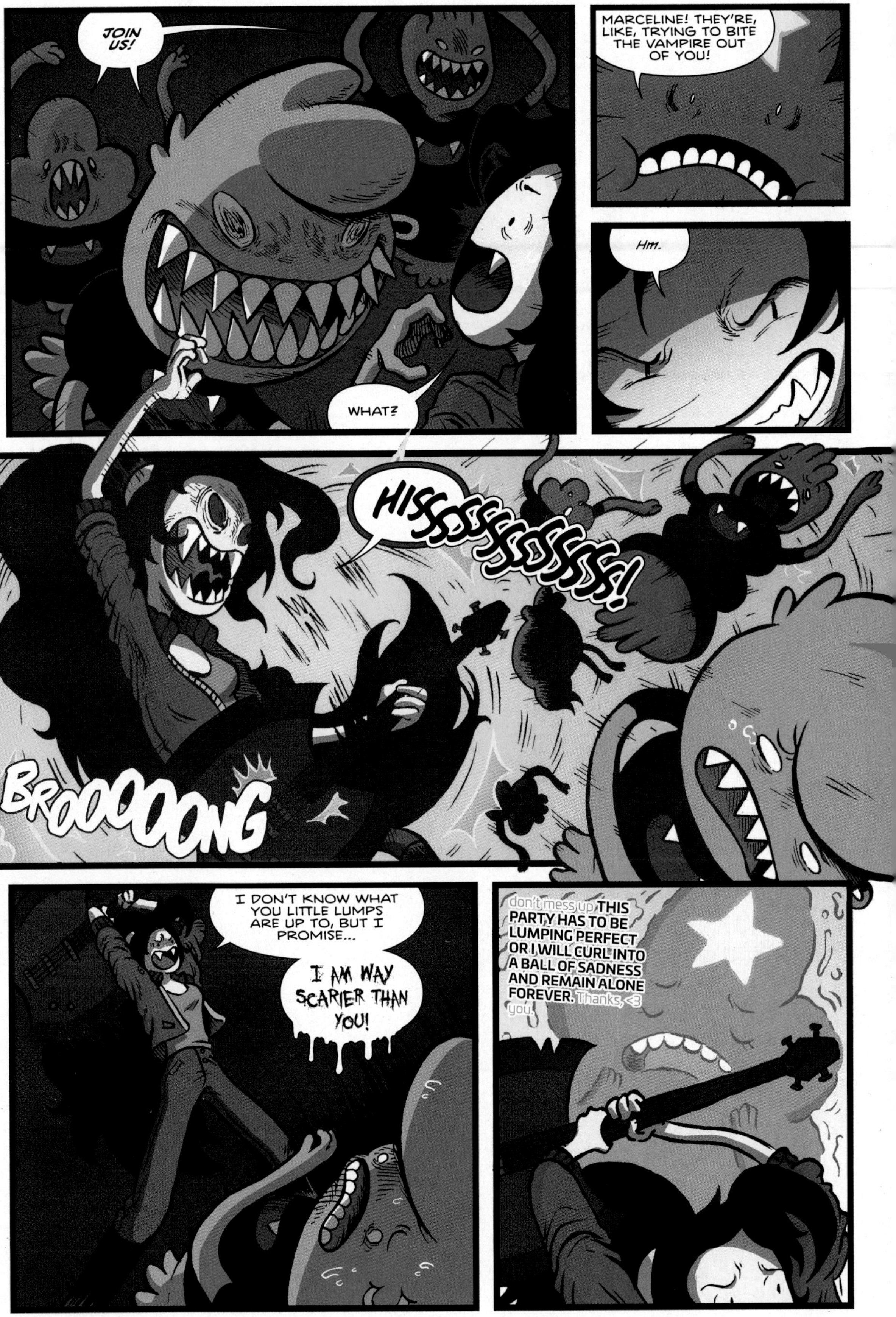
JOIN US!
WHAT?
MARCELINE! THEY'RE, LIKE, TRYING TO BITE THE VAMPIRE OUT OF YOU!
HM.
HISSSSSSSSSSSS!
BROOOOOONG
I DON'T KNOW WHAT YOU LITTLE LUMPS ARE UP TO, BUT I PROMISE...
I AM WAY SCARIER THAN YOU!
don't mess up THIS PARTY HAS TO BE LUMPING PERFECT OR I WILL CURL INTO A BALL OF SADNESS AND REMAIN ALONE FOREVER. Thanks, <3 you.

WHY WERE YOU TRYING TO BITE ME?

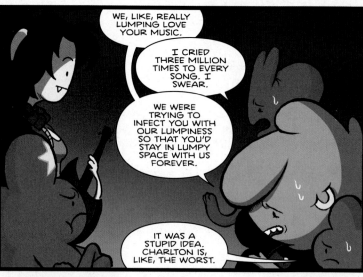

WE, LIKE, REALLY LUMPING LOVE YOUR MUSIC.

I CRIED THREE MILLION TIMES TO EVERY SONG. I SWEAR.

WE WERE TRYING TO INFECT YOU WITH OUR LUMPINESS SO THAT YOU'D STAY IN LUMPY SPACE WITH US FOREVER.

IT WAS A STUPID IDEA. CHARLTON IS, LIKE, THE WORST.

WELL, I GUESS THAT'S KIND OF SWEET.

PART OF ME STILL WANTS TO KICK YOUR LUMPY BEHIND INTO *NIGHTOSPHERE* FOR AN ETERNITY OF TORMENT...

BUT HEY, IN HONOR OF LUMPY SPACE PRINCESS'S AWESOME PARTY, I'M WILLING TO FORGIVE AND FORGET.

SO...WOULD YOU, LIKE, CONSIDER VOLUNTARILY STAYING IN LUMPY SPACE FOR THE REST OF YOUR LIFE?

HECK NO, CHARLTON. BUT...

HOW ABOUT A SPECIAL ENCORE?

FANGS AND LUMPS, IT MAKES SUCH A GOOD PAIR
HANGING IN LUMPY SPACE, SLEEPOVERS BACK AT MY LAIR
ALL WE CAN DO IS PUT FRIENDS FIRST
AT LEAST WE KNOW NOW THAT CHARLTON IS THE WORST.

DID YOU GUYS HEAR THAT? SHE SAID MY NAME! I'M IN THE SONG! THIS IS, LIKE, THE BEST DAY OF MY WHOLE LUMPING LIFE!

YEAAAAAH, CHARLTON IS THE WOOOORST.

THE END

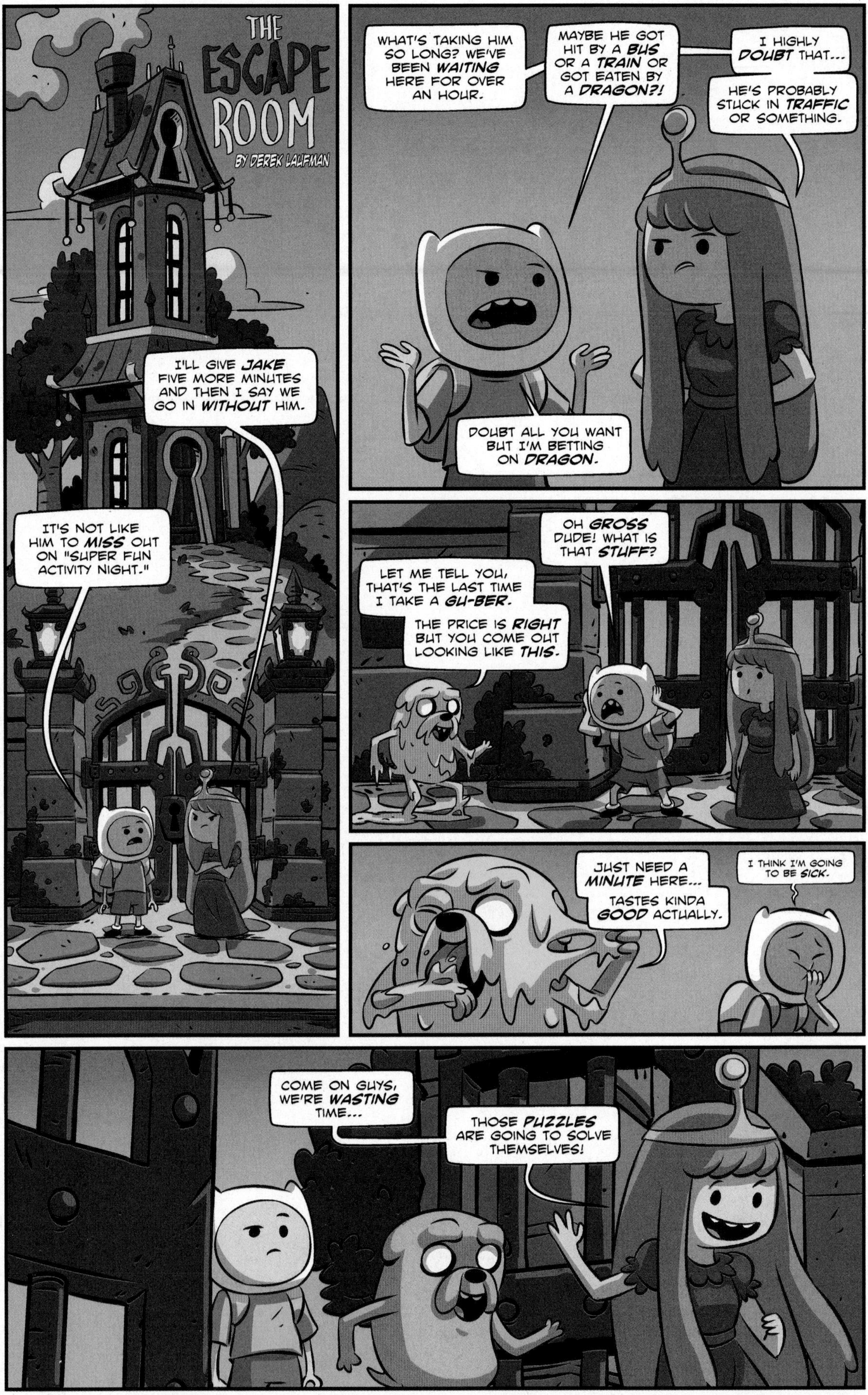
THE ESCAPE ROOM
BY DEREK LAUFMAN
I'LL GIVE JAKE FIVE MORE MINUTES AND THEN I SAY WE GO IN WITHOUT HIM.
IT'S NOT LIKE HIM TO MISS OUT ON "SUPER FUN ACTIVITY NIGHT."
WHAT'S TAKING HIM SO LONG? WE'VE BEEN WAITING HERE FOR OVER AN HOUR.
MAYBE HE GOT HIT BY A BUS OR A TRAIN OR GOT EATEN BY A DRAGON?!
I HIGHLY DOUBT THAT...
HE'S PROBABLY STUCK IN TRAFFIC OR SOMETHING.
DOUBT ALL YOU WANT BUT I'M BETTING ON DRAGON.
LET ME TELL YOU, THAT'S THE LAST TIME I TAKE A GU-BER.
THE PRICE IS RIGHT BUT YOU COME OUT LOOKING LIKE THIS.
OH GROSS DUDE! WHAT IS THAT STUFF?
JUST NEED A MINUTE HERE...
TASTES KINDA GOOD ACTUALLY.
I THINK I'M GOING TO BE SICK.
COME ON GUYS, WE'RE WASTING TIME...
THOSE PUZZLES ARE GOING TO SOLVE THEMSELVES!

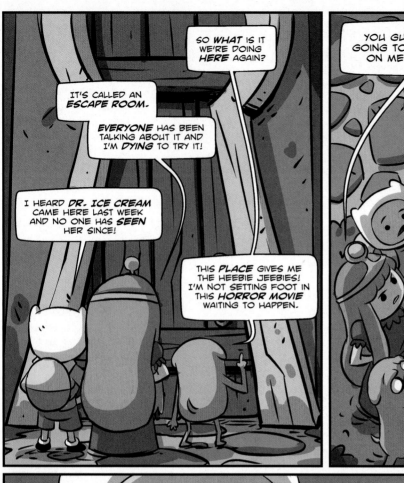

SO **WHAT** IS IT WE'RE DOING **HERE** AGAIN?

IT'S CALLED AN **ESCAPE ROOM.**

EVERYONE HAS BEEN TALKING ABOUT IT AND I'M **DYING** TO TRY IT!

I HEARD **DR. ICE CREAM** CAME HERE LAST WEEK AND NO ONE HAS **SEEN** HER SINCE!

THIS **PLACE** GIVES ME THE HEEBIE JEEBIES! I'M NOT SETTING FOOT IN THIS **HORROR MOVIE** WAITING TO HAPPEN.

YOU GUYS AREN'T GOING TO **WUSS** OUT ON ME ARE YOU?

HEY, DID YOU READ THIS **FINE** PRINT?

FAILED PARTICIPANTS WILL BE TRAPPED FOR **ETERNITY** BUT IF YOU ARE SUCCESSFUL YOU GET A **FREE LOLLIPOP.**

THAT IS **INSANE**--

FREE LOLLIPOPS!

3 FOR THE **ESCAPE ROOM** MY GOOD MAN!

$5 PER PERSON

$20 GROUPS

I HAVE A **BAD** FEELING ABOUT THIS--

STOP **WORRYING,** THIS IS GOING TO BE FUN!

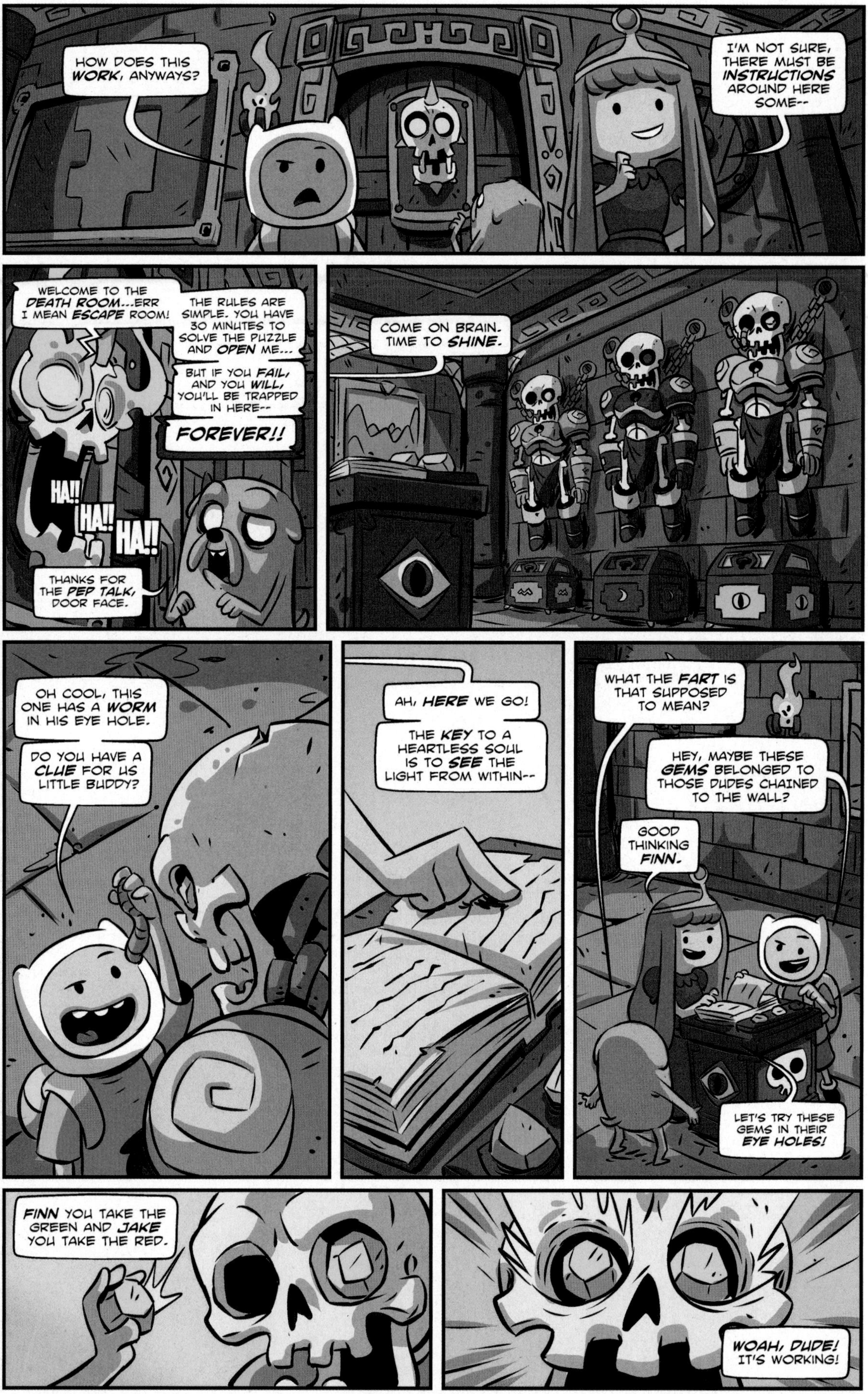

HOW DOES THIS WORK, ANYWAYS?
I'M NOT SURE, THERE MUST BE INSTRUCTIONS AROUND HERE SOME--
WELCOME TO THE DEATH ROOM...ERR I MEAN ESCAPE ROOM!
THE RULES ARE SIMPLE. YOU HAVE 30 MINUTES TO SOLVE THE PUZZLE AND OPEN ME...
BUT IF YOU FAIL, AND YOU WILL, YOU'LL BE TRAPPED IN HERE--
FOREVER!!
HA!! HA!! HA!!
THANKS FOR THE PEP TALK, DOOR FACE.
COME ON BRAIN. TIME TO SHINE.
OH COOL, THIS ONE HAS A WORM IN HIS EYE HOLE.
DO YOU HAVE A CLUE FOR US LITTLE BUDDY?
AH, HERE WE GO!
THE KEY TO A HEARTLESS SOUL IS TO SEE THE LIGHT FROM WITHIN--
WHAT THE FART IS THAT SUPPOSED TO MEAN?
HEY, MAYBE THESE GEMS BELONGED TO THOSE DUDES CHAINED TO THE WALL?
GOOD THINKING FINN.
LET'S TRY THESE GEMS IN THEIR EYE HOLES!
FINN YOU TAKE THE GREEN AND JAKE YOU TAKE THE RED.
WOAH, DUDE! IT'S WORKING!

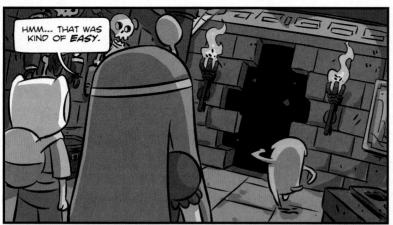

HMM.... THAT WAS KIND OF *EASY.*

PIECE OF *CAKE* GUYS!

SOME *CHALLENGE* THIS TURNED OUT TO BE.

I TAKE IT *BACK!* CLOSE THE DOOR, *CLOSE THE DOOR!*

POP!

SLAM

'SNIFF 'SNIFF SMELLS LIKE *BURNT* BACON IN HERE.

YOU'RE *TELLING* ME.

I'M PRETTY SURE MY BUTT IS *COOKED.*

15 MINUTES UNTIL YOU ARE TRAPPED FOR-- *ETERNITY!*

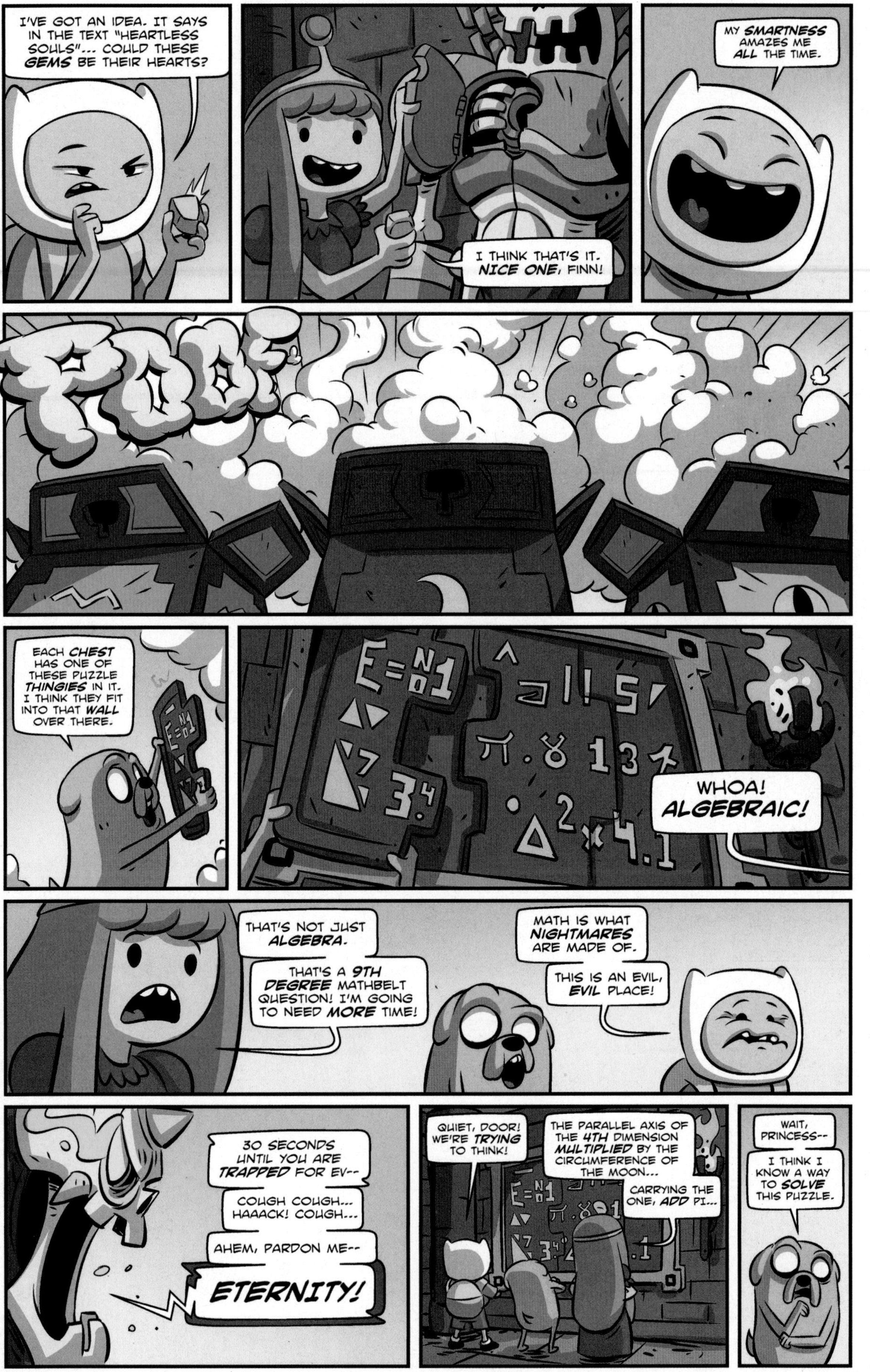
I'VE GOT AN IDEA. IT SAYS IN THE TEXT "HEARTLESS SOULS"... COULD THESE GEMS BE THEIR HEARTS?
I THINK THAT'S IT. NICE ONE, FINN!
MY SMARTNESS AMAZES ME ALL THE TIME.
EACH CHEST HAS ONE OF THESE PUZZLE THINGIES IN IT. I THINK THEY FIT INTO THAT WALL OVER THERE.
WHOA! ALGEBRAIC!
THAT'S NOT JUST ALGEBRA.
THAT'S A 9TH DEGREE MATHBELT QUESTION! I'M GOING TO NEED MORE TIME!
MATH IS WHAT NIGHTMARES ARE MADE OF.
THIS IS AN EVIL, EVIL PLACE!
30 SECONDS UNTIL YOU ARE TRAPPED FOR EV--
COUGH COUGH... HAAACK! COUGH...
AHEM, PARDON ME--
ETERNITY!
QUIET, DOOR! WE'RE TRYING TO THINK!
THE PARALLEL AXIS OF THE 4TH DIMENSION MULTIPLIED BY THE CIRCUMFERENCE OF THE MOON...
CARRYING THE ONE, ADD PI...
WAIT, PRINCESS--
I THINK I KNOW A WAY TO SOLVE THIS PUZZLE.

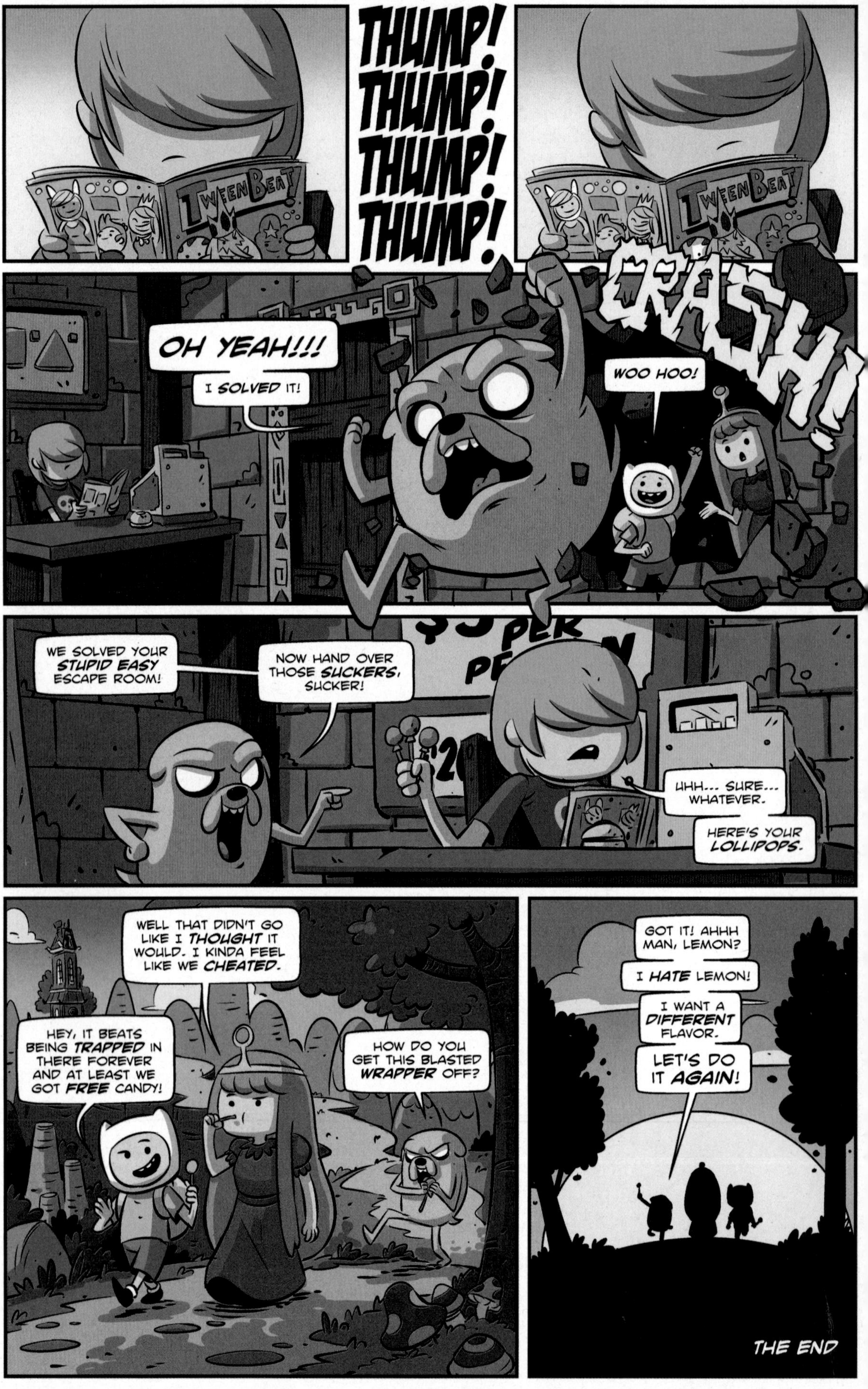

TWEENBEAT!
THUMP! THUMP! THUMP! THUMP!
TWEENBEAT!
CRASH!
OH YEAH!!!
I SOLVED IT!
WOO HOO!
$5 PER PE N
WE SOLVED YOUR STUPID EASY ESCAPE ROOM!
NOW HAND OVER THOSE SUCKERS, SUCKER!
UHH... SURE... WHATEVER.
HERE'S YOUR LOLLIPOPS.
WELL THAT DIDN'T GO LIKE I THOUGHT IT WOULD. I KINDA FEEL LIKE WE CHEATED.
HEY, IT BEATS BEING TRAPPED IN THERE FOREVER AND AT LEAST WE GOT FREE CANDY!
HOW DO YOU GET THIS BLASTED WRAPPER OFF?
GOT IT! AHHH MAN, LEMON?
I HATE LEMON!
I WANT A DIFFERENT FLAVOR.
LET'S DO IT AGAIN!
THE END

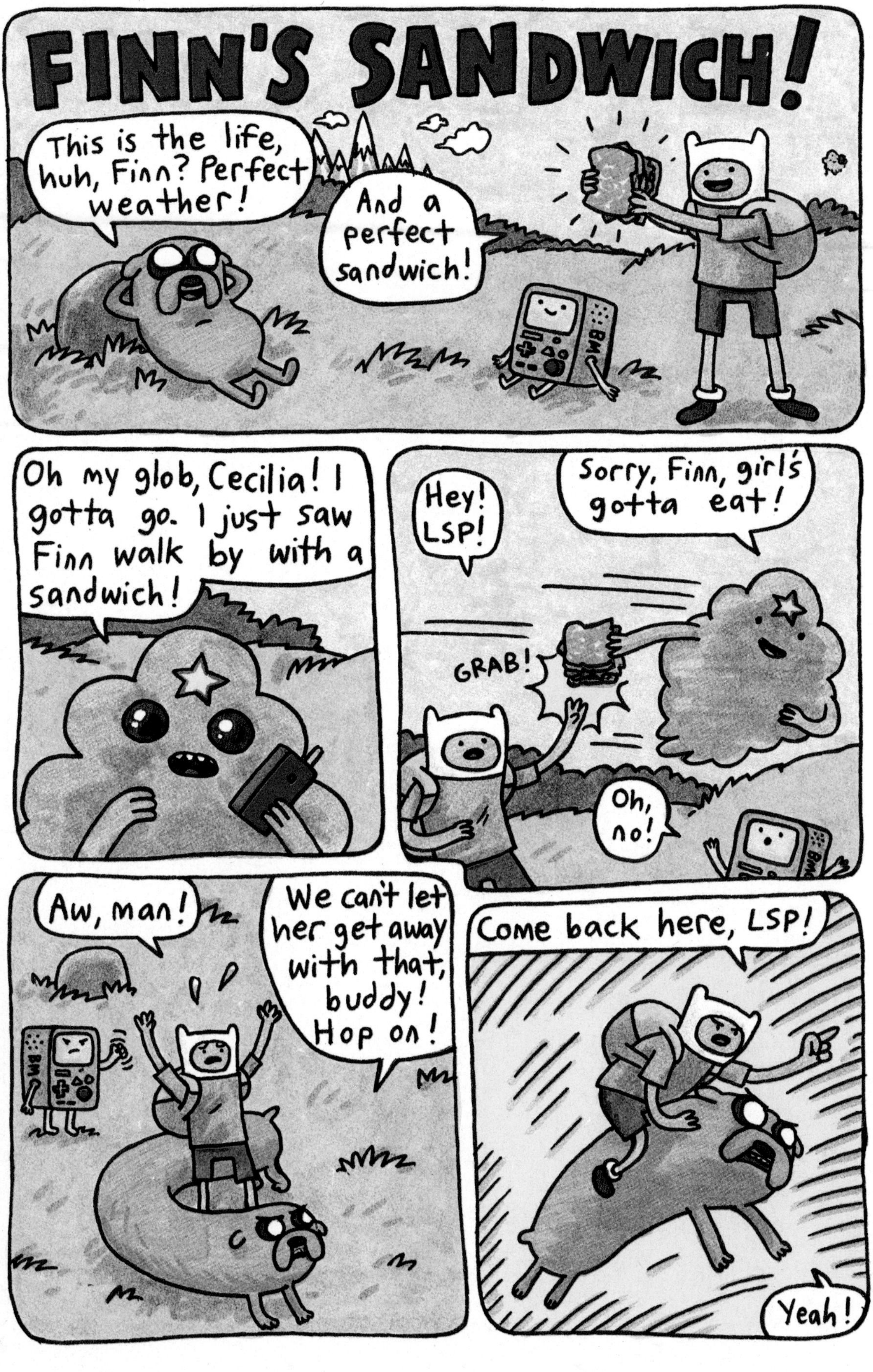
FINN'S SANDWICH!
This is the life, huh, Finn? Perfect weather!
And a perfect sandwich!
Oh my glob, Cecilia! I gotta go. I just saw Finn walk by with a sandwich!
Hey! LSP!
Sorry, Finn, girl's gotta eat!
GRAB!
Oh, no!
BMO
Aw, man!
We can't let her get away with that, buddy! Hop on!
Come back here, LSP!
Yeah!

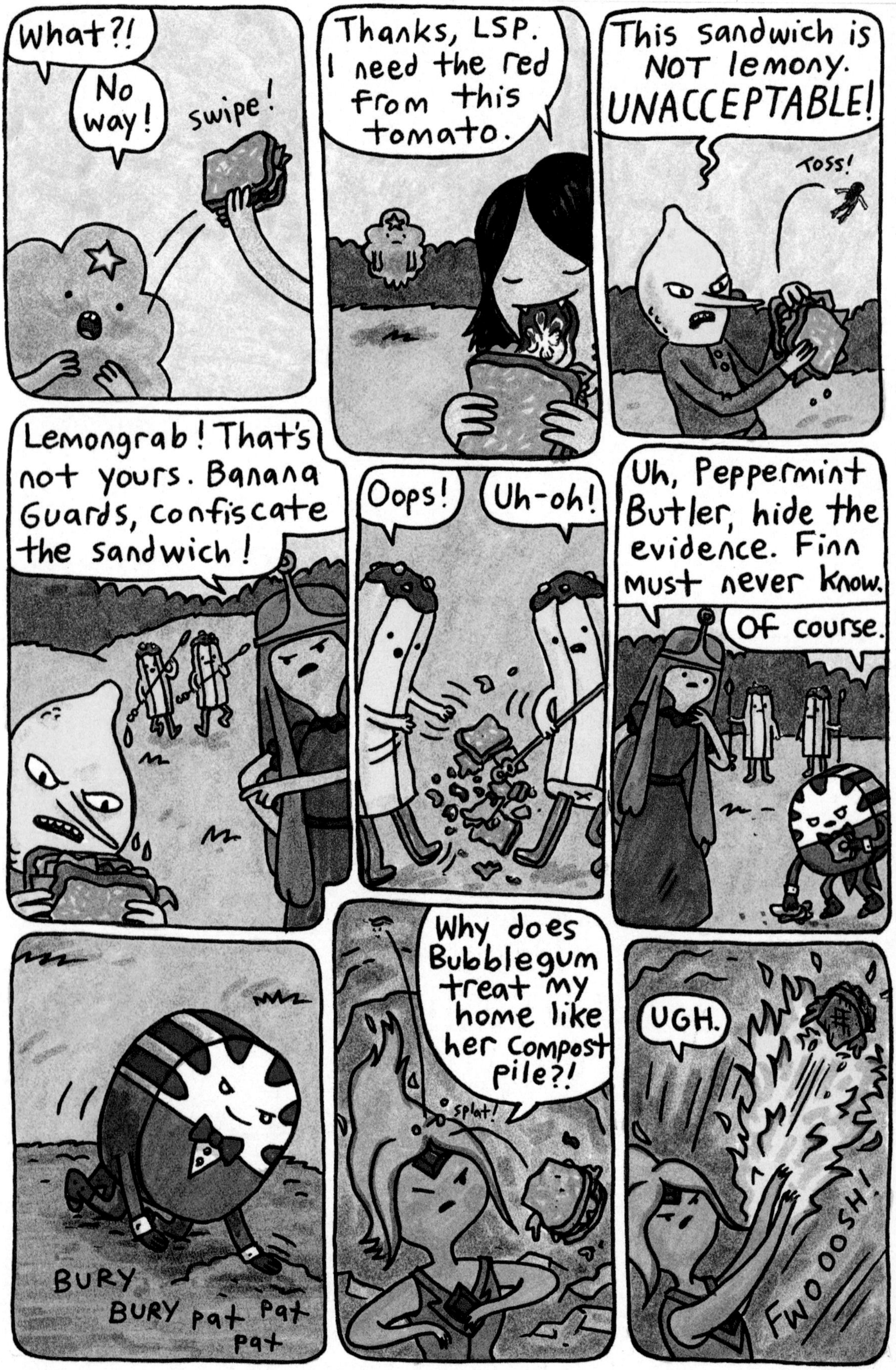

What?!
No way!
swipe!
Thanks, LSP. I need the red from this tomato.
This sandwich is NOT lemony. UNACCEPTABLE!
TOSS!
Lemongrab! That's not yours. Banana Guards, confiscate the sandwich!
Oops!
Uh-oh!
Uh, Peppermint Butler, hide the evidence. Finn must never know.
Of course.
BURY
BURY pat pat
pat
Why does Bubblegum treat my home like her compost pile?!
splat!
UGH.
FWOOOSH!

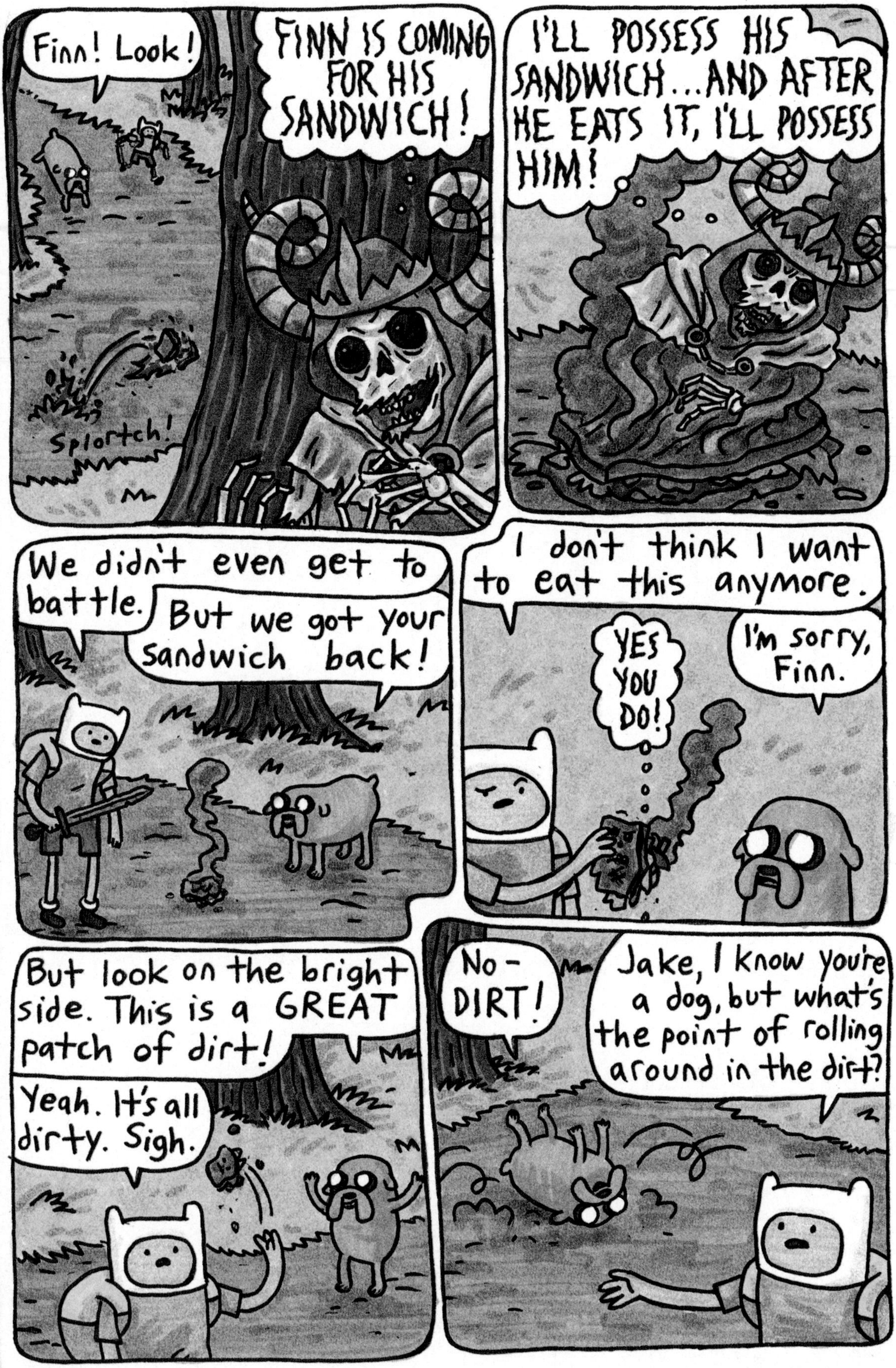
Finn! Look!
FINN IS COMING FOR HIS SANDWICH!
Splortch!
I'LL POSSESS HIS SANDWICH...AND AFTER HE EATS IT, I'LL POSSESS HIM!
We didn't even get to battle.
But we got your sandwich back!
I don't think I want to eat this anymore.
YES YOU DO!
I'm sorry, Finn.
But look on the bright side. This is a GREAT patch of dirt!
Yeah. It's all dirty. Sigh.
No- DIRT!
Jake, I know you're a dog, but what's the point of rolling around in the dirt?

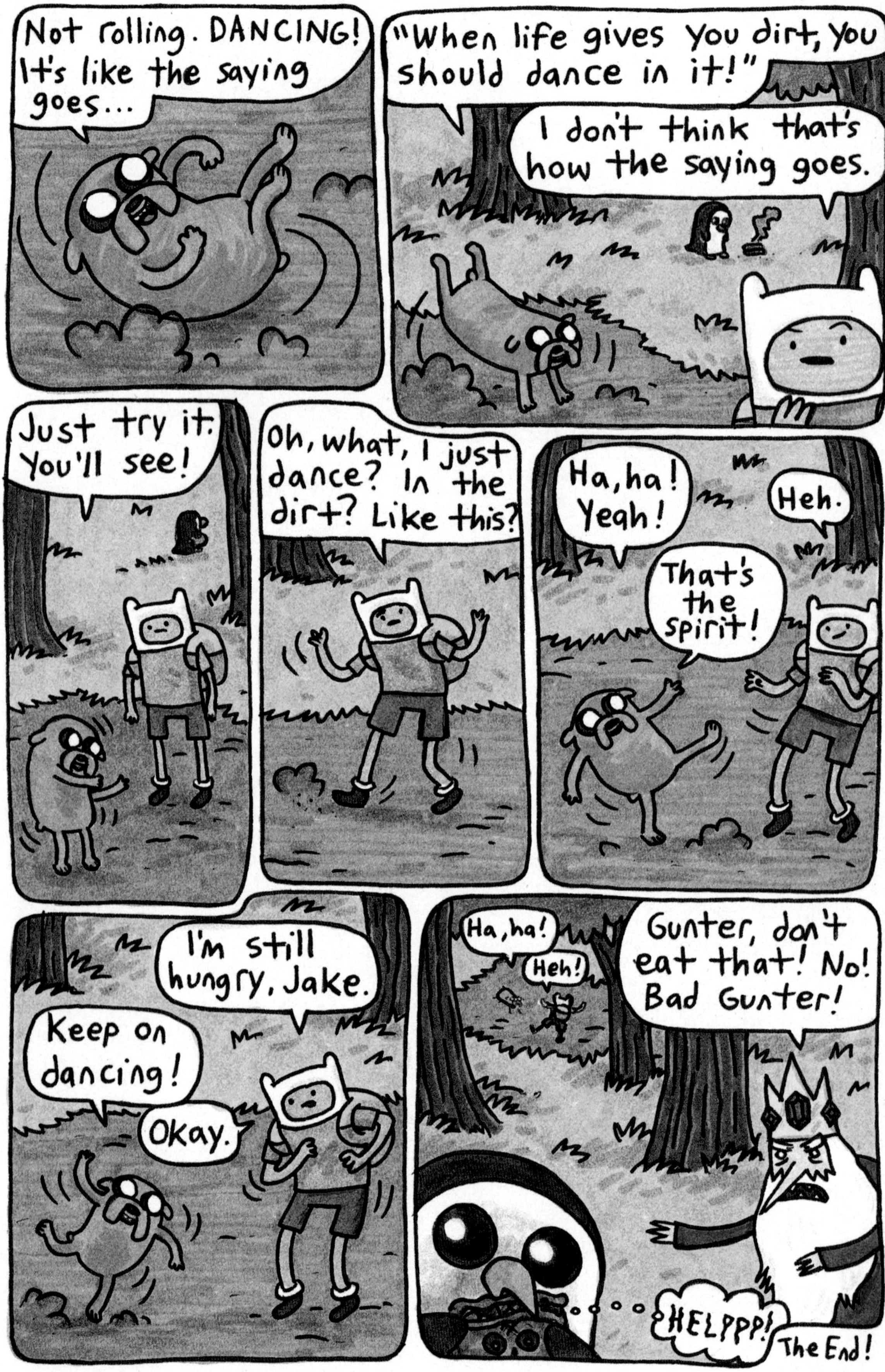
Not rolling. DANCING! It's like the saying goes...
"When life gives you dirt, you should dance in it!"
I don't think that's how the saying goes.
Just try it. You'll see!
Oh, what, I just dance? In the dirt? Like this?
Ha, ha! Yeah!
Heh.
That's the spirit!
I'm still hungry, Jake.
Keep on dancing!
Okay.
Ha, ha!
Heh!
Gunter, don't eat that! No! Bad Gunter!
HELPPP!
The End!

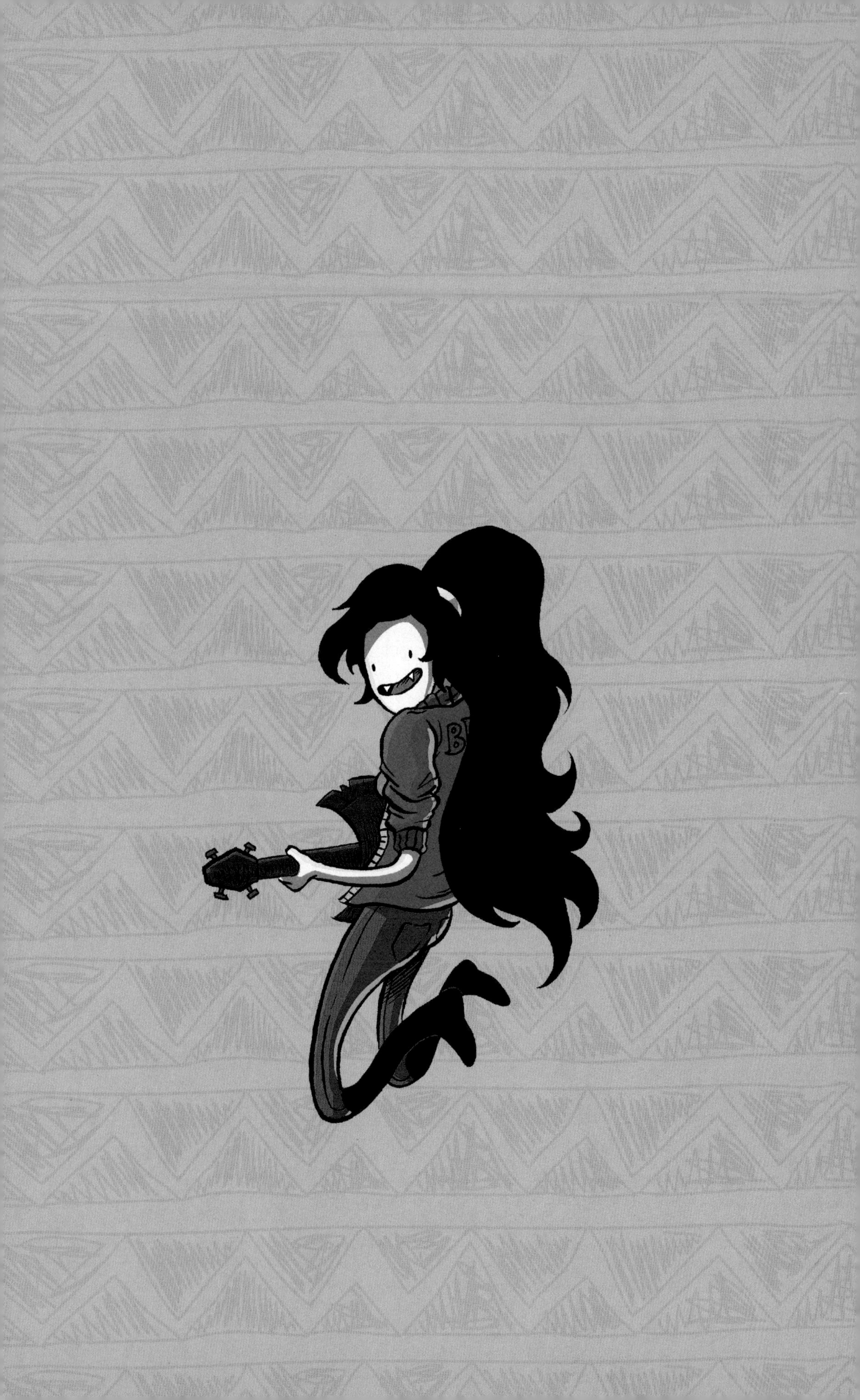

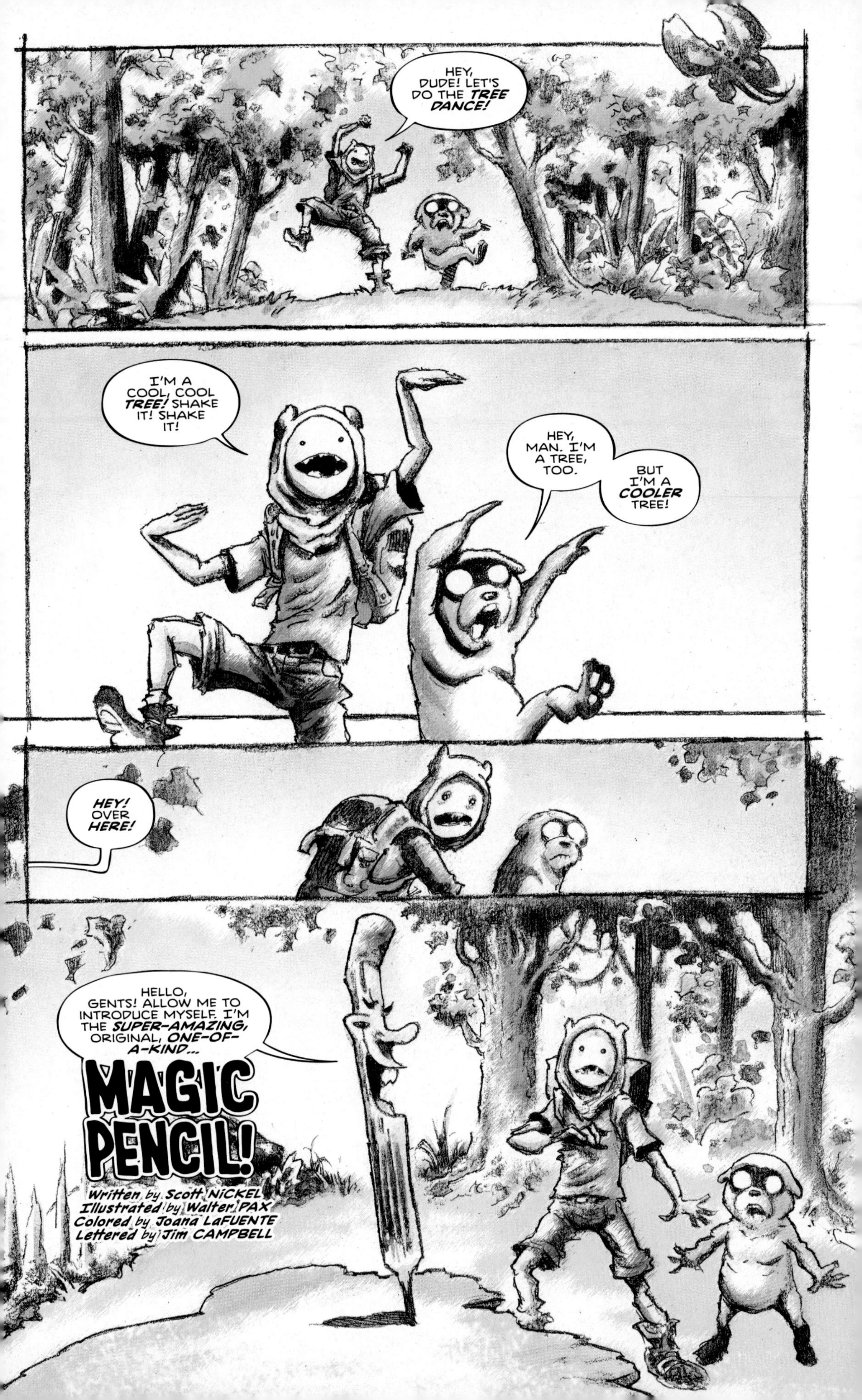
HEY, DUDE! LET'S DO THE TREE DANCE!
I'M A COOL, COOL TREE! SHAKE IT! SHAKE IT!
HEY, MAN. I'M A TREE, TOO.
BUT I'M A COOLER TREE!
HEY! OVER HERE!
HELLO, GENTS! ALLOW ME TO INTRODUCE MYSELF. I'M THE SUPER-AMAZING, ORIGINAL, ONE-OF-A-KIND...
MAGIC PENCIL!
Written by Scott NICKEL
Illustrated by Walter PAX
Colored by Joana LaFUENTE
Lettered by Jim CAMPBELL

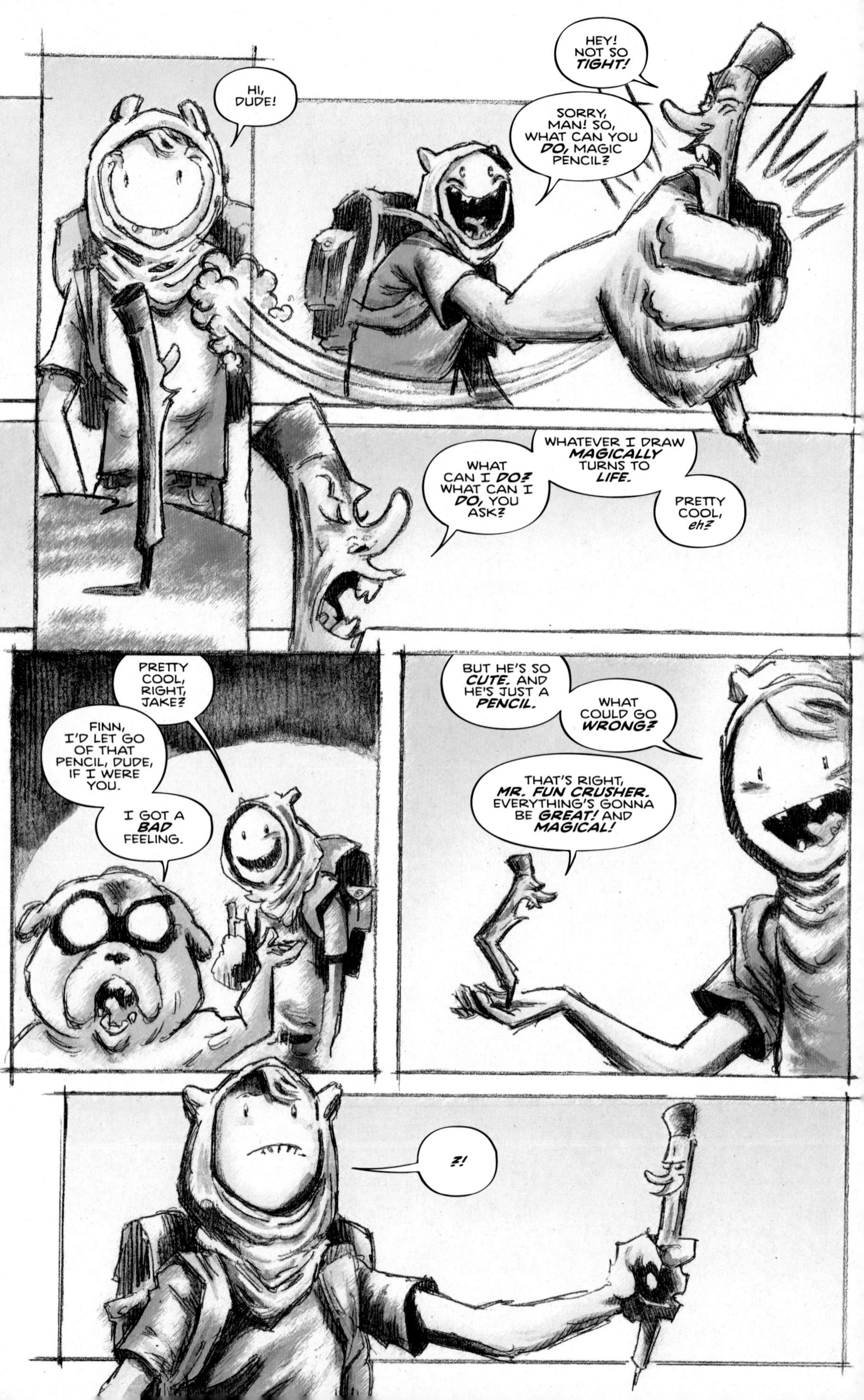
HI, DUDE!
HEY! NOT SO TIGHT!
SORRY, MAN! SO, WHAT CAN YOU DO, MAGIC PENCIL?
WHAT CAN I DO? WHAT CAN I DO, YOU ASK?
WHATEVER I DRAW MAGICALLY TURNS TO LIFE.
PRETTY COOL, eh?
PRETTY COOL, RIGHT, JAKE?
FINN, I'D LET GO OF THAT PENCIL, DUDE, IF I WERE YOU.
I GOT A BAD FEELING.
BUT HE'S SO CUTE. AND HE'S JUST A PENCIL.
WHAT COULD GO WRONG?
THAT'S RIGHT, MR. FUN CRUSHER. EVERYTHING'S GONNA BE GREAT! AND MAGICAL!
?!

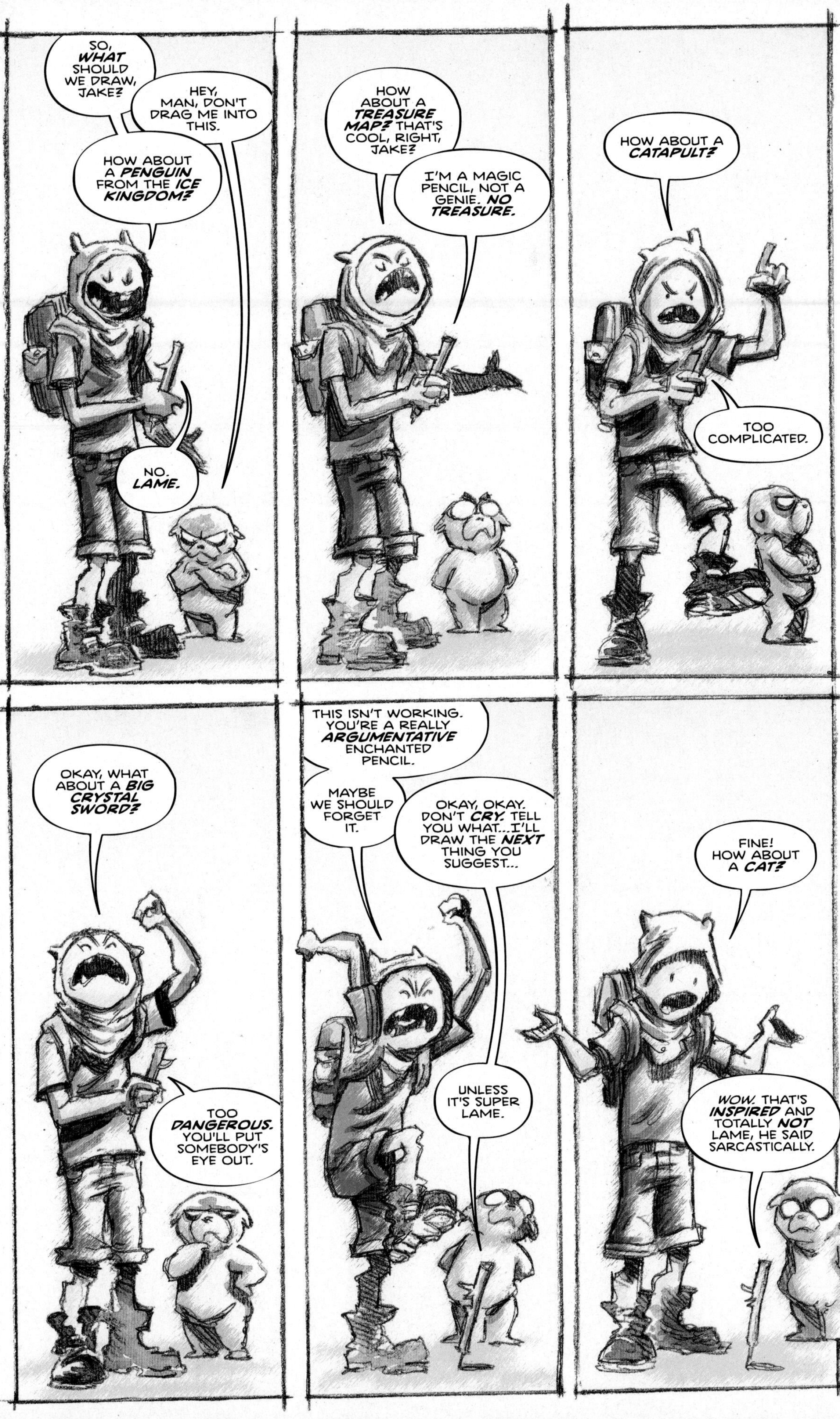
SO, WHAT SHOULD WE DRAW, JAKE?
HEY, MAN, DON'T DRAG ME INTO THIS.
HOW ABOUT A PENGUIN FROM THE ICE KINGDOM?
NO. LAME.
HOW ABOUT A TREASURE MAP? THAT'S COOL, RIGHT, JAKE?
I'M A MAGIC PENCIL, NOT A GENIE. NO TREASURE.
HOW ABOUT A CATAPULT?
TOO COMPLICATED.
OKAY, WHAT ABOUT A BIG CRYSTAL SWORD?
TOO DANGEROUS. YOU'LL PUT SOMEBODY'S EYE OUT.
THIS ISN'T WORKING. YOU'RE A REALLY ARGUMENTATIVE ENCHANTED PENCIL.
MAYBE WE SHOULD FORGET IT.
OKAY, OKAY. DON'T CRY. TELL YOU WHAT...I'LL DRAW THE NEXT THING YOU SUGGEST...
UNLESS IT'S SUPER LAME.
FINE! HOW ABOUT A CAT?
WOW. THAT'S INSPIRED AND TOTALLY NOT LAME, HE SAID SARCASTICALLY.

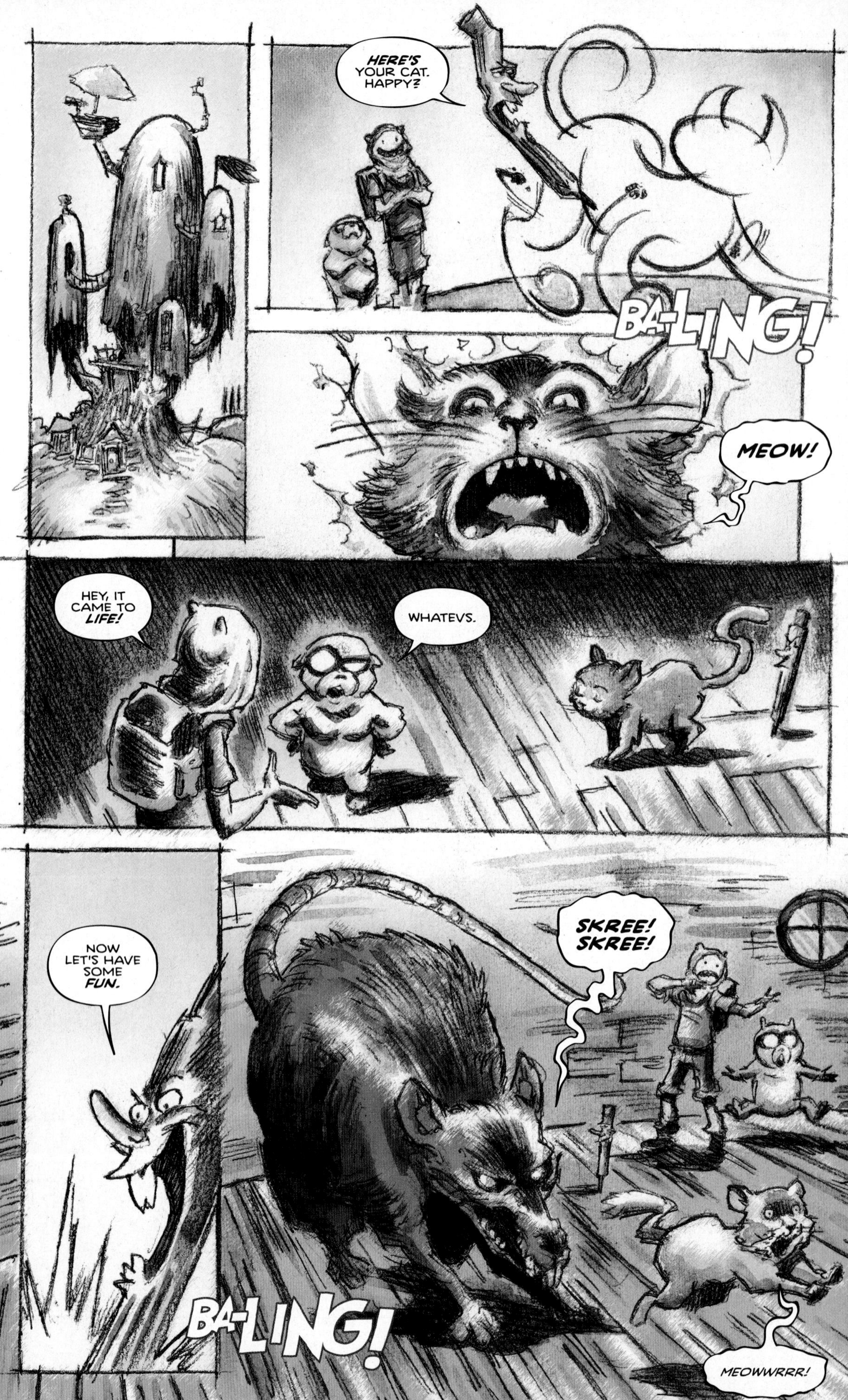
HERE'S YOUR CAT. HAPPY?
BA-LING!
MEOW!
HEY, IT CAME TO LIFE!
WHATEVS.
NOW LET'S HAVE SOME FUN.
SKREE! SKREE!
BA-LING!
MEOWWRRR!

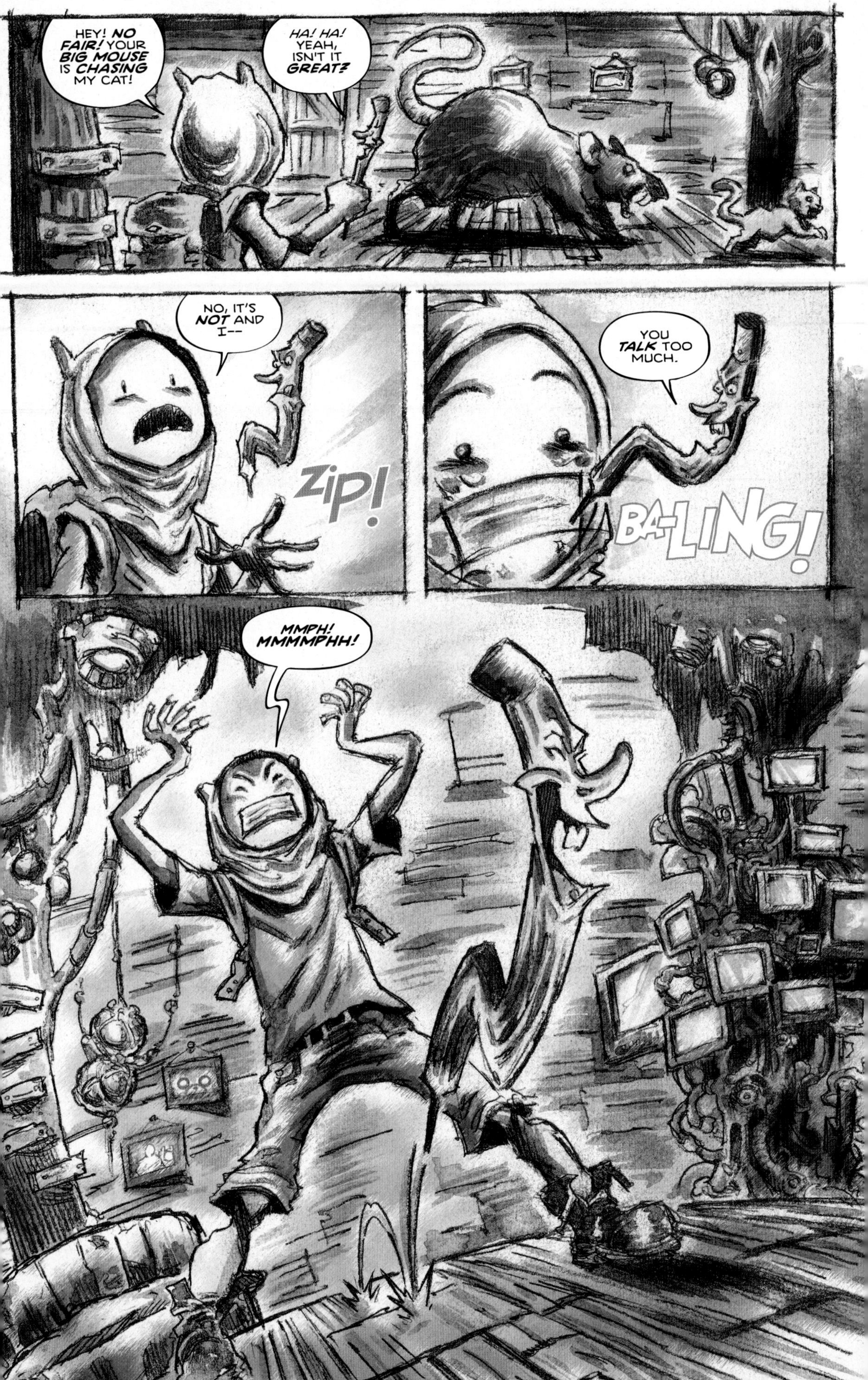
HEY! NO FAIR! YOUR BIG MOUSE IS CHASING MY CAT!
HA! HA! YEAH, ISN'T IT GREAT?
NO, IT'S NOT AND I--
ZIP!
YOU TALK TOO MUCH.
BA-LING!
MMPH! MMMMPHH!

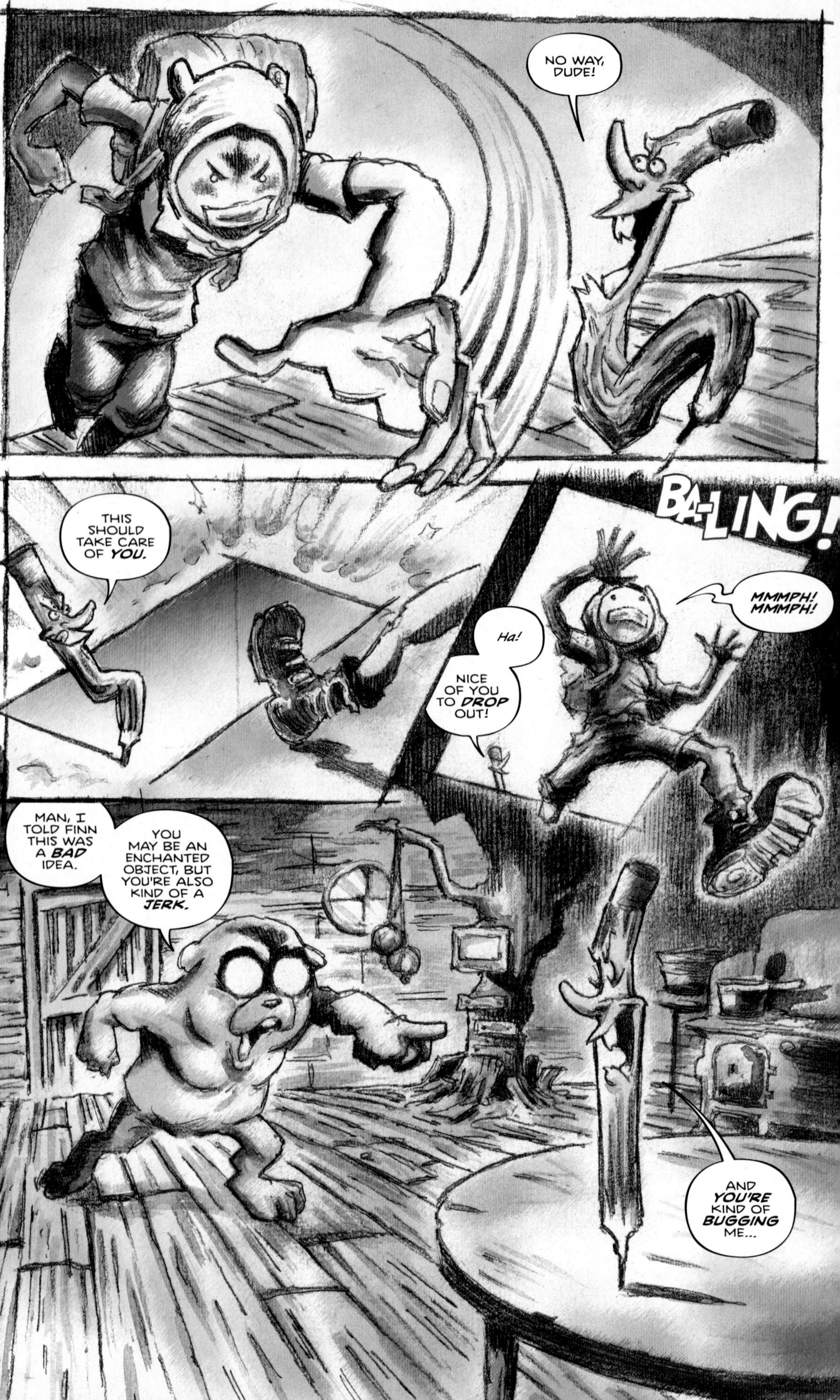
NO WAY, DUDE!
THIS SHOULD TAKE CARE OF *YOU.*
BA-LING!
MMMPH! MMMPH!
Ha!
NICE OF YOU TO *DROP* OUT!
MAN, I TOLD FINN THIS WAS A *BAD* IDEA.
YOU MAY BE AN ENCHANTED OBJECT, BUT YOU'RE ALSO KIND OF A *JERK.*
AND *YOU'RE* KIND OF *BUGGING* ME...

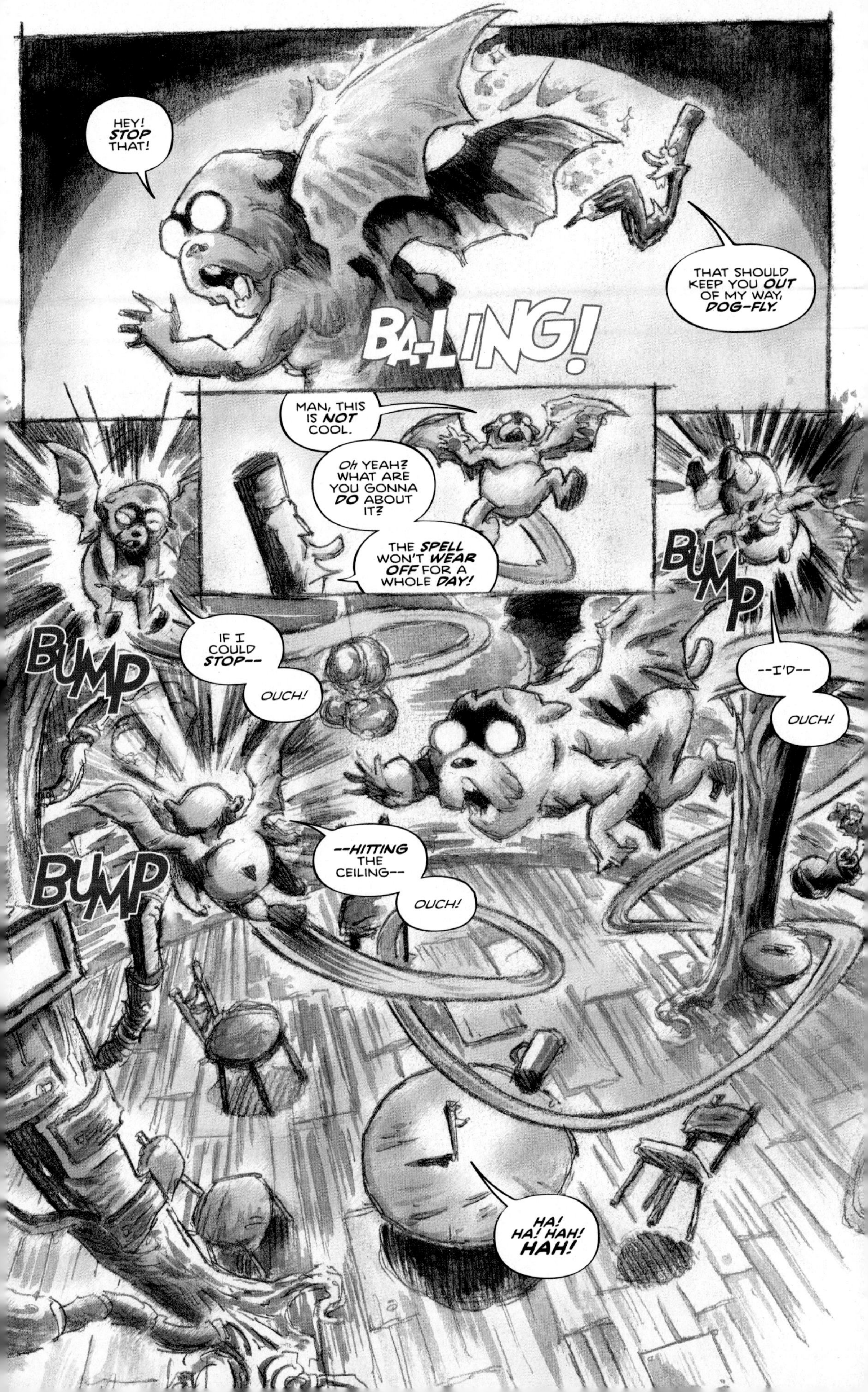
HEY! STOP THAT!
THAT SHOULD KEEP YOU OUT OF MY WAY, DOG-FLY.
BA-LING!
MAN, THIS IS NOT COOL.
Oh YEAH? WHAT ARE YOU GONNA DO ABOUT IT?
THE SPELL WON'T WEAR OFF FOR A WHOLE DAY!
BUMP
IF I COULD STOP--
OUCH!
BUMP
--I'D--
OUCH!
BUMP
--HITTING THE CEILING--
OUCH!
HA! HA! HAH! HAH!

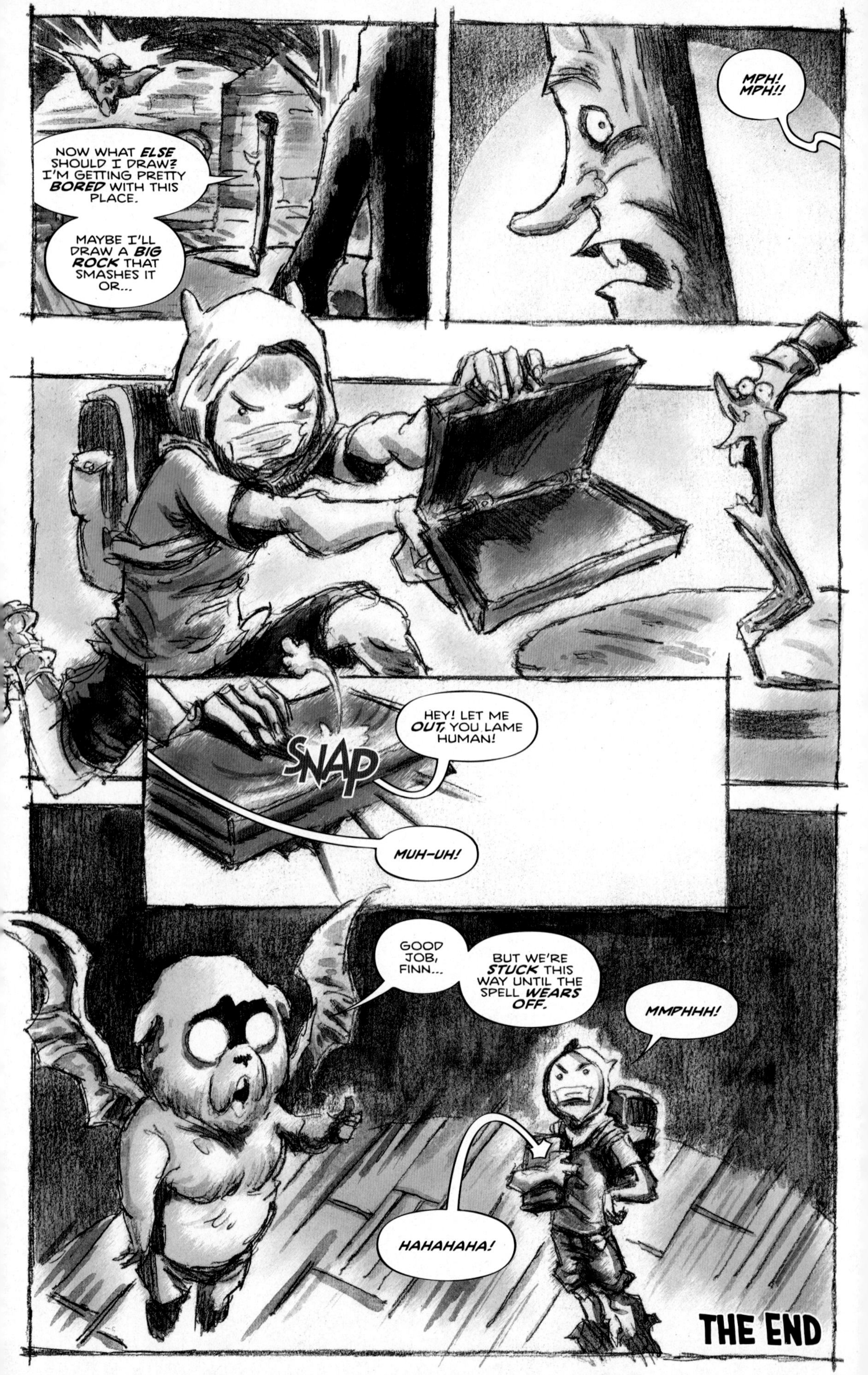

NOW WHAT ELSE SHOULD I DRAW? I'M GETTING PRETTY BORED WITH THIS PLACE.
MAYBE I'LL DRAW A BIG ROCK THAT SMASHES IT OR...
MPH! MPH!!
HEY! LET ME OUT, YOU LAME HUMAN!
SNAP
MUH-UH!
GOOD JOB, FINN...
BUT WE'RE STUCK THIS WAY UNTIL THE SPELL WEARS OFF.
MMPHHH!
HAHAHAHA!
THE END

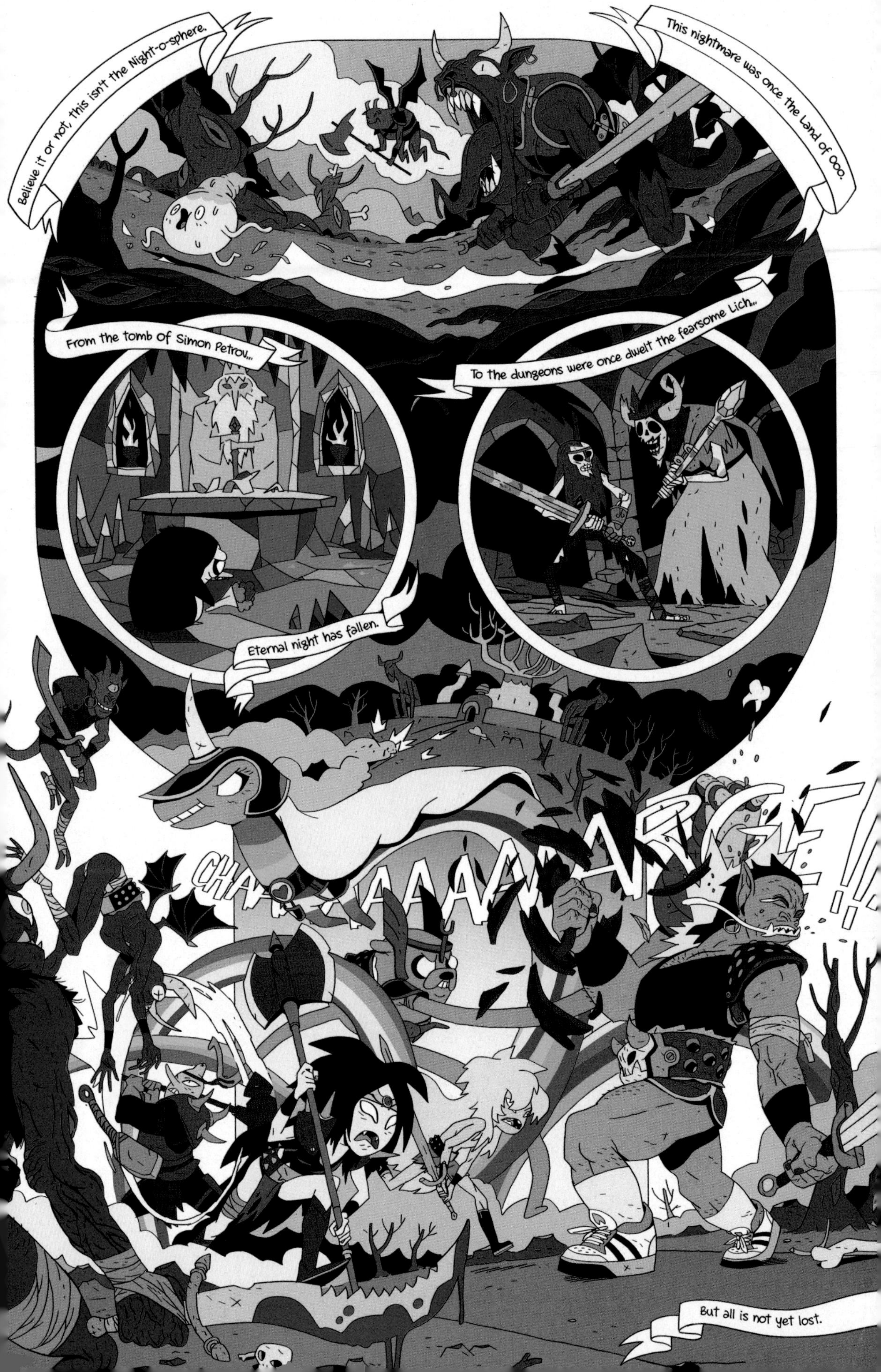

Believe it or not, this isn't the Night-o-sphere.
This nightmare was once the Land of Ooo.
From the tomb of Simon Petrov...
To the dungeons were once dwelt the fearsome Lich...
Eternal night has fallen.
CHAAAAAAARGE!!!
But all is not yet lost.

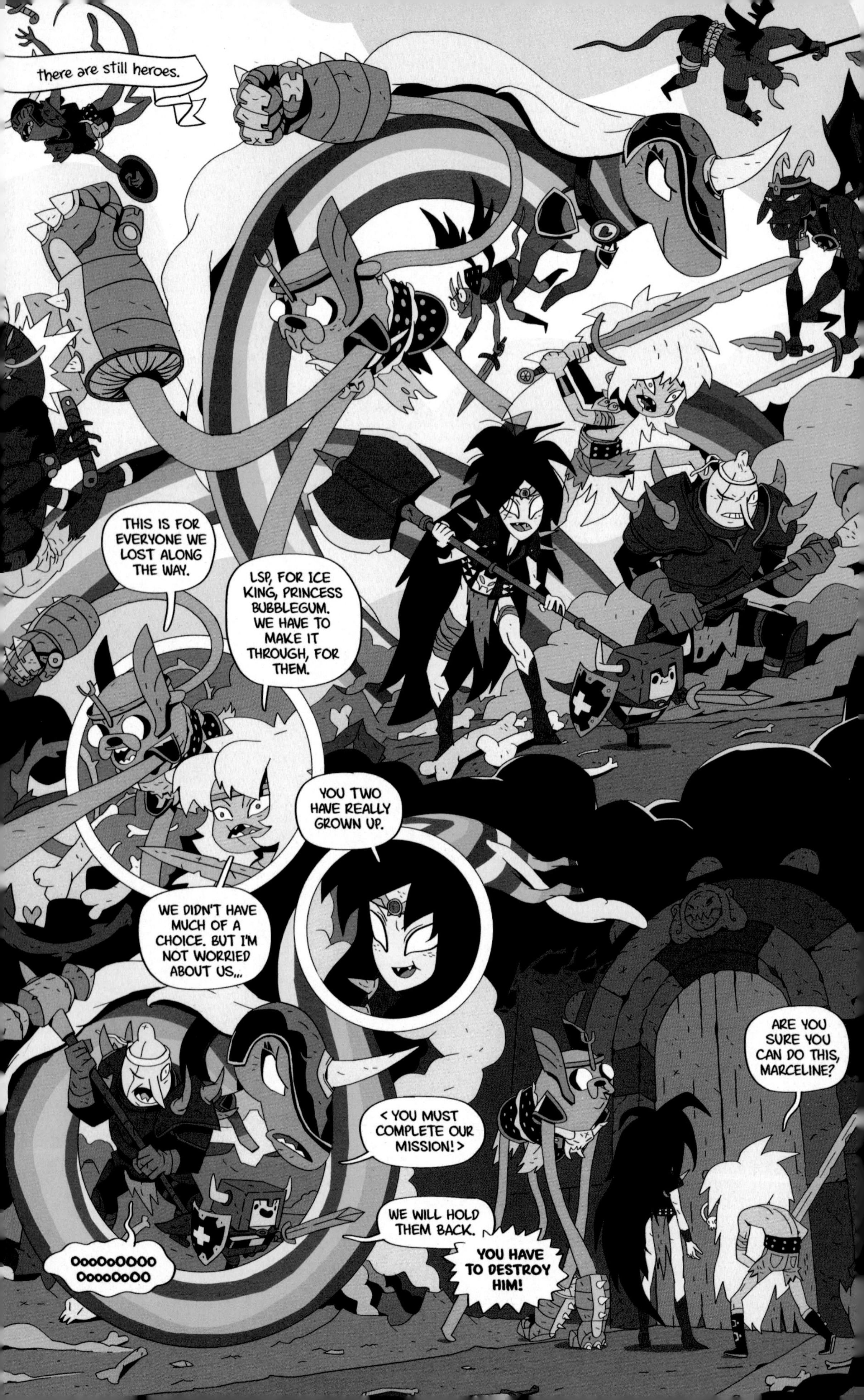
there are still heroes.
THIS IS FOR EVERYONE WE LOST ALONG THE WAY.
LSP, FOR ICE KING, PRINCESS BUBBLEGUM. WE HAVE TO MAKE IT THROUGH, FOR THEM.
YOU TWO HAVE REALLY GROWN UP.
WE DIDN'T HAVE MUCH OF A CHOICE. BUT I'M NOT WORRIED ABOUT US...
ARE YOU SURE YOU CAN DO THIS, MARCELINE?
< YOU MUST COMPLETE OUR MISSION! >
WE WILL HOLD THEM BACK.
YOU HAVE TO DESTROY HIM!
OooOoOOOO OoooOoOO

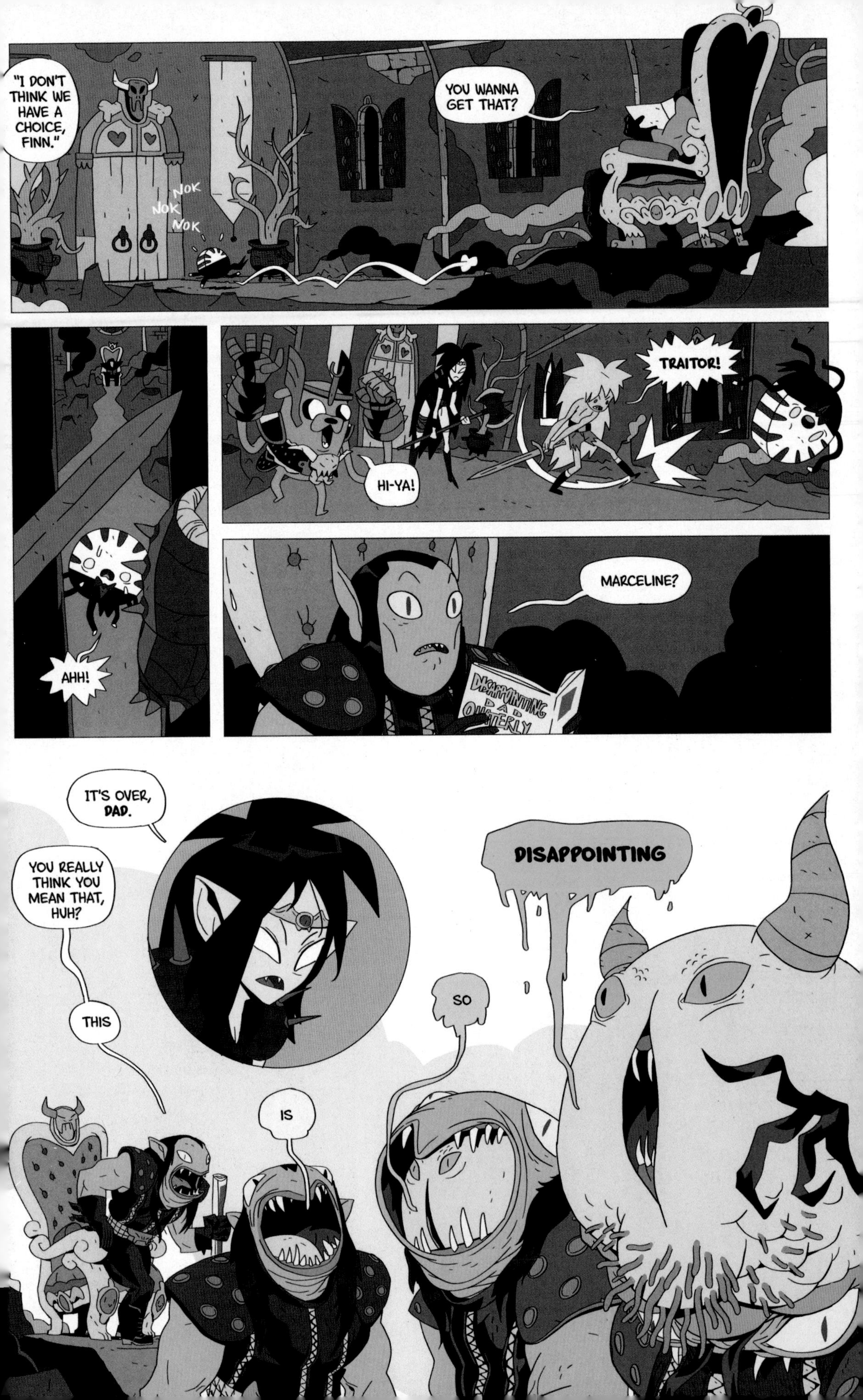
"I DON'T THINK WE HAVE A CHOICE, FINN."
NOK NOK NOK
YOU WANNA GET THAT?
TRAITOR!
HI-YA!
AHH!
MARCELINE?
DISAPPOINTING DAD QUARTERLY
IT'S OVER, DAD.
YOU REALLY THINK YOU MEAN THAT, HUH?
THIS
IS
SO
DISAPPOINTING

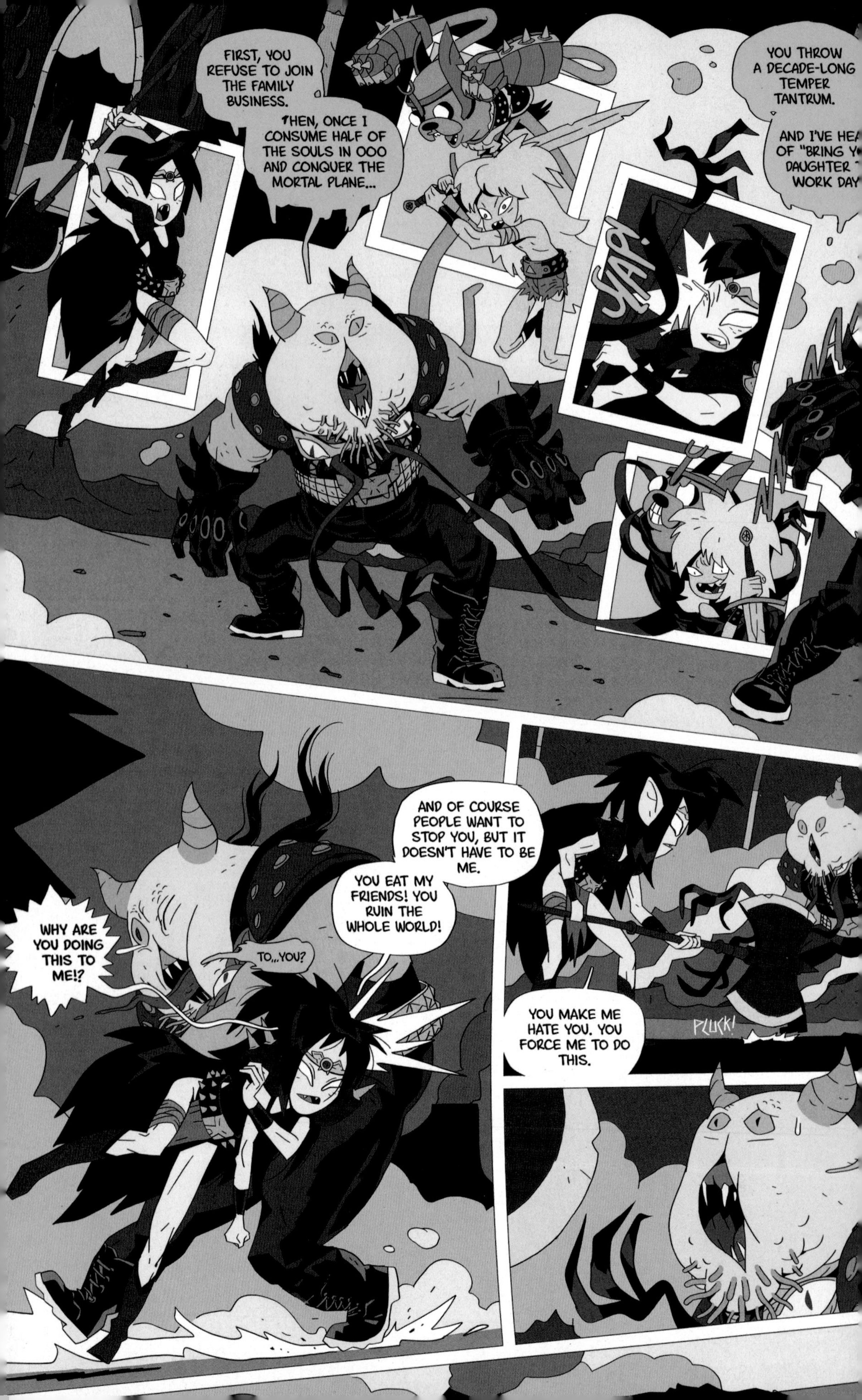
FIRST, YOU REFUSE TO JOIN THE FAMILY BUSINESS.
THEN, ONCE I CONSUME HALF OF THE SOULS IN OOO AND CONQUER THE MORTAL PLANE...
YOU THROW A DECADE-LONG TEMPER TANTRUM.
AND I'VE HEA OF "BRING Y DAUGHTER T WORK DAY
YAP!
WHY ARE YOU DOING THIS TO ME!?
TO...YOU?
YOU EAT MY FRIENDS! YOU RUIN THE WHOLE WORLD!
AND OF COURSE PEOPLE WANT TO STOP YOU, BUT IT DOESN'T HAVE TO BE ME.
YOU MAKE ME HATE YOU. YOU FORCE ME TO DO THIS.
PLUCK!

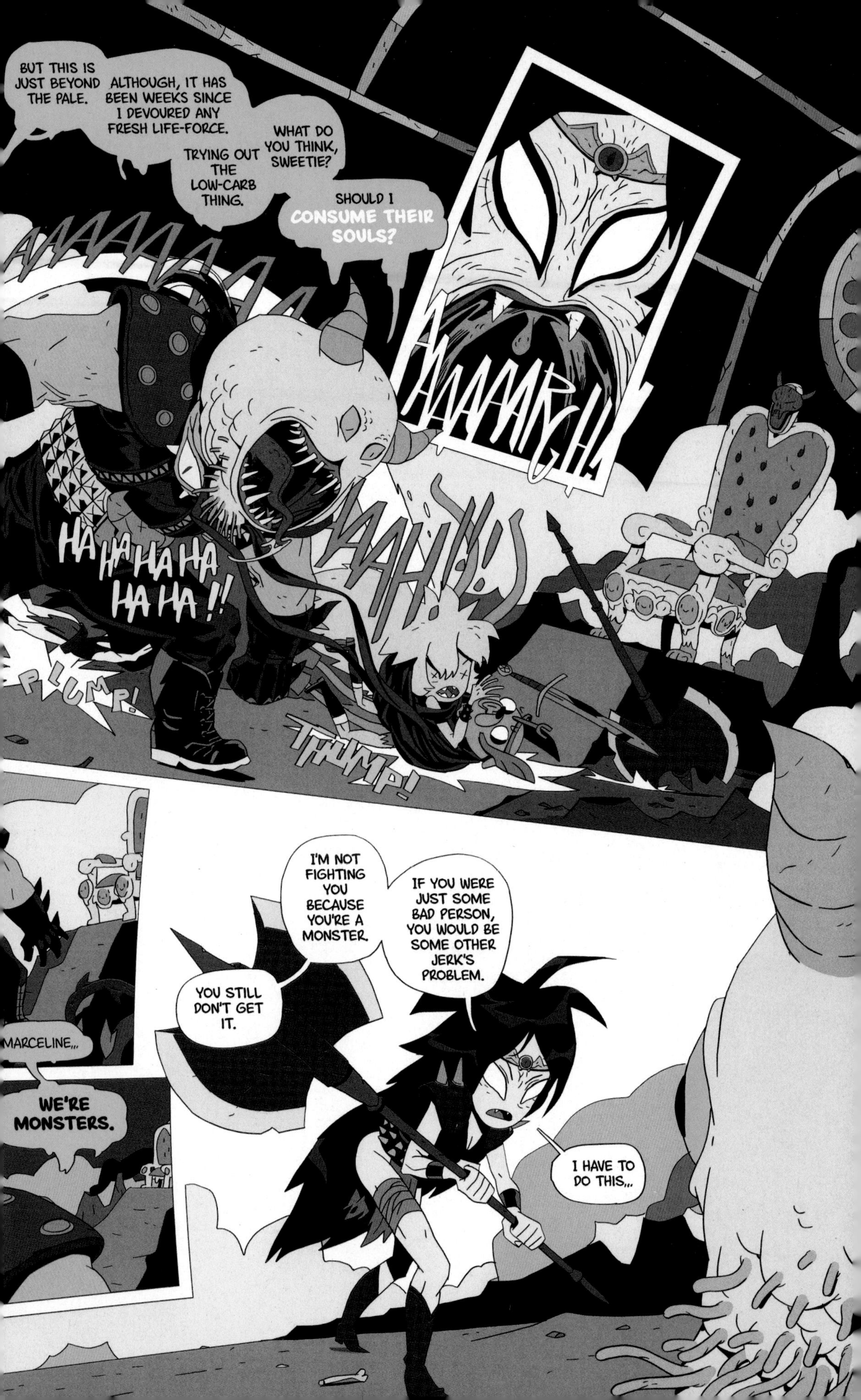

BUT THIS IS JUST BEYOND THE PALE.
ALTHOUGH, IT HAS BEEN WEEKS SINCE I DEVOURED ANY FRESH LIFE-FORCE.
TRYING OUT THE LOW-CARB THING.
WHAT DO YOU THINK, SWEETIE?
SHOULD I CONSUME THEIR SOULS?
AAAAAAAAAA
AAAAARGH!
AAAHH!!
HA HA HA HA HA HA HA !!
PLUMP!
THUMP!
I'M NOT FIGHTING YOU BECAUSE YOU'RE A MONSTER.
IF YOU WERE JUST SOME BAD PERSON, YOU WOULD BE SOME OTHER JERK'S PROBLEM.
YOU STILL DON'T GET IT.
MARCELINE...
WE'RE MONSTERS.
I HAVE TO DO THIS...

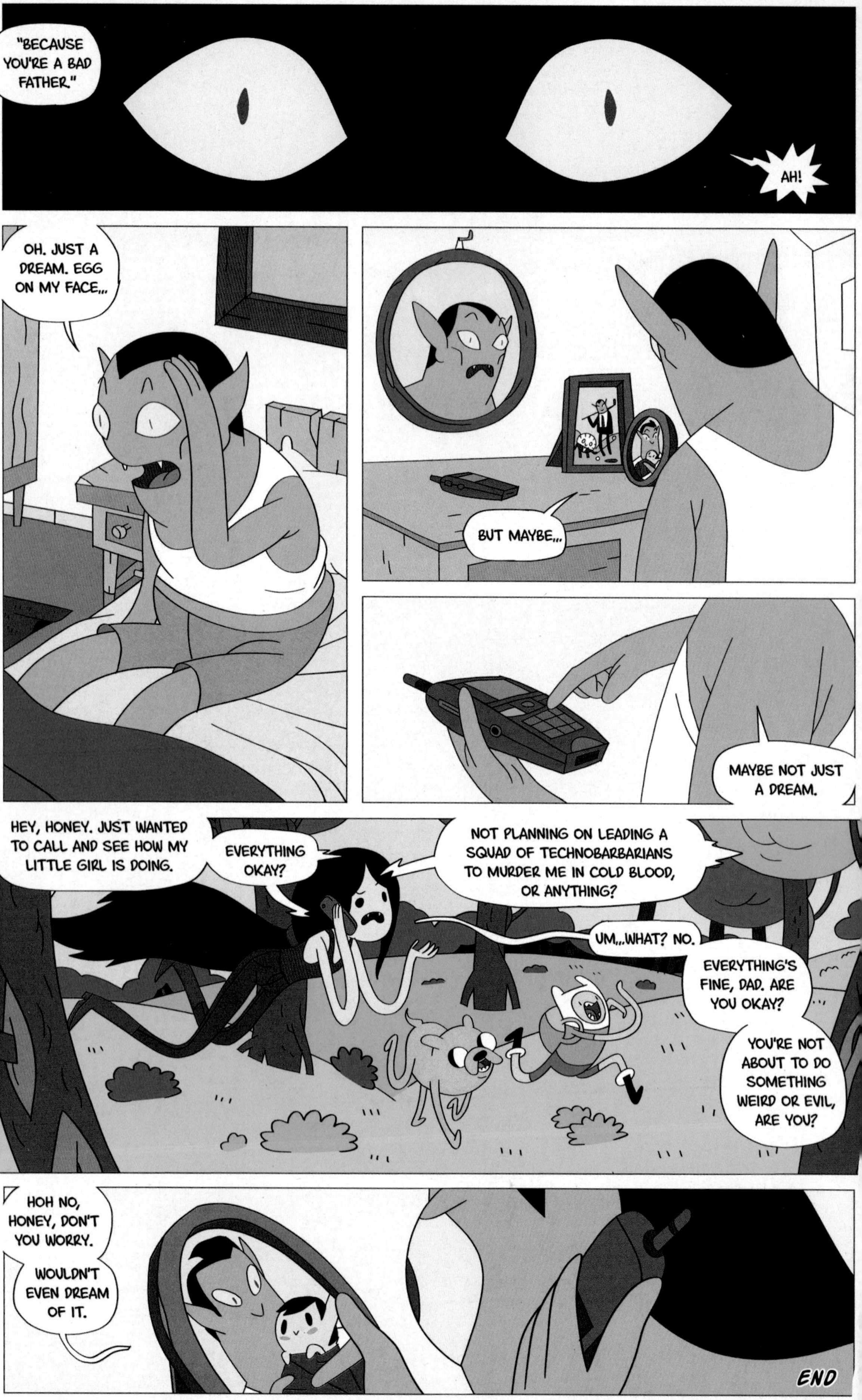
"BECAUSE YOU'RE A BAD FATHER."
AH!
OH. JUST A DREAM. EGG ON MY FACE...
BUT MAYBE...
MAYBE NOT JUST A DREAM.
HEY, HONEY. JUST WANTED TO CALL AND SEE HOW MY LITTLE GIRL IS DOING.
EVERYTHING OKAY?
NOT PLANNING ON LEADING A SQUAD OF TECHNOBARBARIANS TO MURDER ME IN COLD BLOOD, OR ANYTHING?
UM...WHAT? NO.
EVERYTHING'S FINE, DAD. ARE YOU OKAY?
YOU'RE NOT ABOUT TO DO SOMETHING WEIRD OR EVIL, ARE YOU?
HOH NO, HONEY, DON'T YOU WORRY.
WOULDN'T EVEN DREAM OF IT.
END

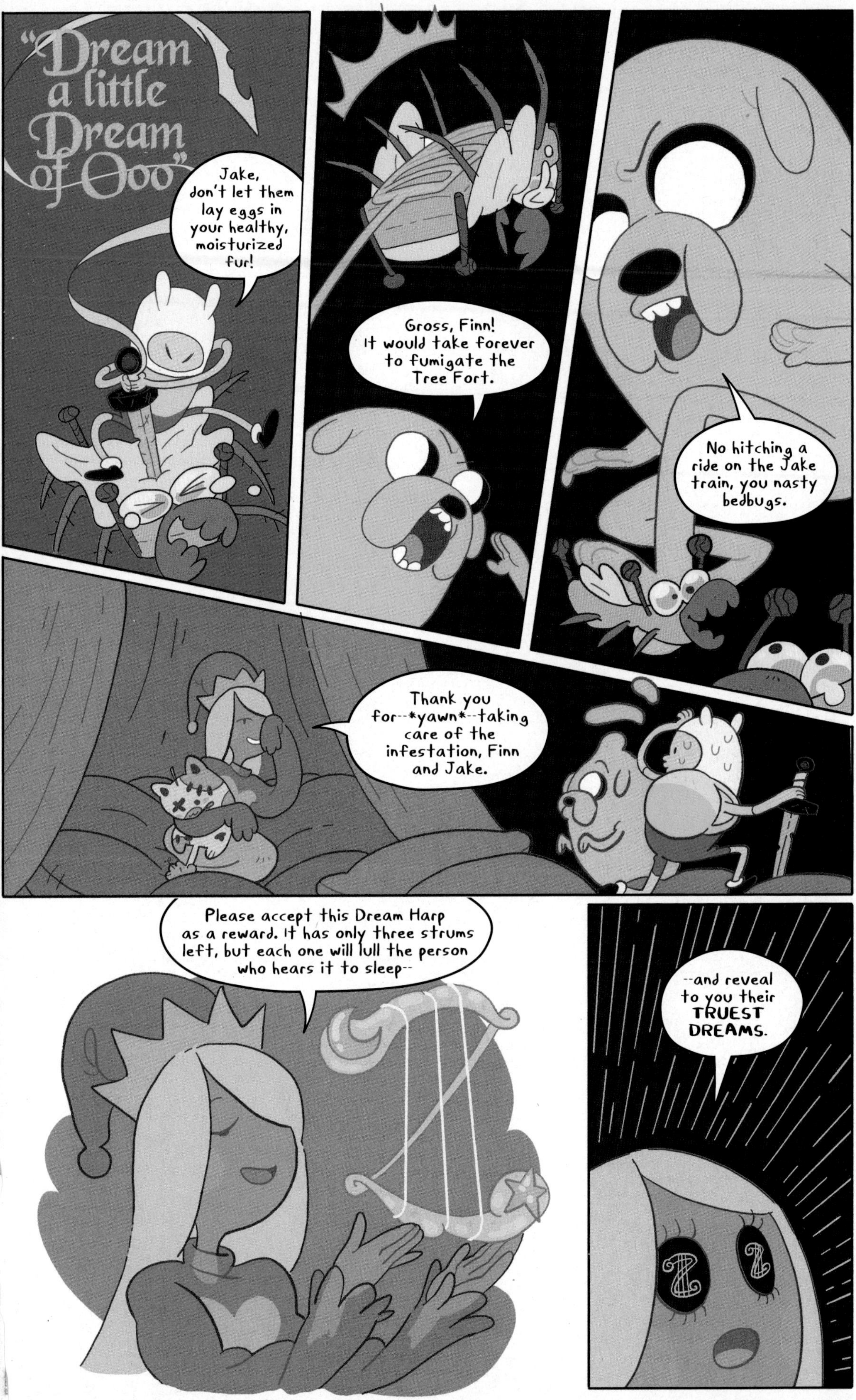
"Dream a little Dream of Ooo"
Jake, don't let them lay eggs in your healthy, moisturized fur!
Gross, Finn! It would take forever to fumigate the Tree Fort.
No hitching a ride on the Jake train, you nasty bedbugs.
Thank you for--*yawn*--taking care of the infestation, Finn and Jake.
Please accept this Dream Harp as a reward. It has only three strums left, but each one will lull the person who hears it to sleep--
--and reveal to you their TRUEST DREAMS.

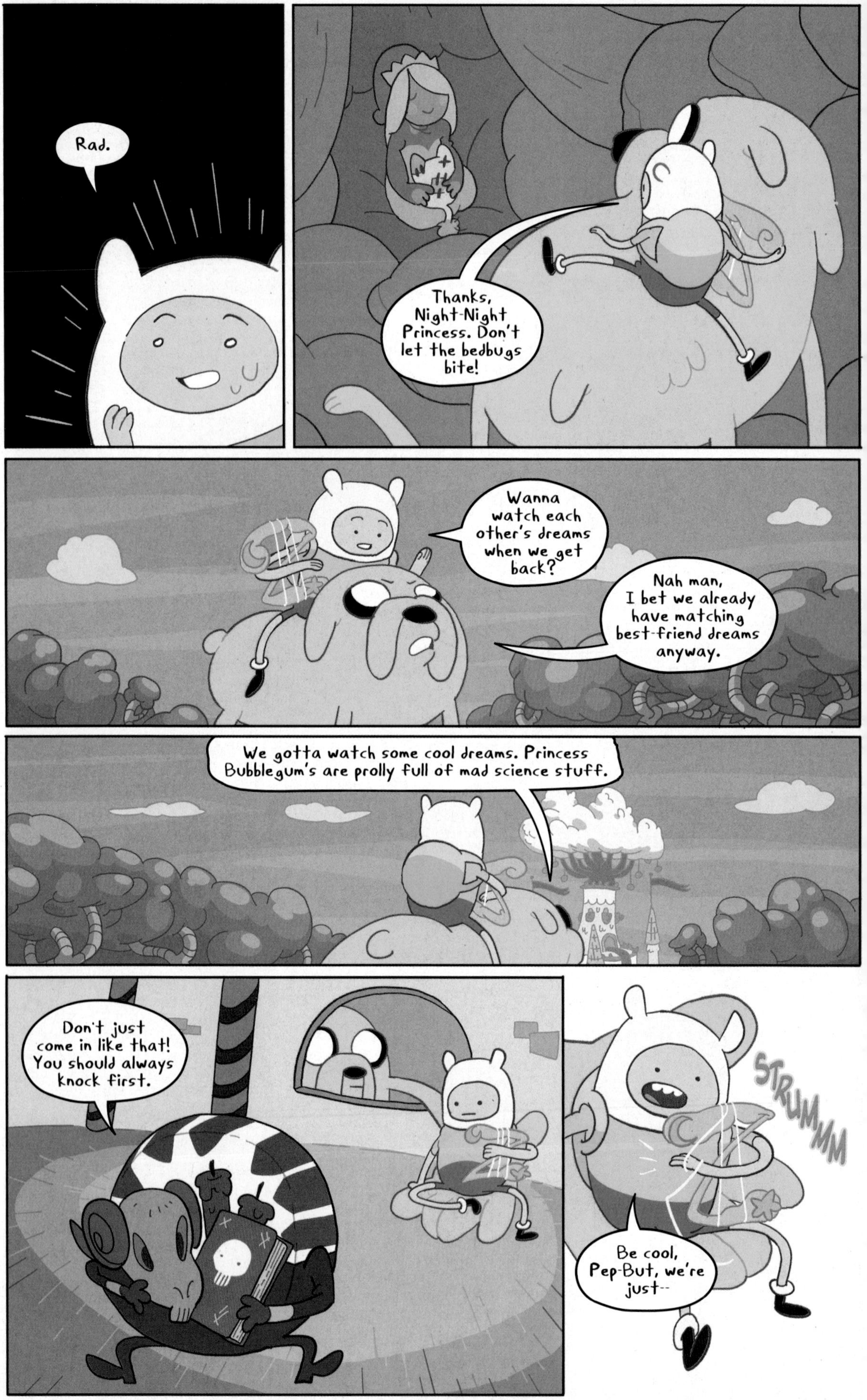
Rad.
Thanks, Night-Night Princess. Don't let the bedbugs bite!
Wanna watch each other's dreams when we get back?
Nah man, I bet we already have matching best-friend dreams anyway.
We gotta watch some cool dreams. Princess Bubblegum's are prolly full of mad science stuff.
Don't just come in like that! You should always knock first.
STRUMMM
Be cool, Pep-But, we're just--

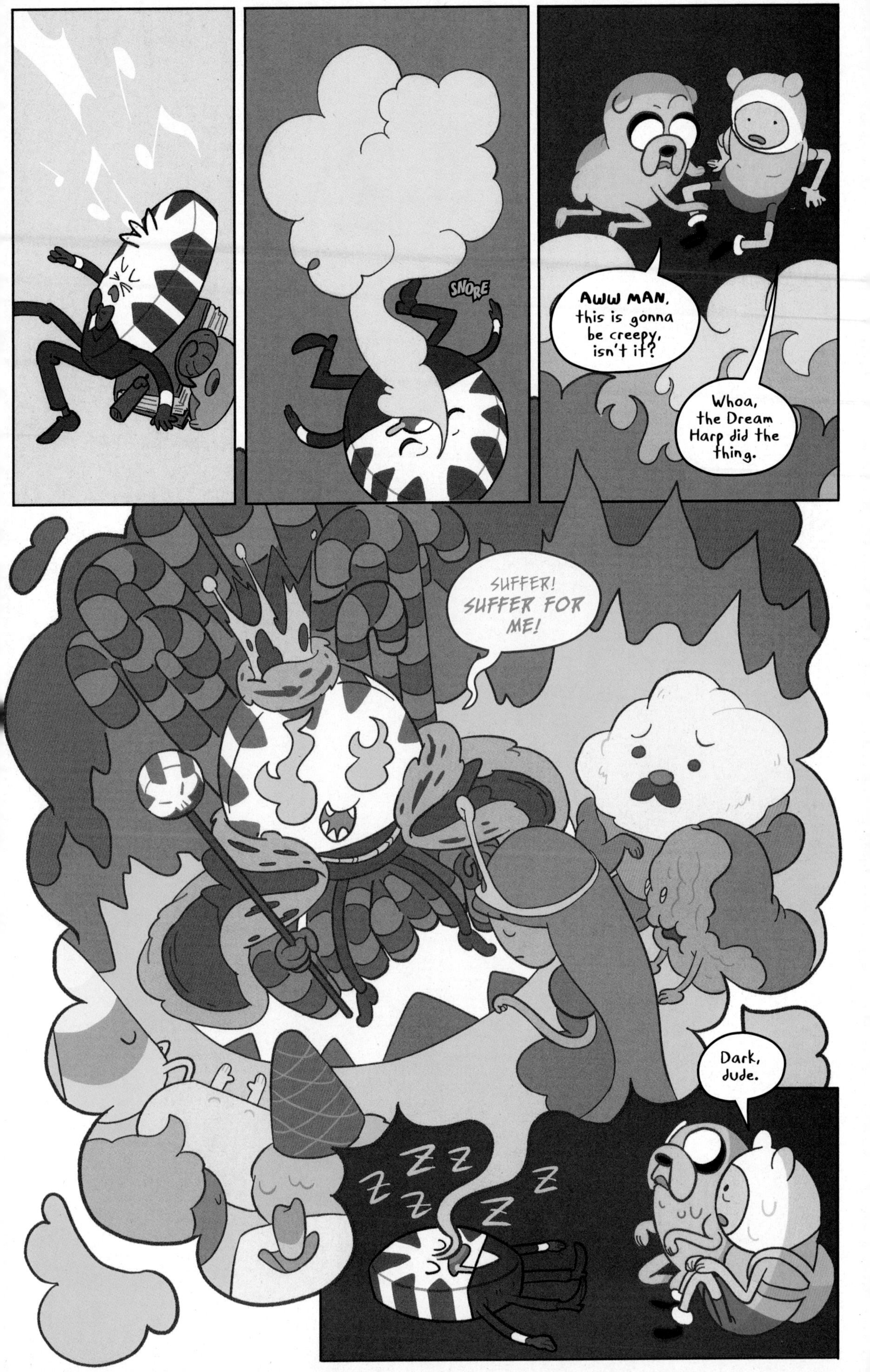
SNORE
AWW MAN, this is gonna be creepy, isn't it?
Whoa, the Dream Harp did the thing.
SUFFER! SUFFER FOR ME!
Dark, dude.
Z Z Z Z Z Z

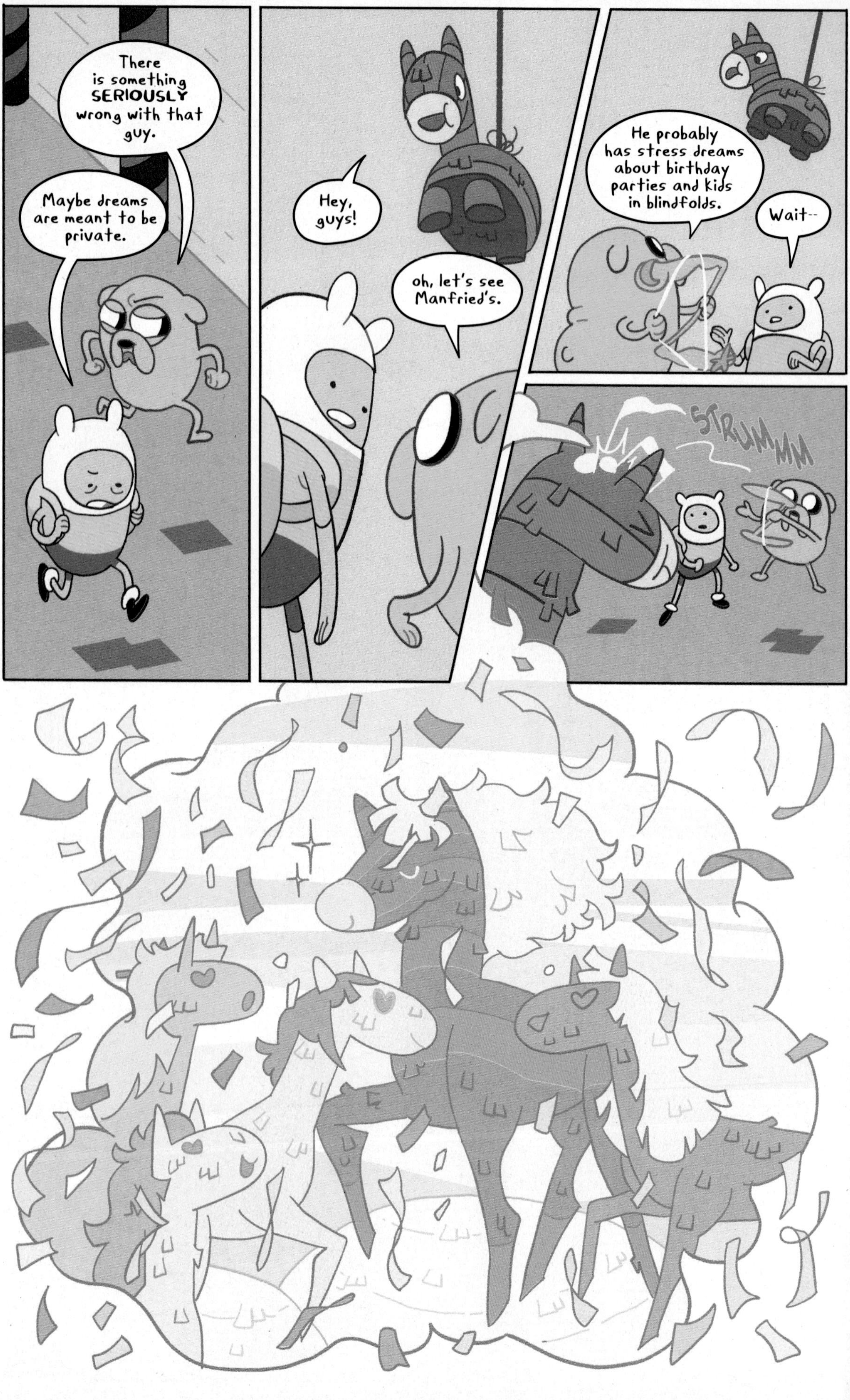

There is something SERIOUSLY wrong with that guy.
Maybe dreams are meant to be private.
Hey, guys!
oh, let's see Manfried's.
He probably has stress dreams about birthday parties and kids in blindfolds.
Wait--
STRUMMM

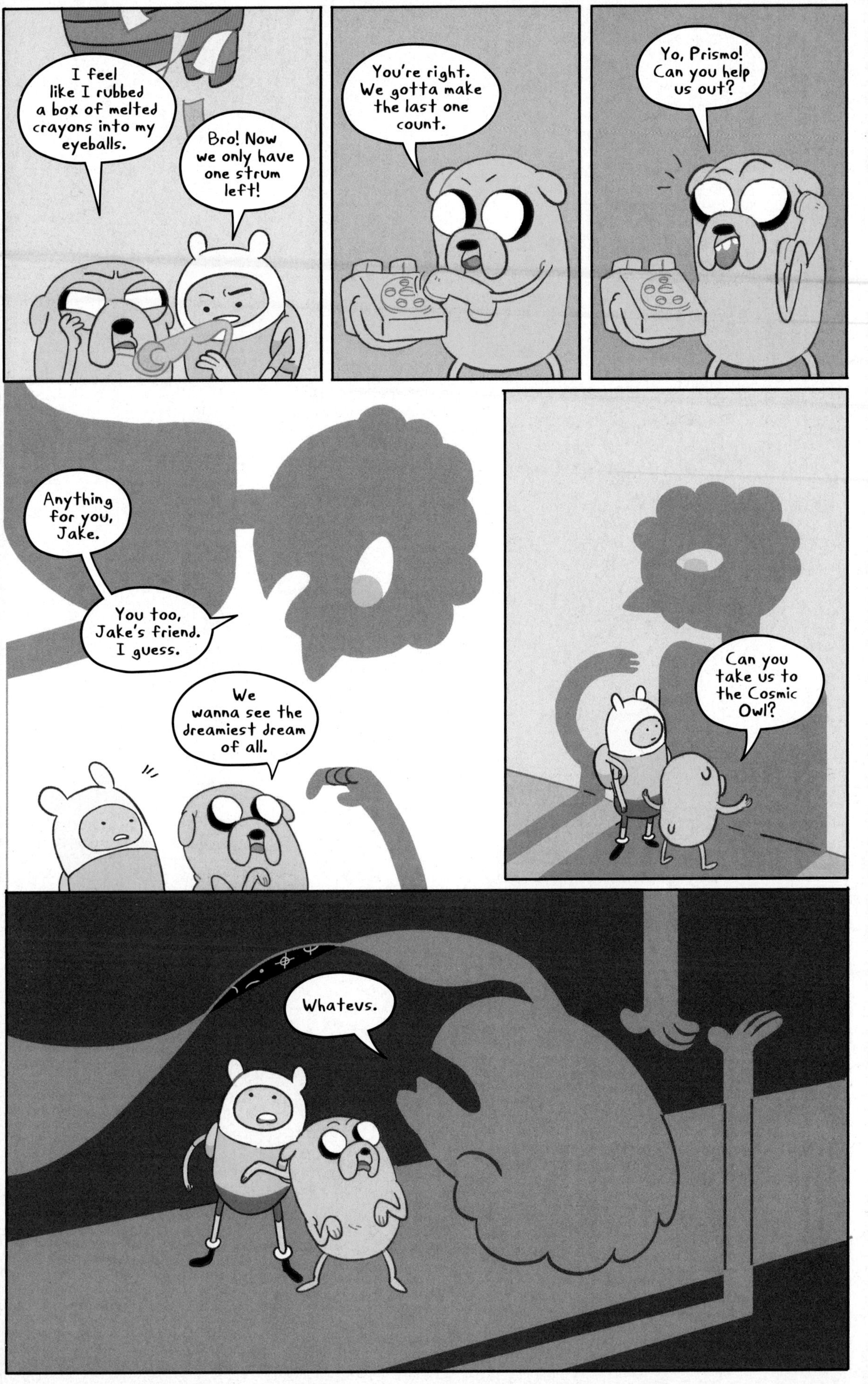
I feel like I rubbed a box of melted crayons into my eyeballs.
Bro! Now we only have one strum left!
You're right. We gotta make the last one count.
Yo, Prismo! Can you help us out?
Anything for you, Jake.
You too, Jake's friend. I guess.
We wanna see the dreamiest dream of all.
Can you take us to the Cosmic Owl?
Whatevs.

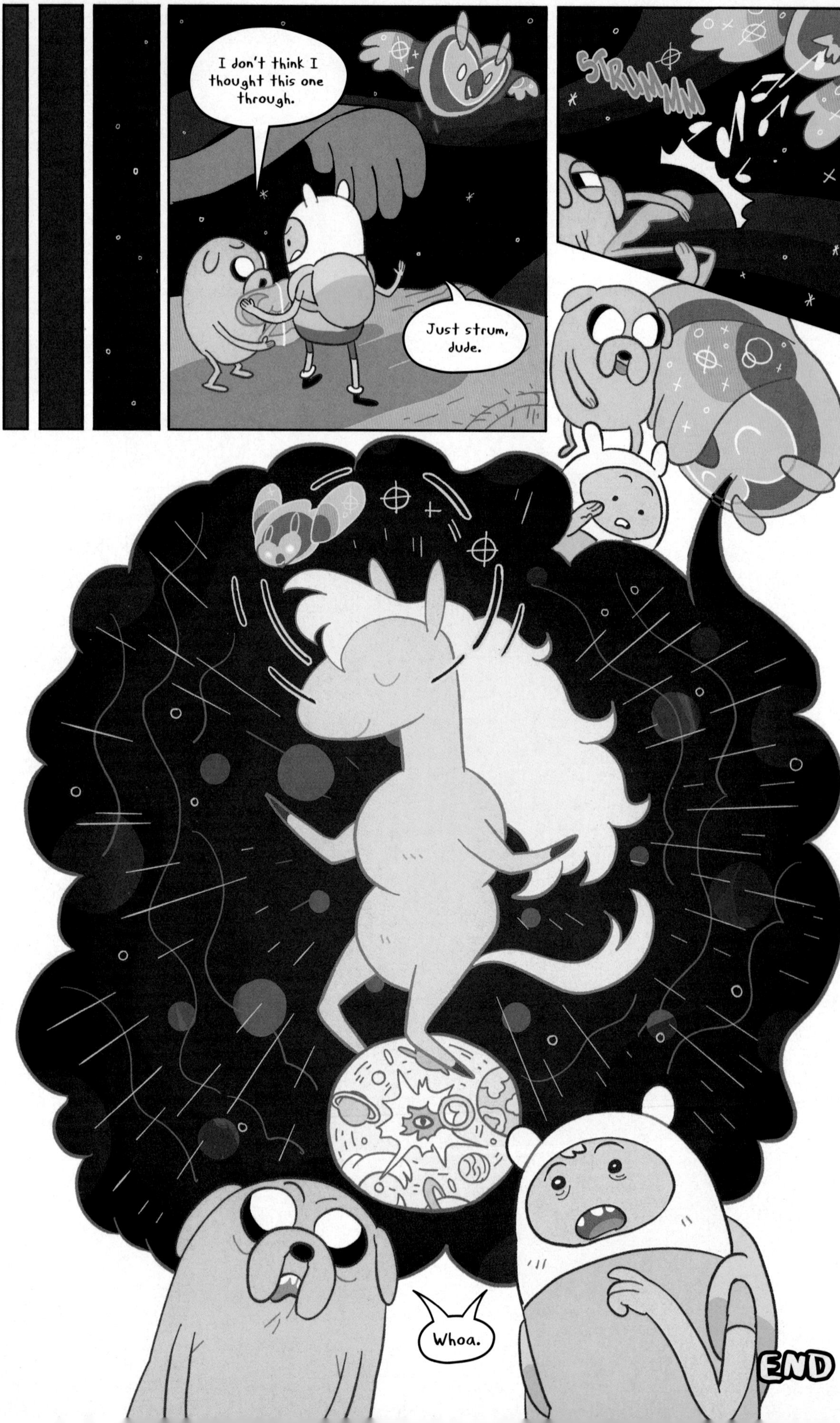
I don't think I thought this one through.
Just strum, dude.
STRUMMM
Whoa.
END

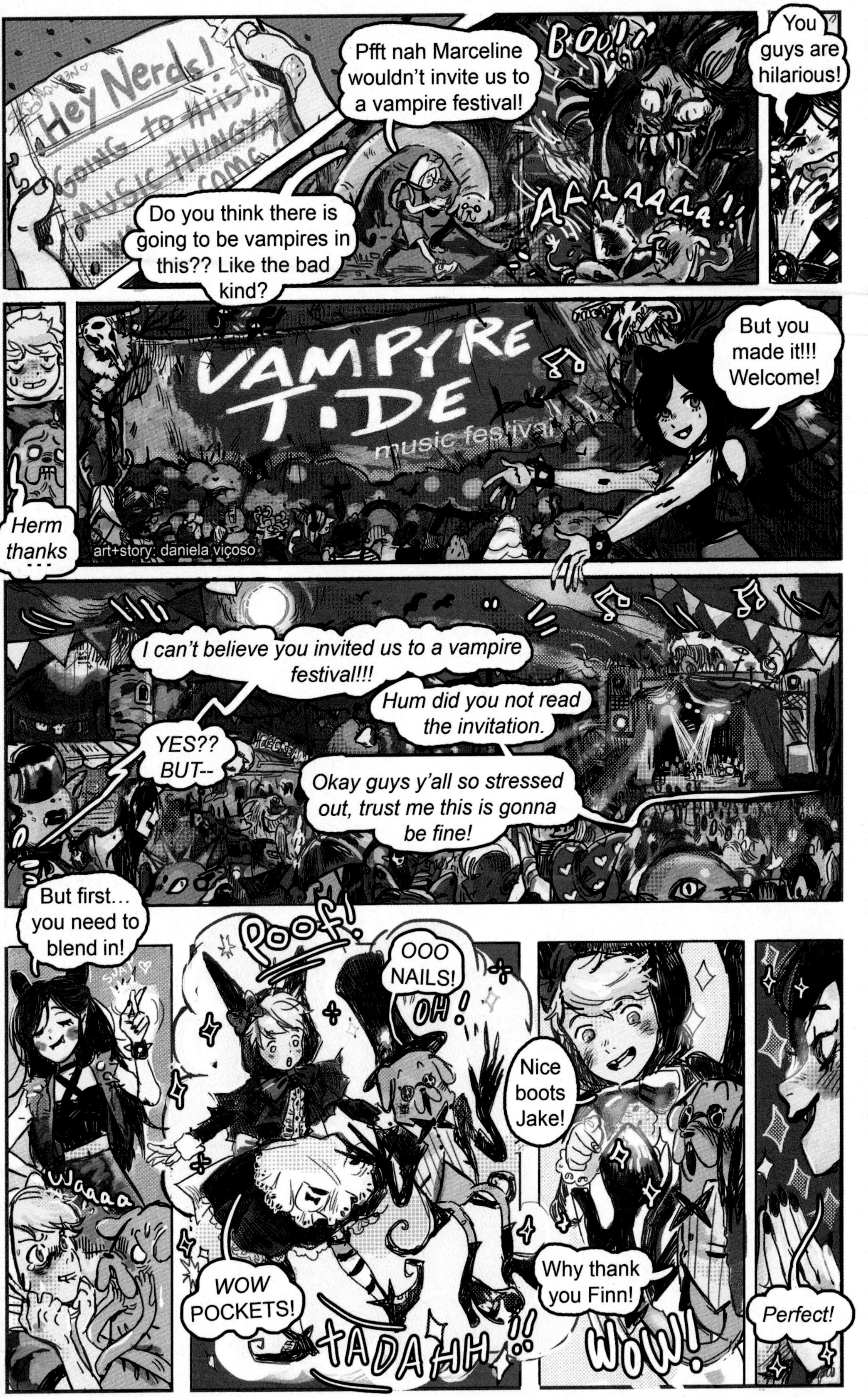
Hey Nerds!
GOING TO THIS MUSIC THING!! COME
Pfft nah Marceline wouldn't invite us to a vampire festival!
Do you think there is going to be vampires in this?? Like the bad kind?
BOO!!
AAAAAAA!!
You guys are hilarious!
VAMPYRE TIDE
music festival
But you made it!!! Welcome!
Herm thanks . . .
art+story: daniela viçoso
I can't believe you invited us to a vampire festival!!!
YES?? BUT--
Hum did you not read the invitation.
Okay guys y'all so stressed out, trust me this is gonna be fine!
But first… you need to blend in!
Waaaa
Poof!
OOO NAILS!
OH!
WOW POCKETS!
TADAHH!!
Nice boots Jake!
Why thank you Finn!
WOW!
Perfect!

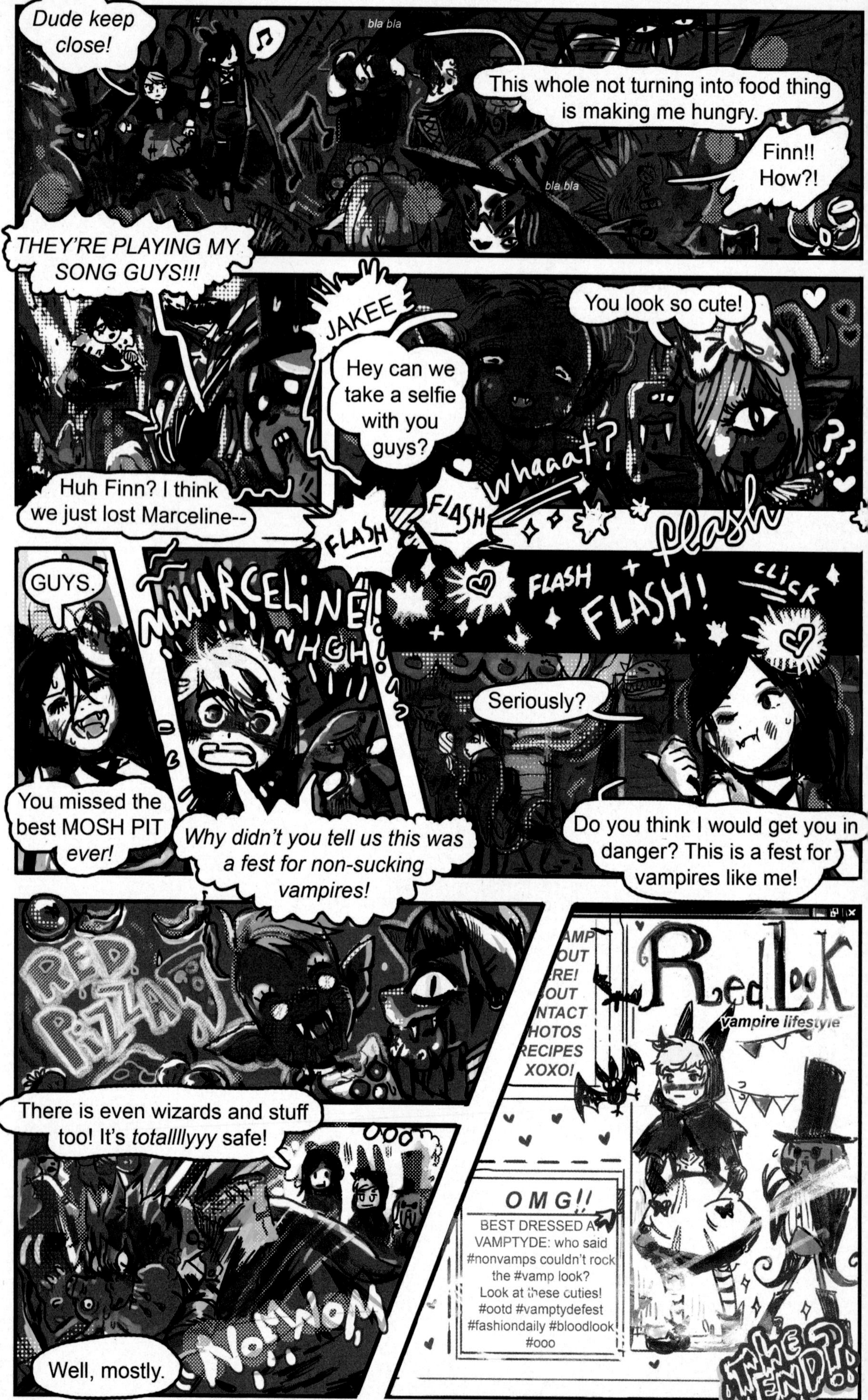
Dude keep close!
bla bla
This whole not turning into food thing is making me hungry.
Finn!! How?!
bla bla
THEY'RE PLAYING MY SONG GUYS!!!
JAKEE
Hey can we take a selfie with you guys?
You look so cute!
whaaat?
Huh Finn? I think we just lost Marceline--
FLASH
FLASH
flash
GUYS.
MAAARCELINE!
NHGH!
FLASH
FLASH!
CLICK
Seriously?
You missed the best MOSH PIT ever!
Why didn't you tell us this was a fest for non-sucking vampires!
Do you think I would get you in danger? This is a fest for vampires like me!
RED PIZZA
RedLook
vampire lifestyle
VAMP
OUT
RE!
OUT
NTACT
HOTOS
RECIPES
XOXO!
There is even wizards and stuff too! It's totallllyyy safe!
OOO
OMG!!
BEST DRESSED AT VAMPTYDE: who said #nonvamps couldn't rock the #vamp look? Look at these cuties! #ootd #vamptydefest #fashiondaily #bloodlook #ooo
Well, mostly.
NOM NOM
THE END?!

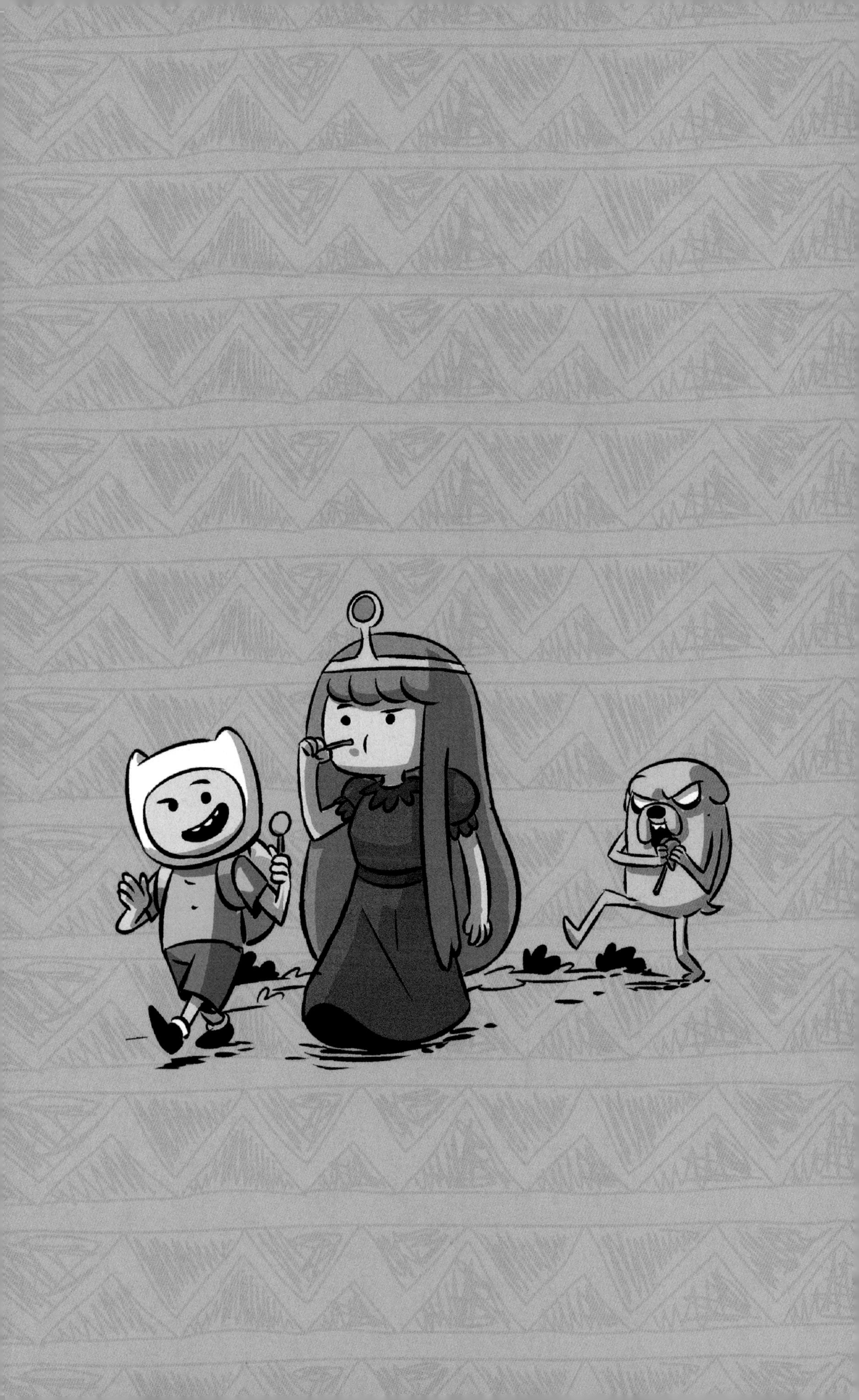

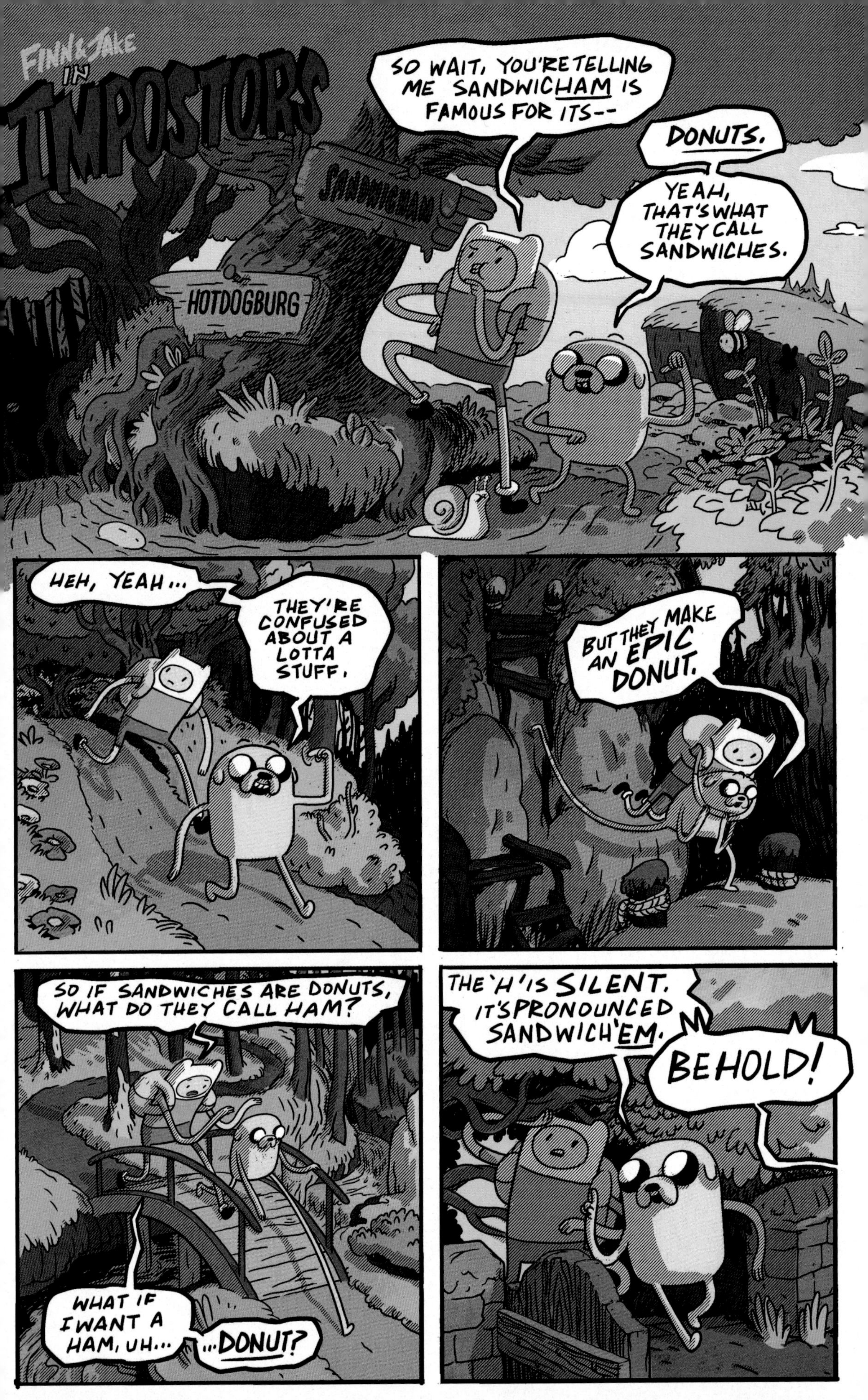
FINN & JAKE
IN
IMPOSTORS
SO WAIT, YOU'RE TELLING ME SANDWICHAM IS FAMOUS FOR ITS--
DONUTS.
YEAH, THAT'S WHAT THEY CALL SANDWICHES.
SANDWICHAM
HOTDOGBURG
HEH, YEAH...
THEY'RE CONFUSED ABOUT A LOTTA STUFF.
BUT THEY MAKE AN EPIC DONUT.
SO IF SANDWICHES ARE DONUTS, WHAT DO THEY CALL HAM?
WHAT IF I WANT A HAM, UH...
...DONUT?
THE 'H' IS SILENT. IT'S PRONOUNCED SANDWICH'EM.
BEHOLD!

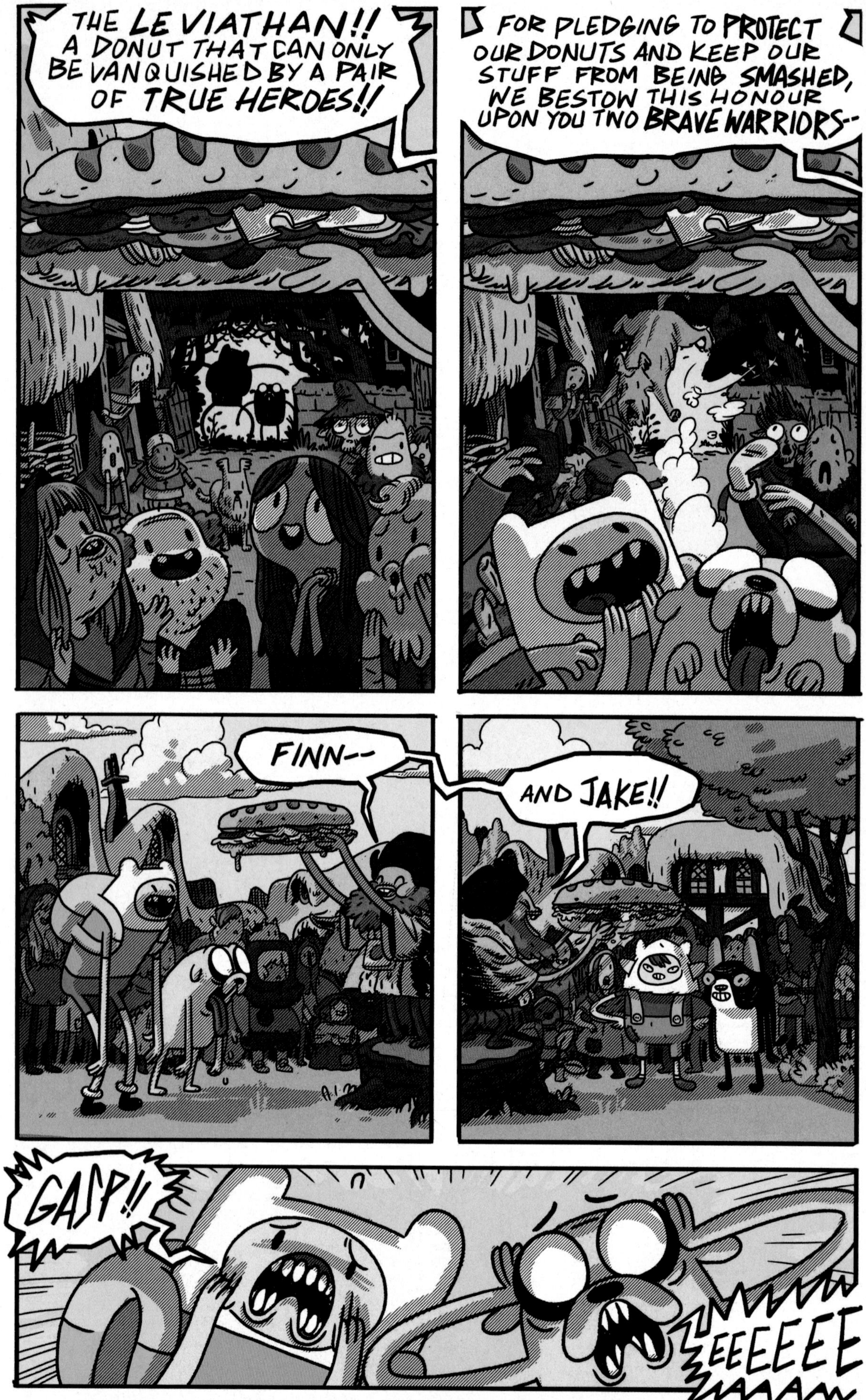
THE LEVIATHAN!! A DONUT THAT CAN ONLY BE VANQUISHED BY A PAIR OF TRUE HEROES!!
FOR PLEDGING TO PROTECT OUR DONUTS AND KEEP OUR STUFF FROM BEING SMASHED, WE BESTOW THIS HONOUR UPON YOU TWO BRAVE WARRIORS--
FINN--
AND JAKE!!
GASP!!
EEEEEE

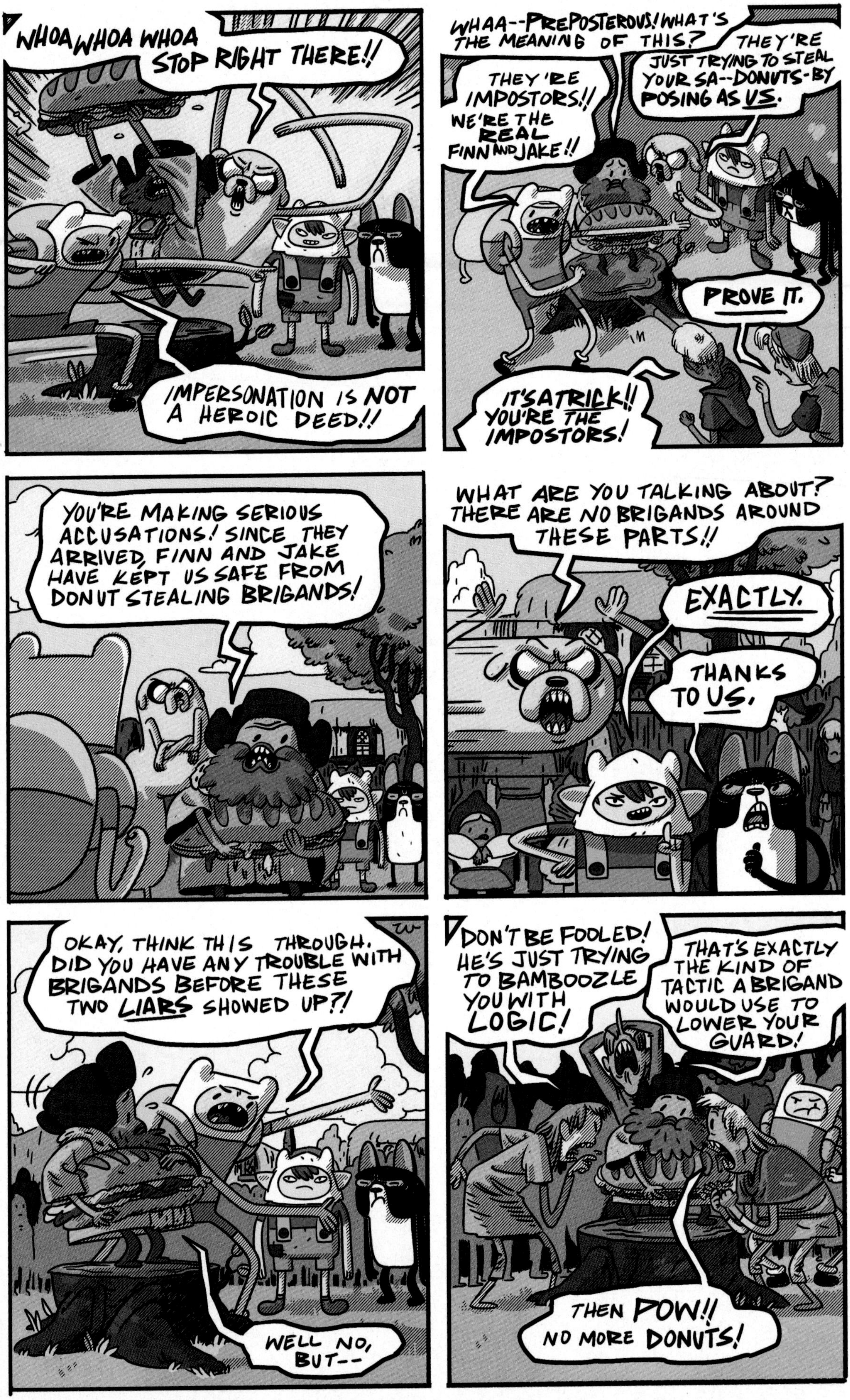
WHOA WHOA WHOA STOP RIGHT THERE!!
IMPERSONATION IS NOT A HEROIC DEED!!
WHAA--PREPOSTEROUS! WHAT'S THE MEANING OF THIS?
THEY'RE IMPOSTORS!! WE'RE THE REAL FINN AND JAKE!!
THEY'RE JUST TRYING TO STEAL YOUR SA--DONUTS-BY POSING AS US.
PROVE IT.
IT'S A TRICK!! YOU'RE THE IMPOSTORS!
YOU'RE MAKING SERIOUS ACCUSATIONS! SINCE THEY ARRIVED, FINN AND JAKE HAVE KEPT US SAFE FROM DONUT STEALING BRIGANDS!
WHAT ARE YOU TALKING ABOUT? THERE ARE NO BRIGANDS AROUND THESE PARTS!!
EXACTLY.
THANKS TO US.
OKAY, THINK THIS THROUGH. DID YOU HAVE ANY TROUBLE WITH BRIGANDS BEFORE THESE TWO LIARS SHOWED UP?!
WELL NO, BUT--
DON'T BE FOOLED! HE'S JUST TRYING TO BAMBOOZLE YOU WITH LOGIC!
THAT'S EXACTLY THE KIND OF TACTIC A BRIGAND WOULD USE TO LOWER YOUR GUARD!
THEN POW!! NO MORE DONUTS!

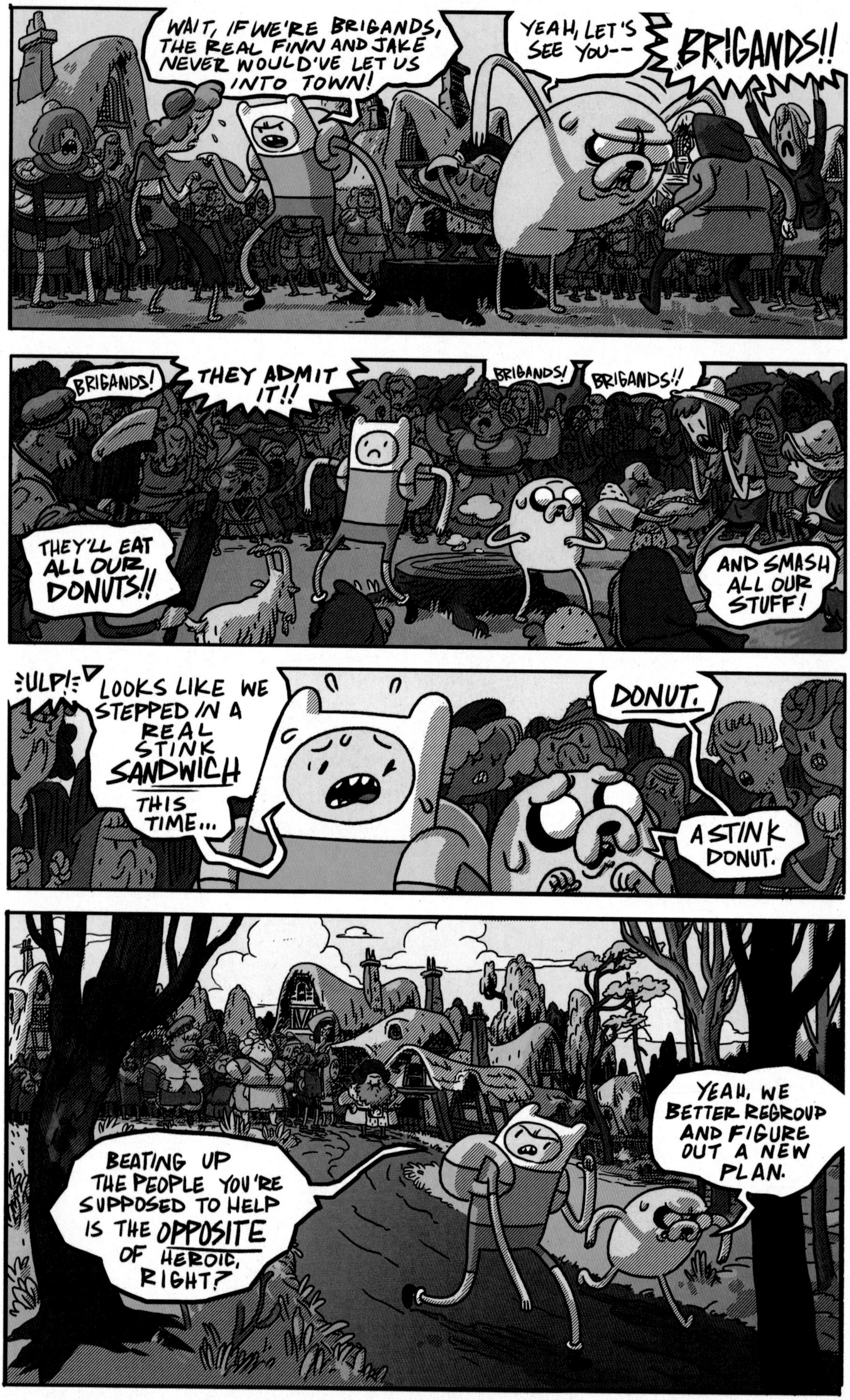

WAIT, IF WE'RE BRIGANDS, THE REAL FINN AND JAKE NEVER WOULD'VE LET US INTO TOWN!
YEAH, LET'S SEE YOU--
BRIGANDS!!
BRIGANDS!
THEY ADMIT IT!!
BRIGANDS!
BRIGANDS!!
THEY'LL EAT ALL OUR DONUTS!!
AND SMASH ALL OUR STUFF!
ULP!
LOOKS LIKE WE STEPPED IN A REAL STINK SANDWICH THIS TIME...
DONUT.
A STINK DONUT.
BEATING UP THE PEOPLE YOU'RE SUPPOSED TO HELP IS THE OPPOSITE OF HEROIC, RIGHT?
YEAH, WE BETTER REGROUP AND FIGURE OUT A NEW PLAN.

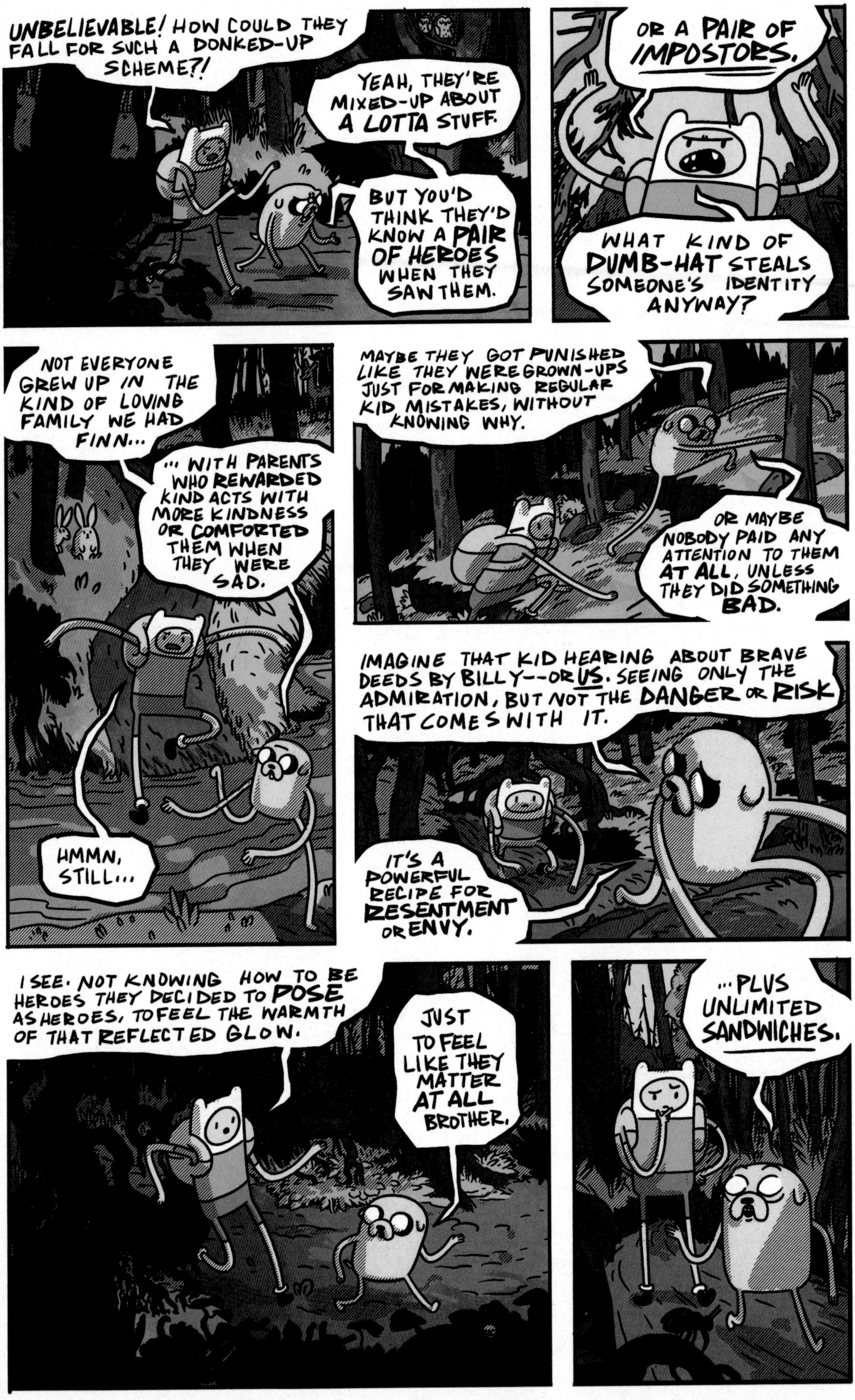
UNBELIEVABLE! HOW COULD THEY FALL FOR SUCH A DONKED-UP SCHEME?!
YEAH, THEY'RE MIXED-UP ABOUT A LOTTA STUFF.
BUT YOU'D THINK THEY'D KNOW A PAIR OF HEROES WHEN THEY SAW THEM.
OR A PAIR OF IMPOSTORS.
WHAT KIND OF DUMB-HAT STEALS SOMEONE'S IDENTITY ANYWAY?
NOT EVERYONE GREW UP IN THE KIND OF LOVING FAMILY WE HAD FINN...
...WITH PARENTS WHO REWARDED KIND ACTS WITH MORE KINDNESS OR COMFORTED THEM WHEN THEY WERE SAD.
HMMN, STILL...
MAYBE THEY GOT PUNISHED LIKE THEY WERE GROWN-UPS JUST FOR MAKING REGULAR KID MISTAKES, WITHOUT KNOWING WHY.
OR MAYBE NOBODY PAID ANY ATTENTION TO THEM AT ALL, UNLESS THEY DID SOMETHING BAD.
IMAGINE THAT KID HEARING ABOUT BRAVE DEEDS BY BILLY--OR US. SEEING ONLY THE ADMIRATION, BUT NOT THE DANGER OR RISK THAT COMES WITH IT.
IT'S A POWERFUL RECIPE FOR RESENTMENT OR ENVY.
I SEE. NOT KNOWING HOW TO BE HEROES THEY DECIDED TO POSE AS HEROES, TO FEEL THE WARMTH OF THAT REFLECTED GLOW.
JUST TO FEEL LIKE THEY MATTER AT ALL BROTHER.
...PLUS UNLIMITED SANDWICHES.

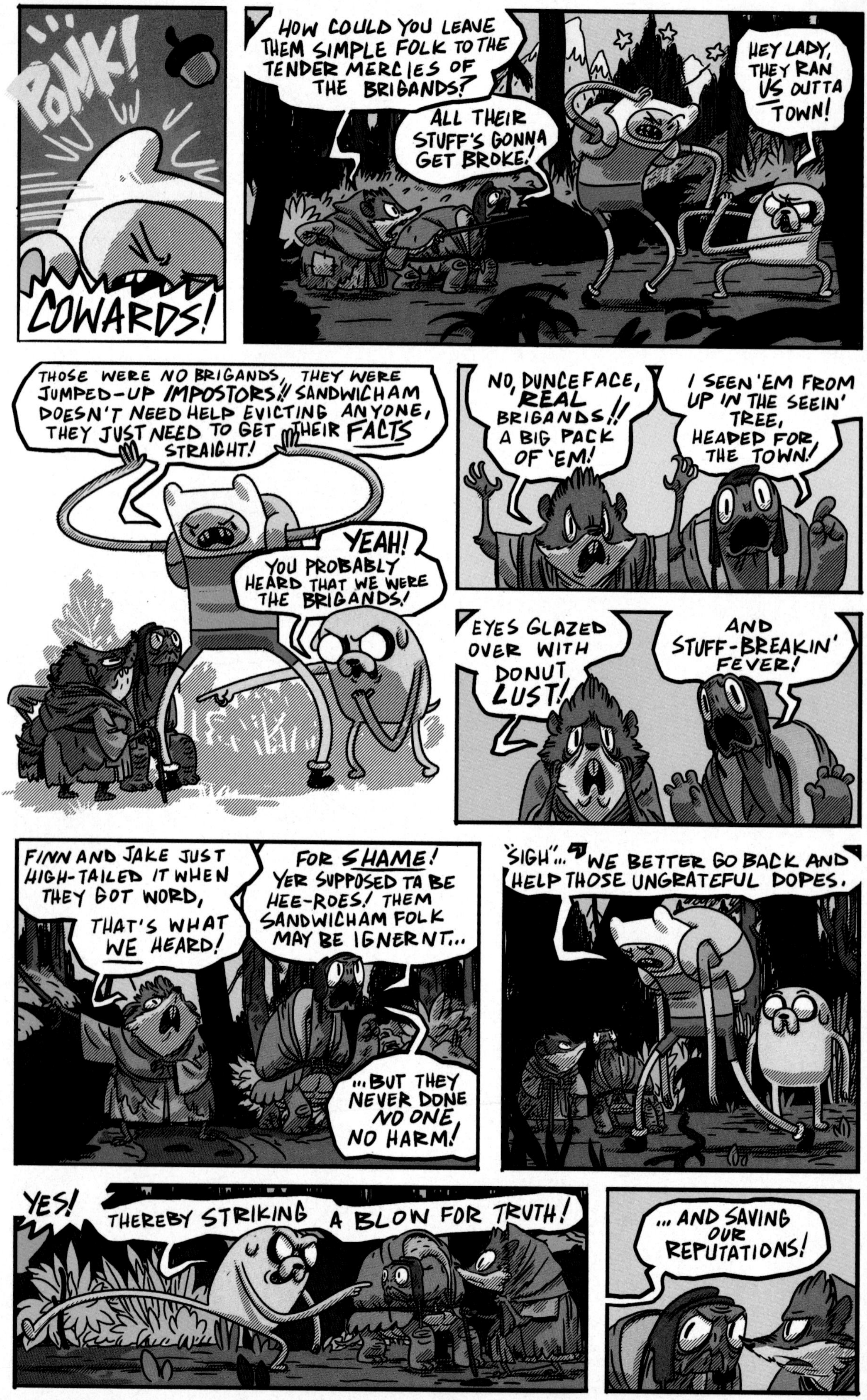
PONK!
COWARDS!
HOW COULD YOU LEAVE THEM SIMPLE FOLK TO THE TENDER MERCIES OF THE BRIGANDS?
ALL THEIR STUFF'S GONNA GET BROKE!
HEY LADY, THEY RAN US OUTTA TOWN!
THOSE WERE NO BRIGANDS, THEY WERE JUMPED-UP IMPOSTORS!! SANDWICHAM DOESN'T NEED HELP EVICTING ANYONE, THEY JUST NEED TO GET THEIR FACTS STRAIGHT!
YEAH! YOU PROBABLY HEARD THAT WE WERE THE BRIGANDS!
NO, DUNCEFACE, REAL BRIGANDS!! A BIG PACK OF 'EM!
I SEEN 'EM FROM UP IN THE SEEIN' TREE, HEADED FOR THE TOWN!
EYES GLAZED OVER WITH DONUT LUST!
AND STUFF-BREAKIN' FEVER!
FINN AND JAKE JUST HIGH-TAILED IT WHEN THEY GOT WORD,
THAT'S WHAT WE HEARD!
FOR SHAME! YER SUPPOSED TA BE HEE-ROES! THEM SANDWICHAM FOLK MAY BE IGNERNT...
...BUT THEY NEVER DONE NO ONE NO HARM!
"SIGH"... WE BETTER GO BACK AND HELP THOSE UNGRATEFUL DOPES.
YES!
THEREBY STRIKING A BLOW FOR TRUTH!
...AND SAVING OUR REPUTATIONS!

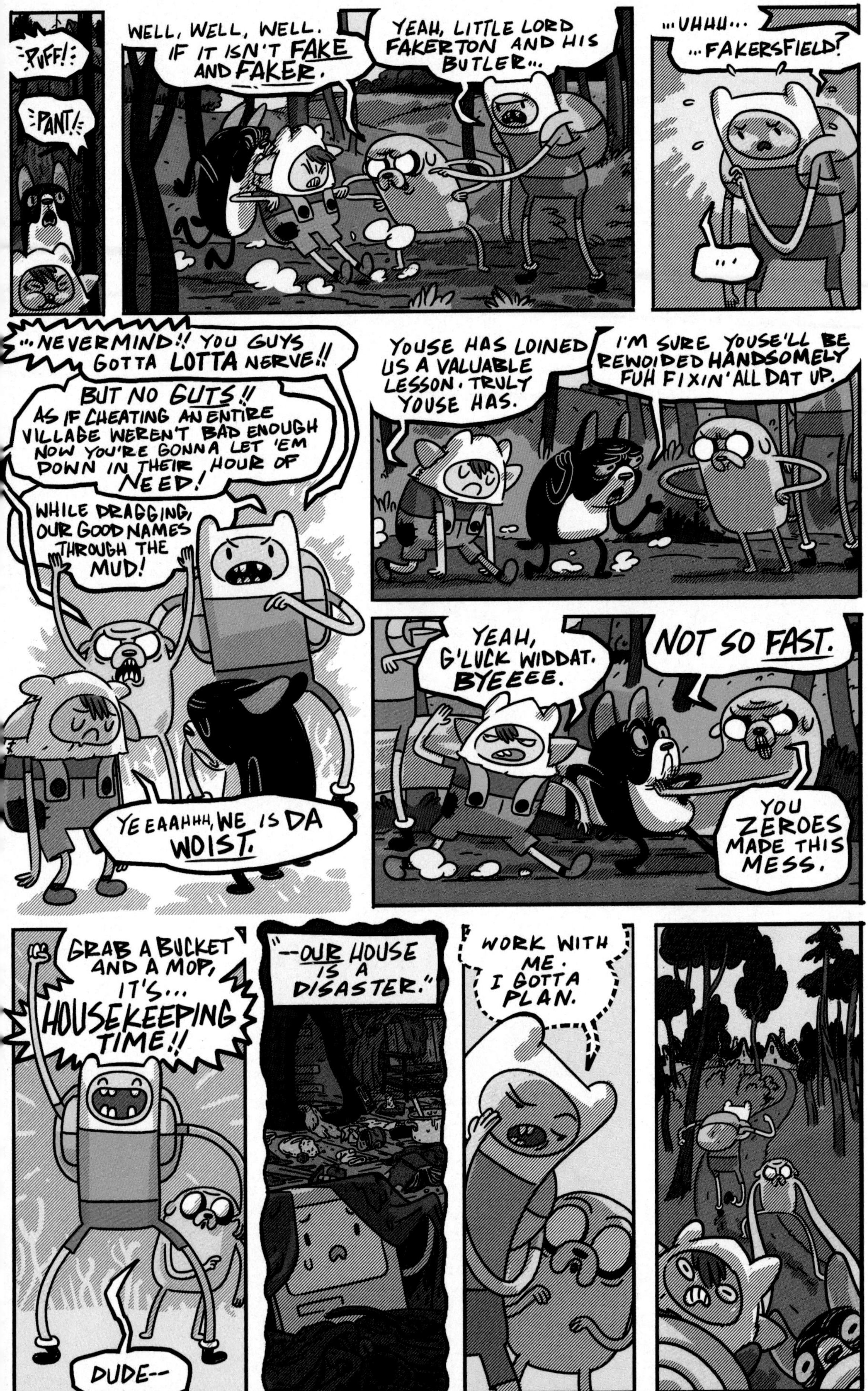
PUFF!
PANT!
WELL, WELL, WELL. IF IT ISN'T FAKE AND FAKER.
YEAH, LITTLE LORD FAKERTON AND HIS BUTLER...
...UHHH... ...FAKERSFIELD?
...
...NEVERMIND!! YOU GUYS GOTTA LOTTA NERVE!!
BUT NO GUTS!! AS IF CHEATING AN ENTIRE VILLAGE WEREN'T BAD ENOUGH NOW YOU'RE GONNA LET 'EM DOWN IN THEIR HOUR OF NEED!
WHILE DRAGGING OUR GOOD NAMES THROUGH THE MUD!
YEEAAHHH, WE IS DA WOIST.
YOUSE HAS LOINED US A VALUABLE LESSON. TRULY YOUSE HAS.
I'M SURE YOUSE'LL BE REWOIDED HANDSOMELY FUH FIXIN' ALL DAT UP.
YEAH, G'LUCK WIDDAT. BYEEEEE.
NOT SO FAST.
YOU ZEROES MADE THIS MESS.
GRAB A BUCKET AND A MOP, IT'S... HOUSEKEEPING TIME!!
DUDE--
"--OUR HOUSE IS A DISASTER."
WORK WITH ME. I GOTTA PLAN.

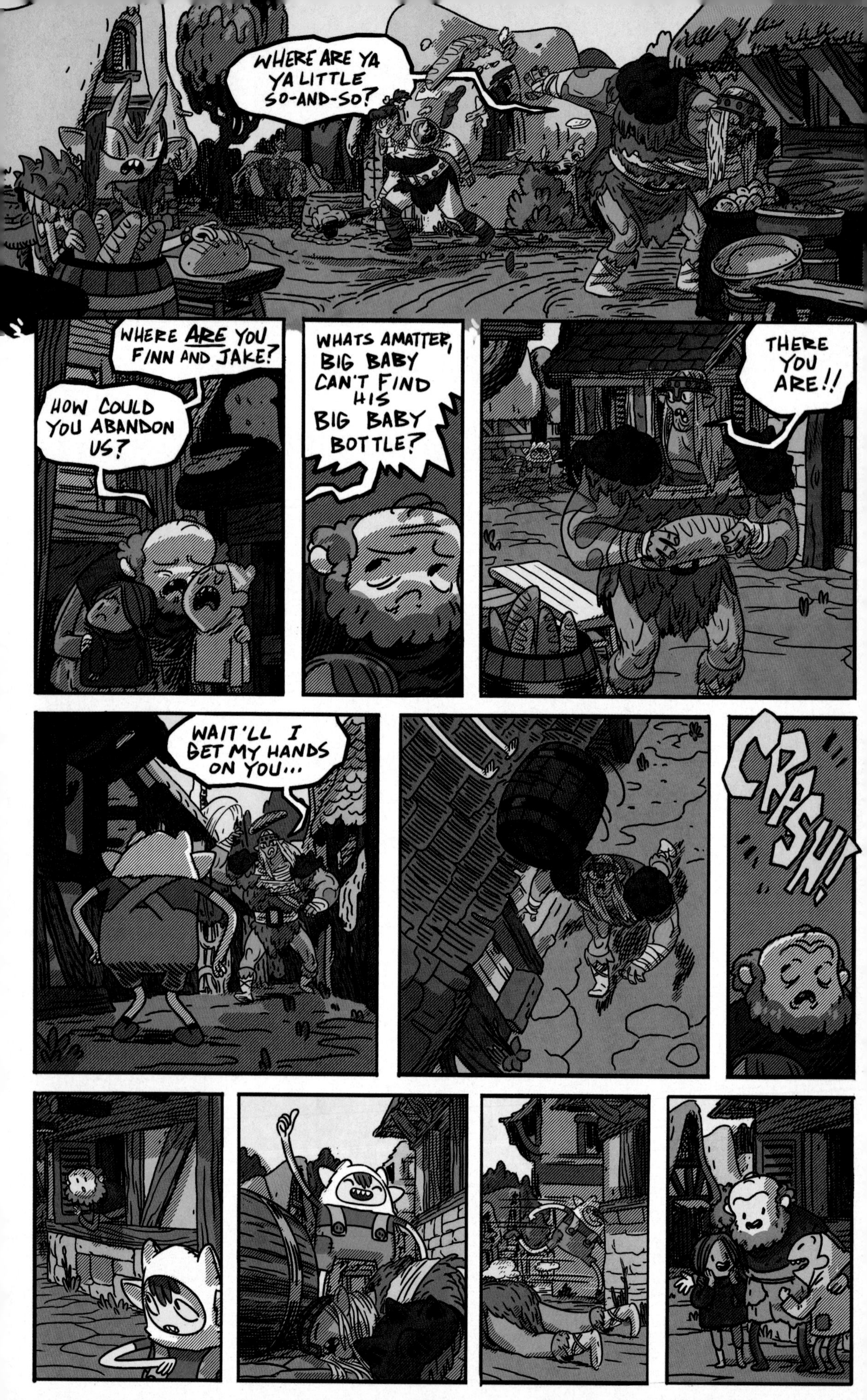
WHERE ARE YA YA LITTLE SO-AND-SO?
WHERE ARE YOU FINN AND JAKE?
HOW COULD YOU ABANDON US?
WHATS AMATTER, BIG BABY CAN'T FIND HIS BIG BABY BOTTLE?
THERE YOU ARE!!
WAIT'LL I GET MY HANDS ON YOU...
CRASH!

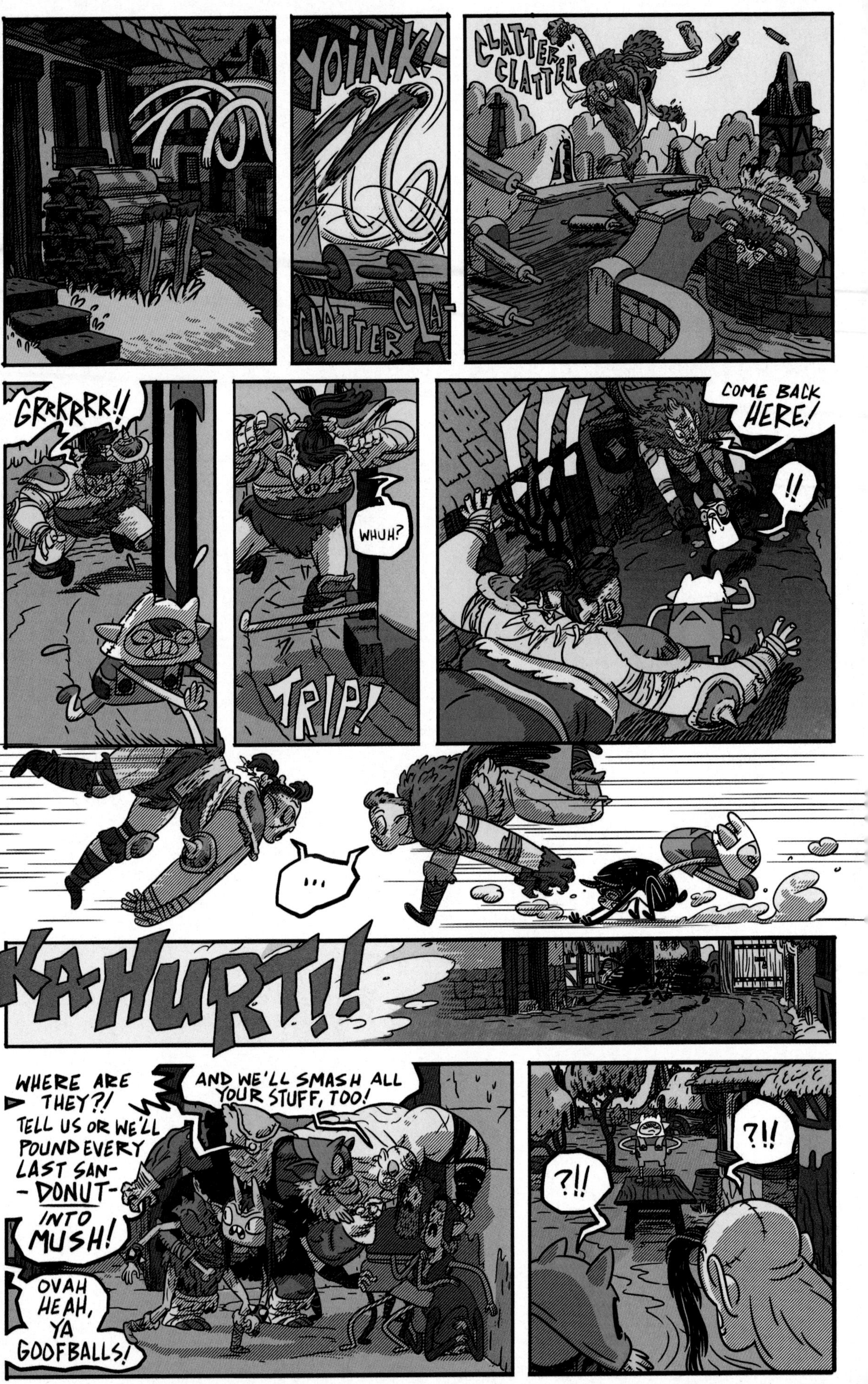
YOINK!
CLATTER CLA-
CLATTER CLATTER
GRRRRRR!!
WHUH?
TRIP!
!!!
COME BACK HERE!
!!
...
KAHURT!!
WHERE ARE THEY?! TELL US OR WE'LL POUND EVERY LAST SAN- - DONUT- INTO MUSH!
AND WE'LL SMASH ALL YOUR STUFF, TOO!
OVAH HEAH, YA GOOFBALLS!
?!!
?!!

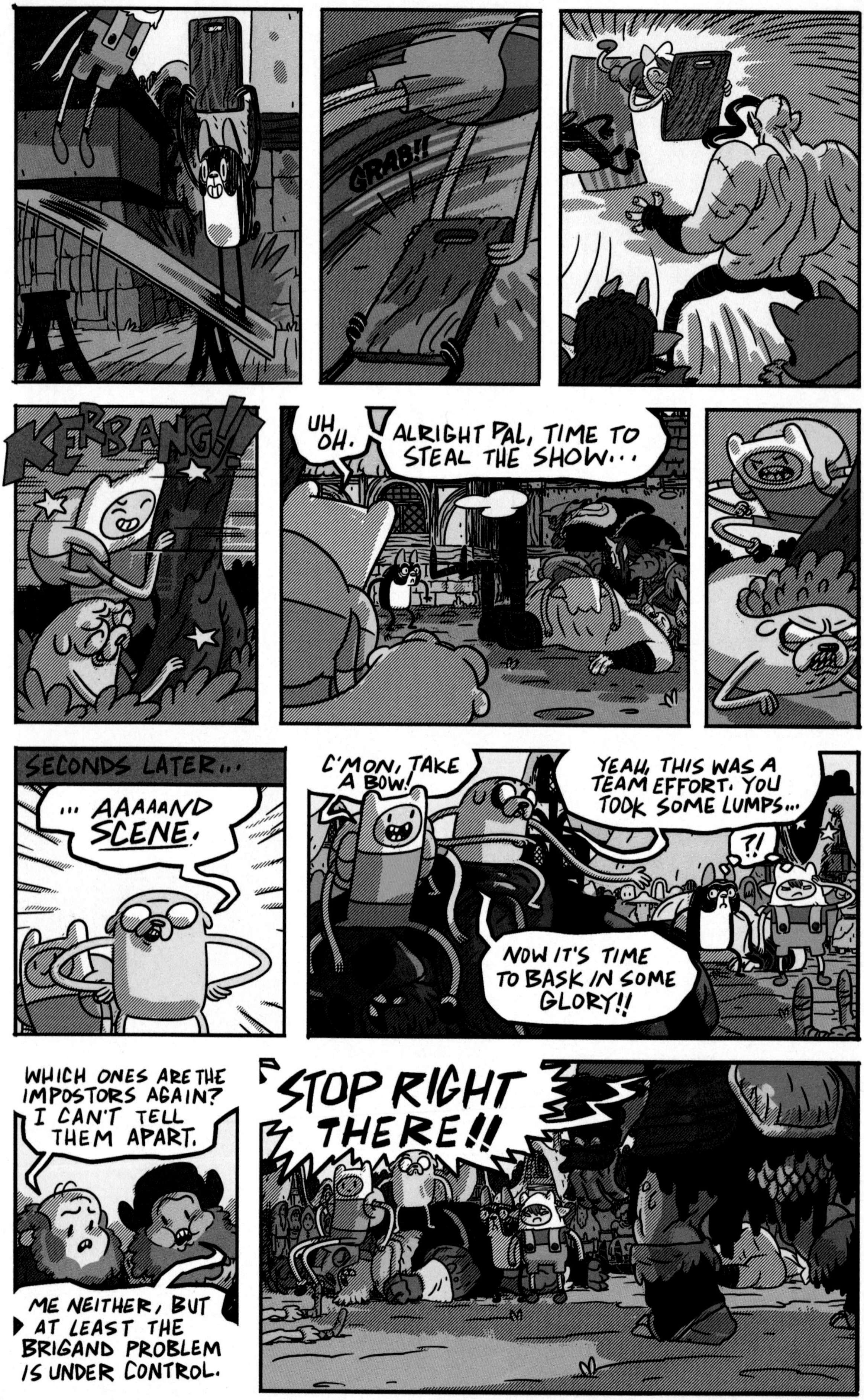
GRAB!!
KERBANG!!
UH OH.
ALRIGHT PAL, TIME TO STEAL THE SHOW...
SECONDS LATER...
... AAAAAND SCENE.
C'MON, TAKE A BOW!
YEAH, THIS WAS A TEAM EFFORT. YOU TOOK SOME LUMPS...
?!
NOW IT'S TIME TO BASK IN SOME GLORY!!
WHICH ONES ARE THE IMPOSTORS AGAIN? I CAN'T TELL THEM APART.
ME NEITHER, BUT AT LEAST THE BRIGAND PROBLEM IS UNDER CONTROL.
STOP RIGHT THERE!!

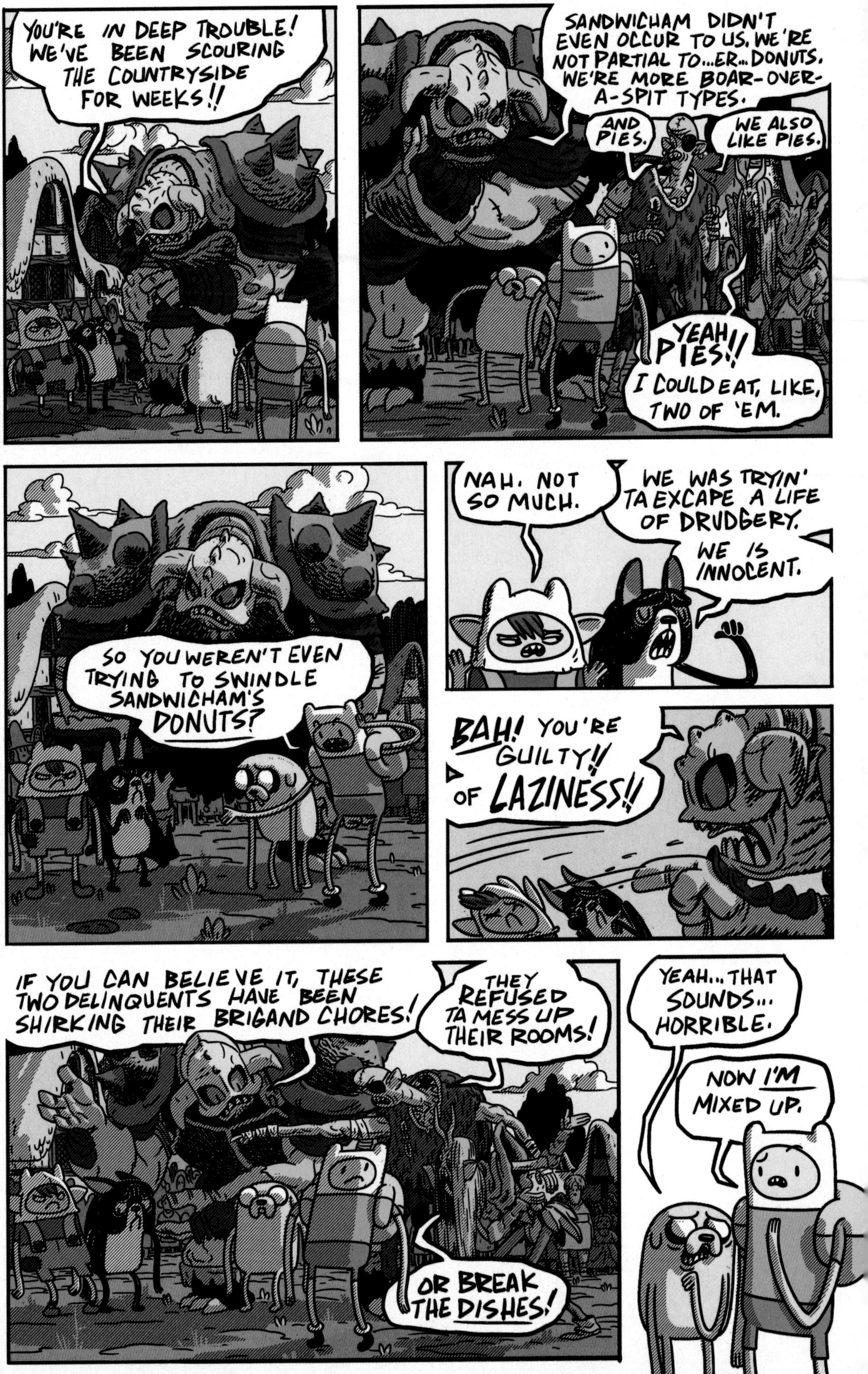
YOU'RE IN DEEP TROUBLE! WE'VE BEEN SCOURING THE COUNTRYSIDE FOR WEEKS!!
SANDWICHAM DIDN'T EVEN OCCUR TO US. WE'RE NOT PARTIAL TO...ER...DONUTS. WE'RE MORE BOAR-OVER-A-SPIT TYPES.
AND PIES.
WE ALSO LIKE PIES.
YEAH PIES!! I COULD EAT, LIKE, TWO OF 'EM.
SO YOU WEREN'T EVEN TRYING TO SWINDLE SANDWICHAM'S DONUTS?
NAH. NOT SO MUCH.
WE WAS TRYIN' TA EXCAPE A LIFE OF DRUDGERY.
WE IS INNOCENT.
BAH! YOU'RE GUILTY!! OF LAZINESS!!
IF YOU CAN BELIEVE IT, THESE TWO DELINQUENTS HAVE BEEN SHIRKING THEIR BRIGAND CHORES!
THEY REFUSED TA MESS UP THEIR ROOMS!
OR BREAK THE DISHES!
YEAH... THAT SOUNDS... HORRIBLE.
NOW I'M MIXED UP.

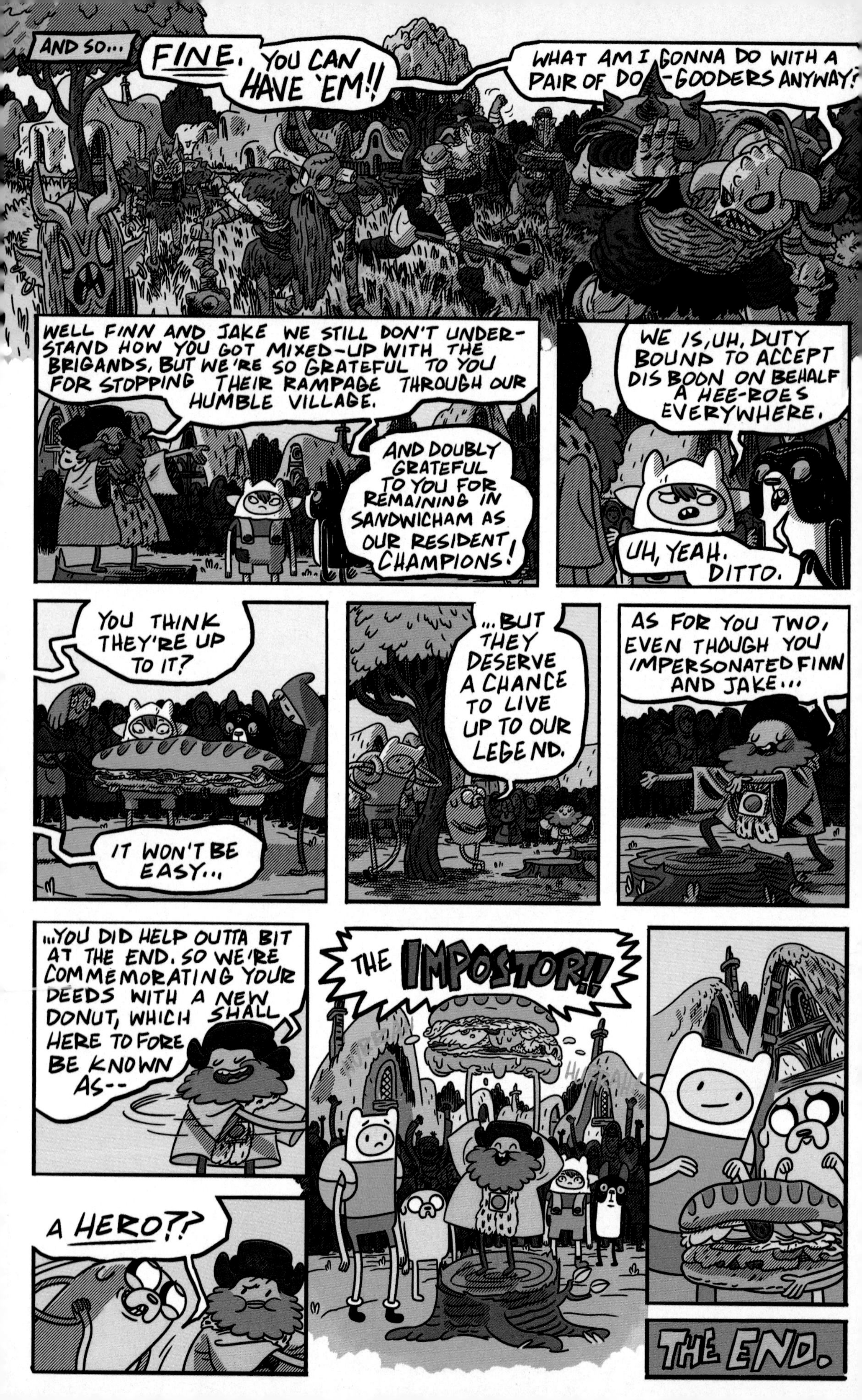
AND SO...
FINE. YOU CAN HAVE 'EM!!
WHAT AM I GONNA DO WITH A PAIR OF DO-GOODERS ANYWAY?
WELL FINN AND JAKE WE STILL DON'T UNDERSTAND HOW YOU GOT MIXED-UP WITH THE BRIGANDS, BUT WE'RE SO GRATEFUL TO YOU FOR STOPPING THEIR RAMPAGE THROUGH OUR HUMBLE VILLAGE.
AND DOUBLY GRATEFUL TO YOU FOR REMAINING IN SANDWICHAM AS OUR RESIDENT CHAMPIONS!
WE IS, UH, DUTY BOUND TO ACCEPT DIS BOON ON BEHALF A HEE-ROES EVERYWHERE.
UH, YEAH. DITTO.
YOU THINK THEY'RE UP TO IT?
IT WON'T BE EASY...
...BUT THEY DESERVE A CHANCE TO LIVE UP TO OUR LEGEND.
AS FOR YOU TWO, EVEN THOUGH YOU IMPERSONATED FINN AND JAKE...
...YOU DID HELP OUTTA BIT AT THE END. SO WE'RE COMMEMORATING YOUR DEEDS WITH A NEW DONUT, WHICH SHALL HERE TO FORE BE KNOWN AS--
A HERO??
THE IMPOSTOR!!
HURRAH!
HURRAH!
THE END.

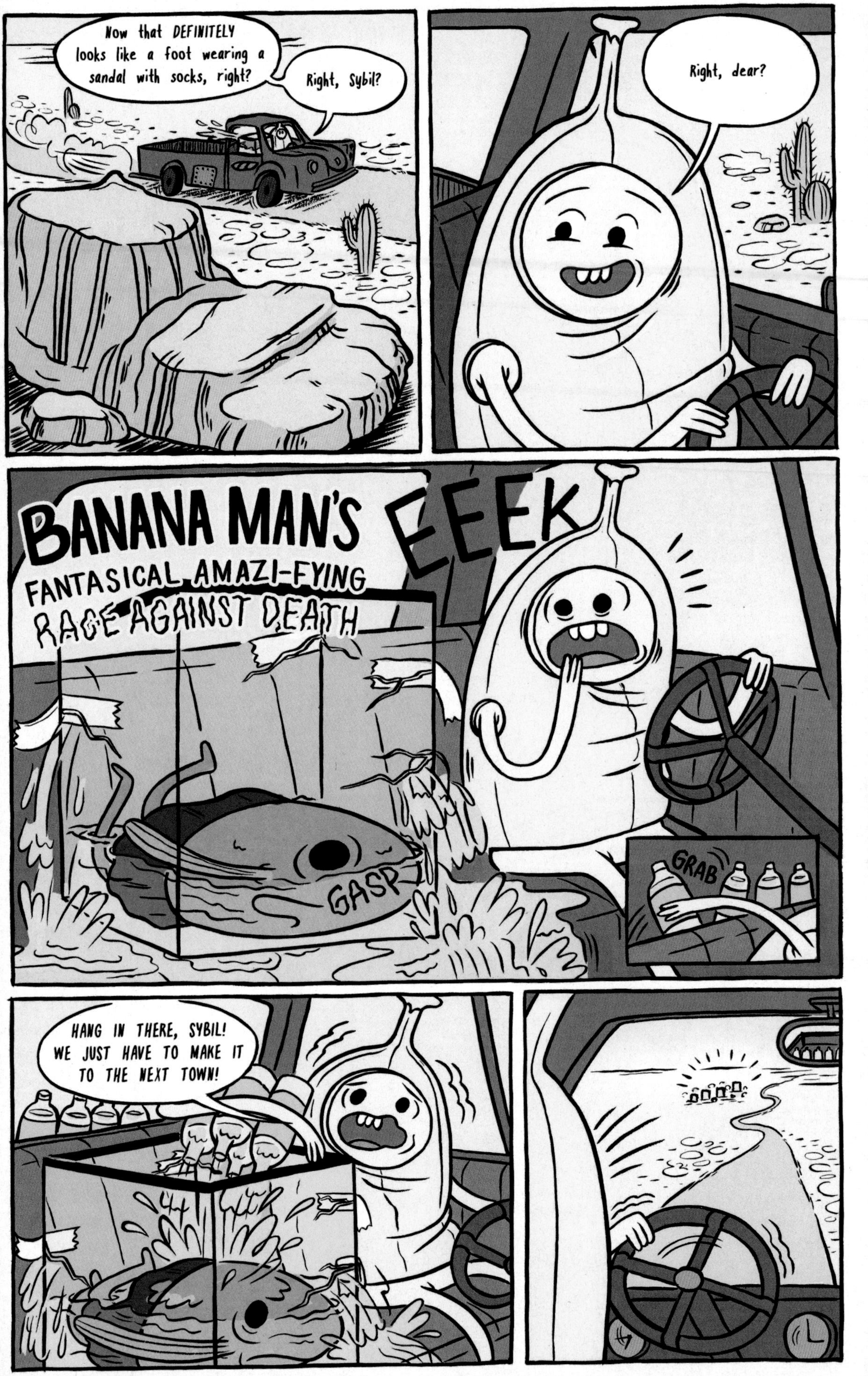
Now that DEFINITELY looks like a foot wearing a sandal with socks, right?
Right, Sybil?
Right, dear?
BANANA MAN'S
FANTASICAL AMAZI-FYING
RAGE AGAINST DEATH
EEEK
GASP
GRAB
HANG IN THERE, SYBIL! WE JUST HAVE TO MAKE IT TO THE NEXT TOWN!

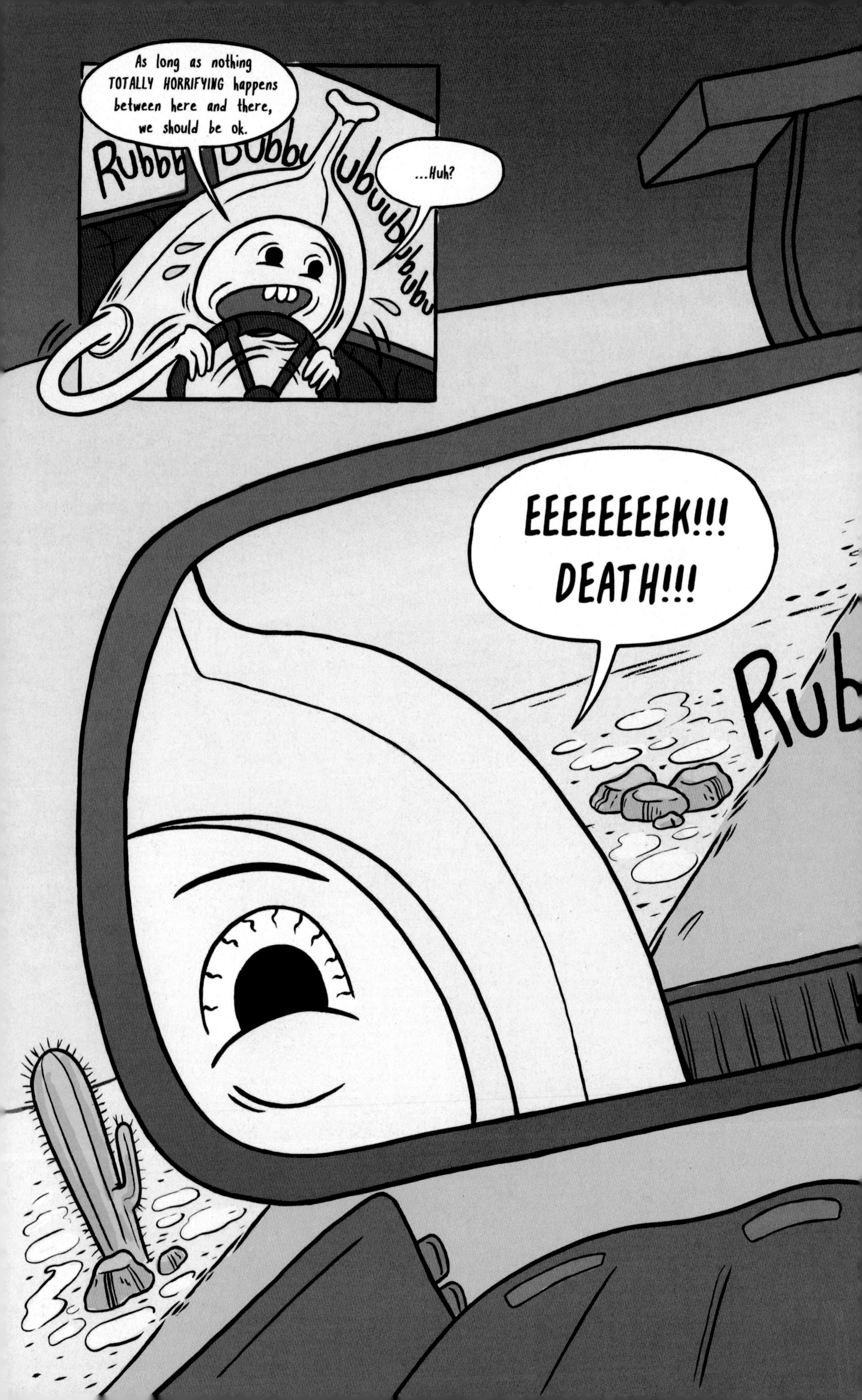
As long as nothing TOTALLY HORRIFYING happens between here and there, we should be ok.
Rubbb bubbu ubuub ubbubu
...Huh?
EEEEEEEEK!!! DEATH!!!
Rub

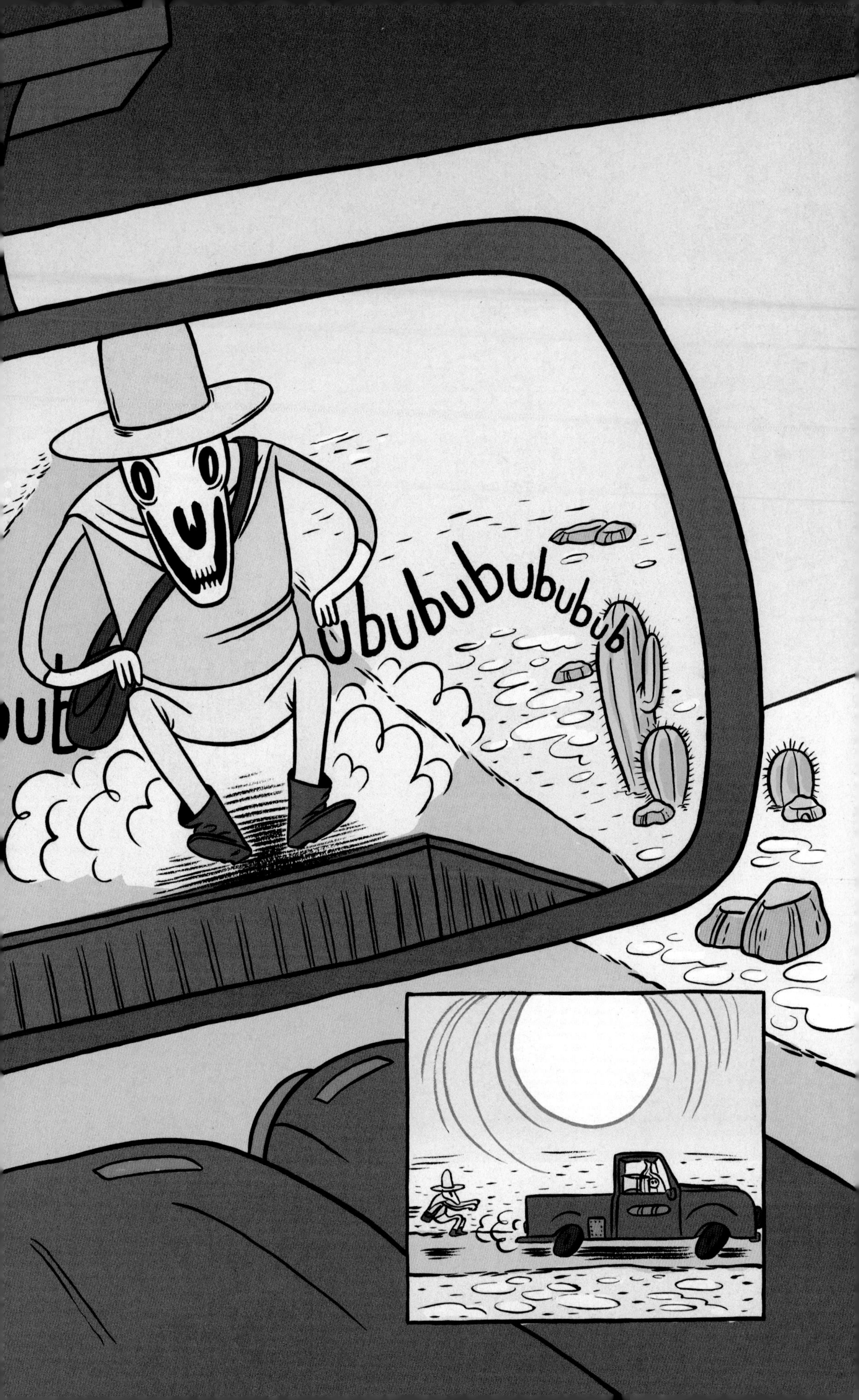
ububububububub
ub

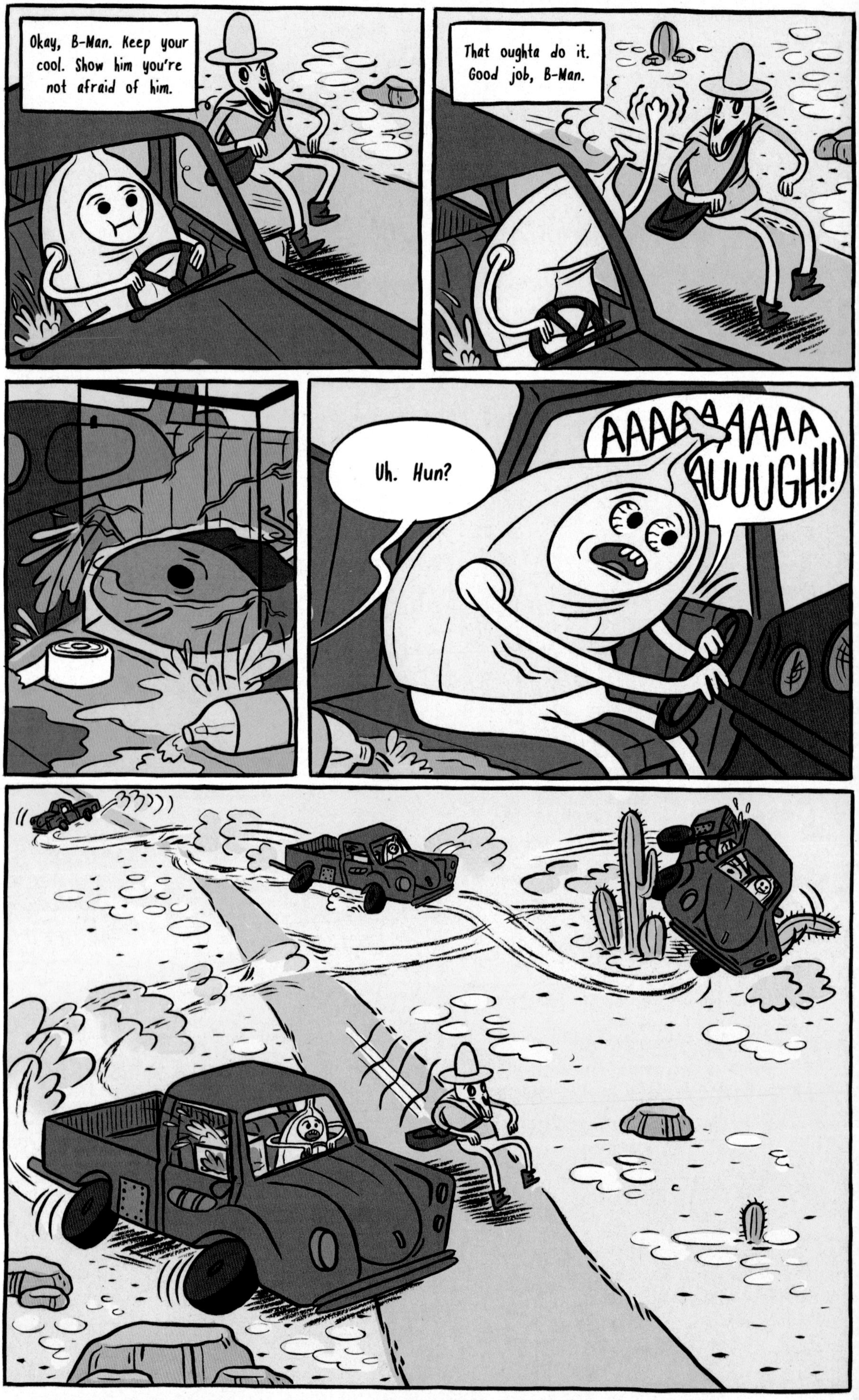
Okay, B-Man. Keep your cool. Show him you're not afraid of him.
That oughta do it. Good job, B-Man.
Uh. Hun?
AAAAAAAAA AUUUGH!!

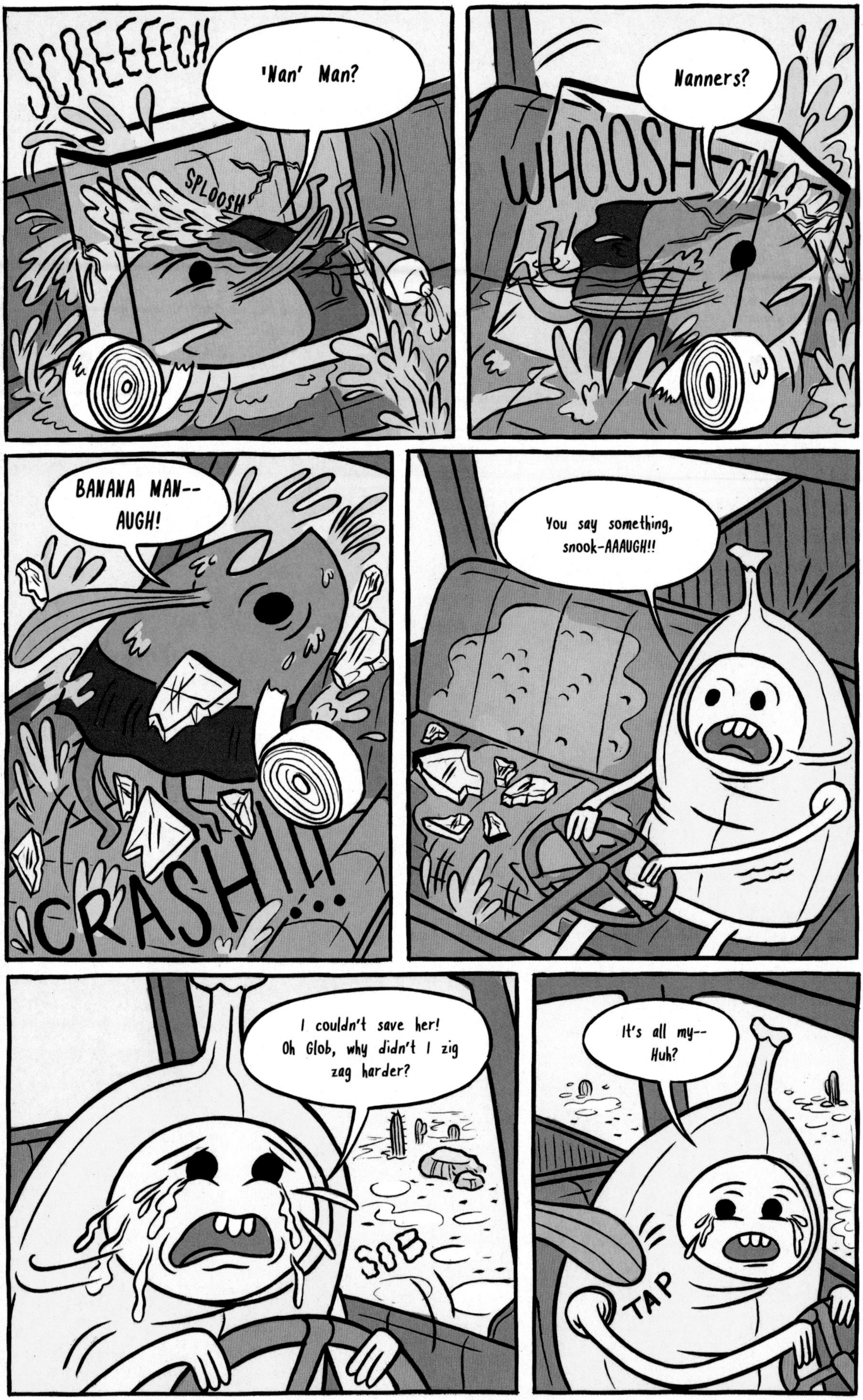
SCREEEECH
'Nan' Man?
SPLOOSH
Nanners?
WHOOSH
BANANA MAN--
AUGH!
CRASH!!!...
You say something, snook-AAAUGH!!
I couldn't save her! Oh Glob, why didn't I zig zag harder?
SOB
It's all my-- Huh?
TAP

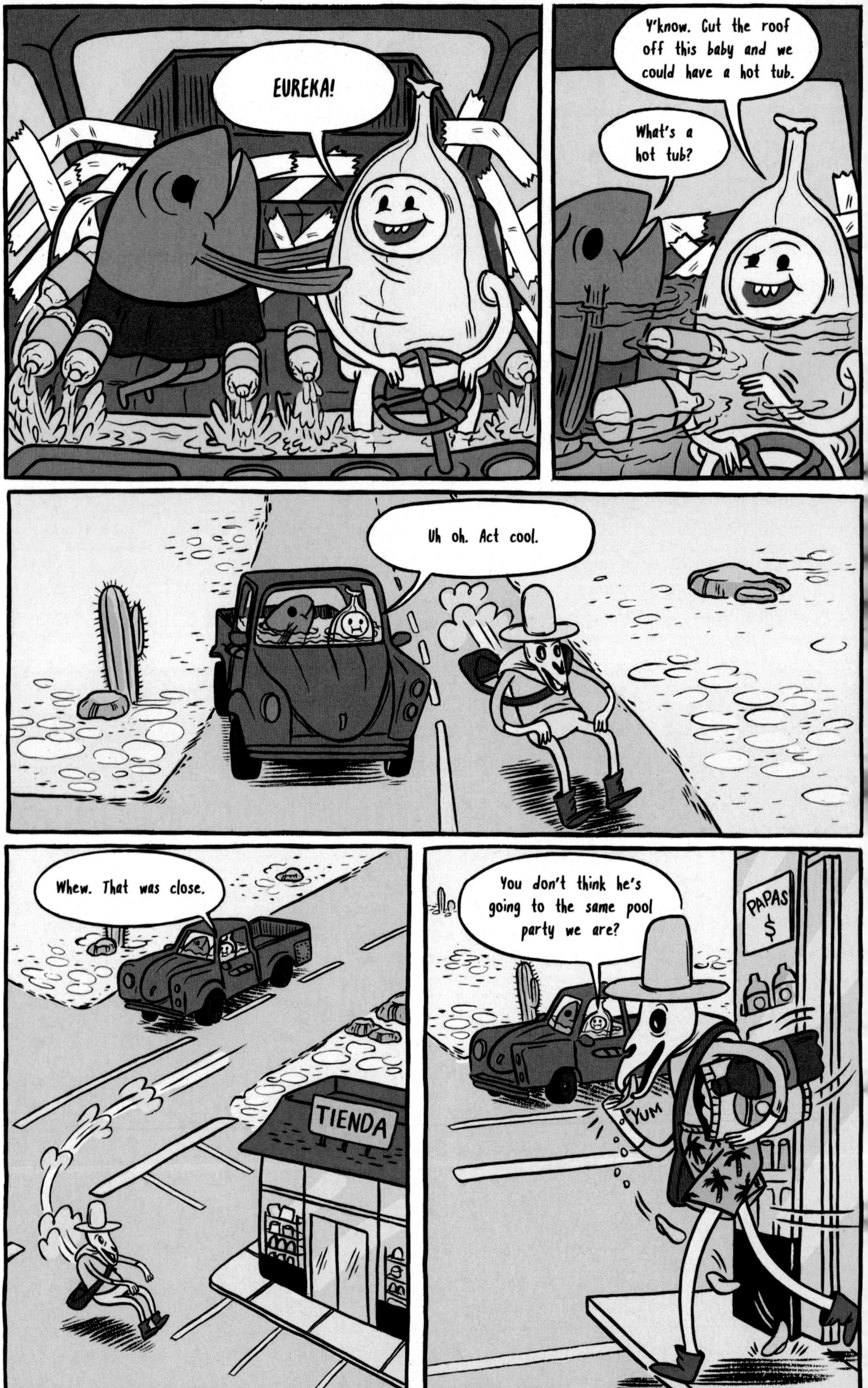
EUREKA!
Y'know. Cut the roof off this baby and we could have a hot tub.
What's a hot tub?
Uh oh. Act cool.
Whew. That was close.
TIENDA
You don't think he's going to the same pool party we are?
PAPAS $
YUM

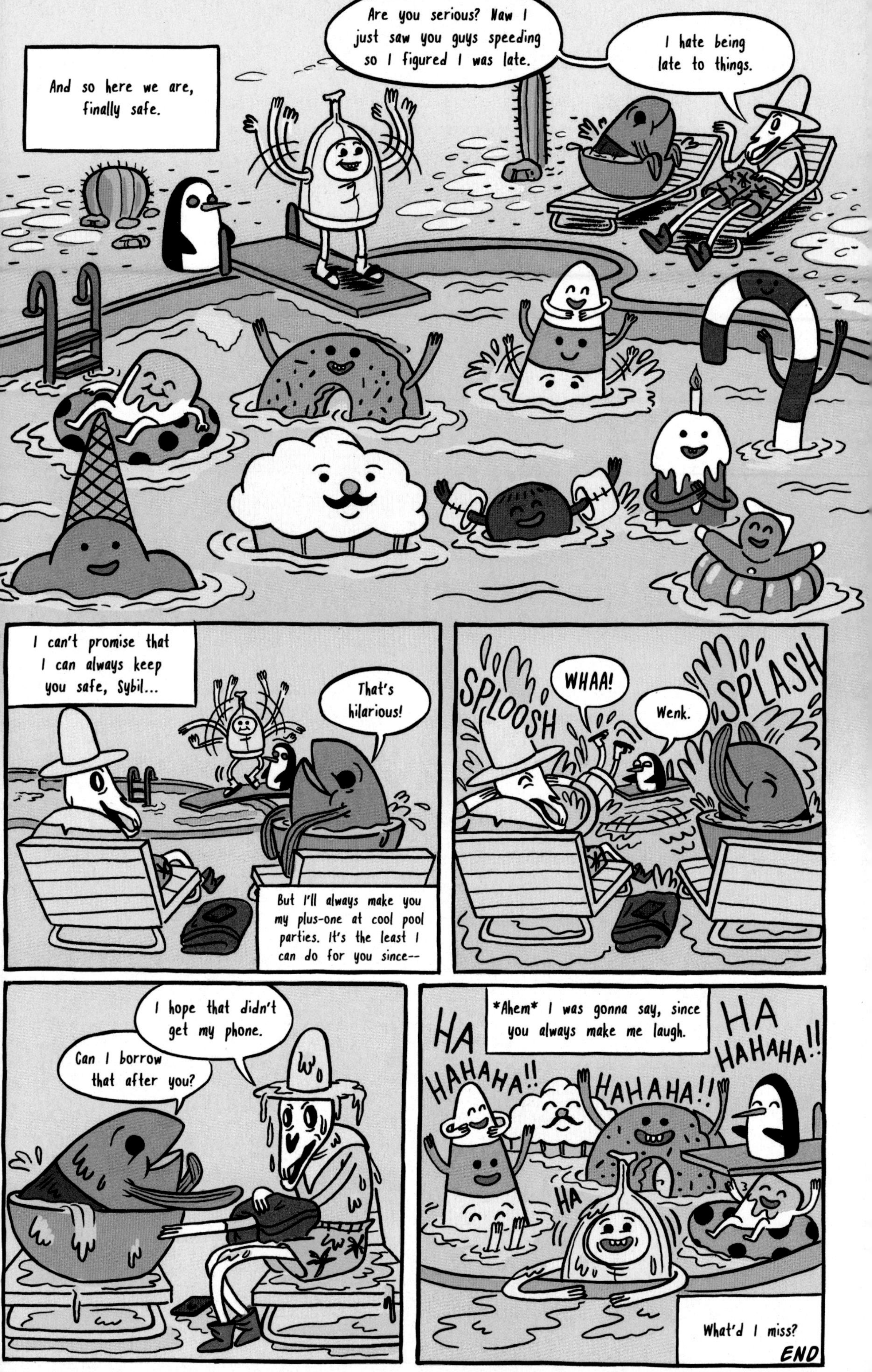
And so here we are, finally safe.
Are you serious? Naw I just saw you guys speeding so I figured I was late.
I hate being late to things.
I can't promise that I can always keep you safe, Sybil...
That's hilarious!
But I'll always make you my plus-one at cool pool parties. It's the least I can do for you since--
SPLOOSH
WHAA!
Wenk.
SPLASH
Can I borrow that after you?
I hope that didn't get my phone.
HA
HAHAHA!!
Ahem I was gonna say, since you always make me laugh.
HAHAHA!!
HA
HA
HAHAHA!!
What'd I miss?
END

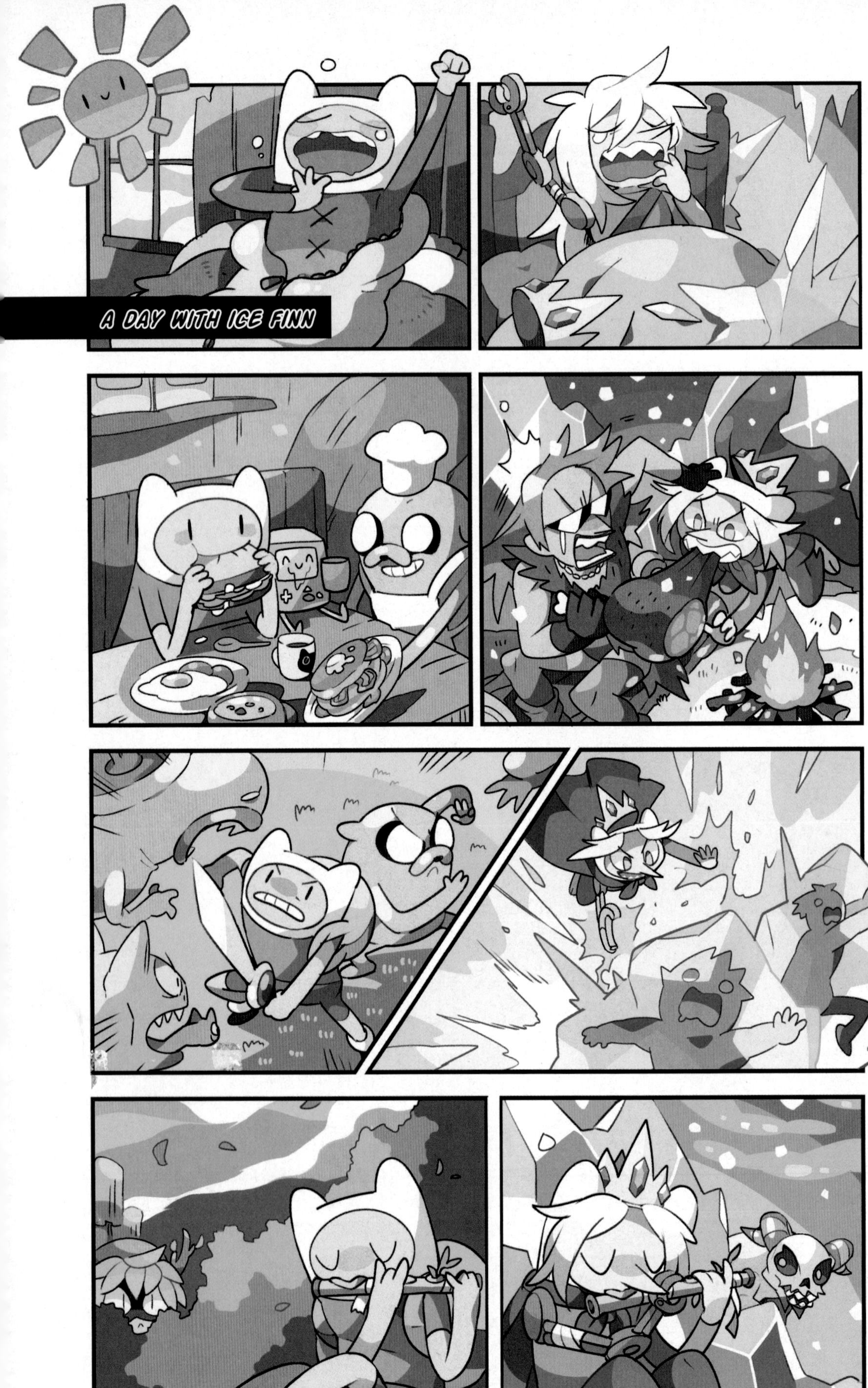
A DAY WITH ICE FINN

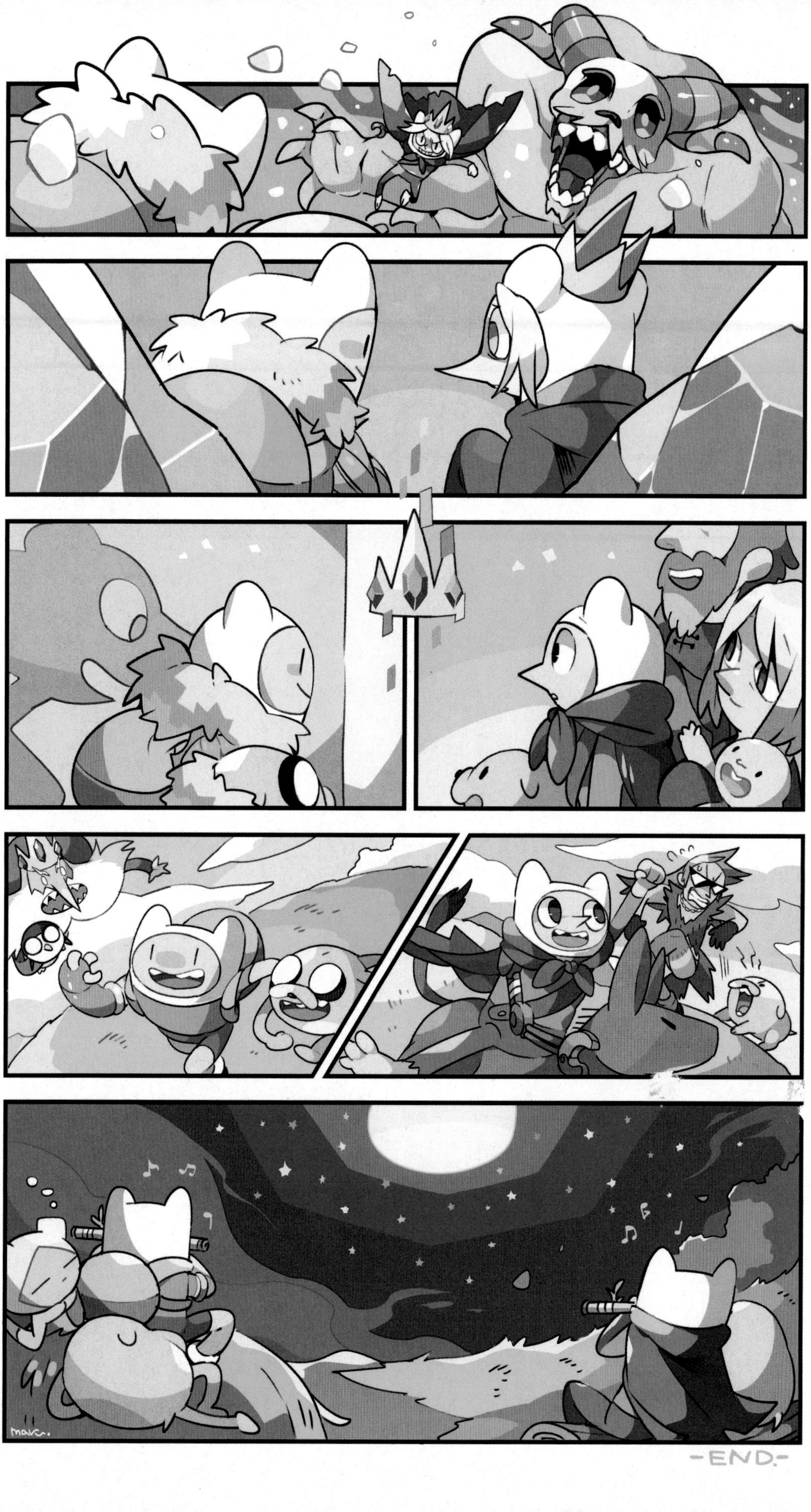

-END-

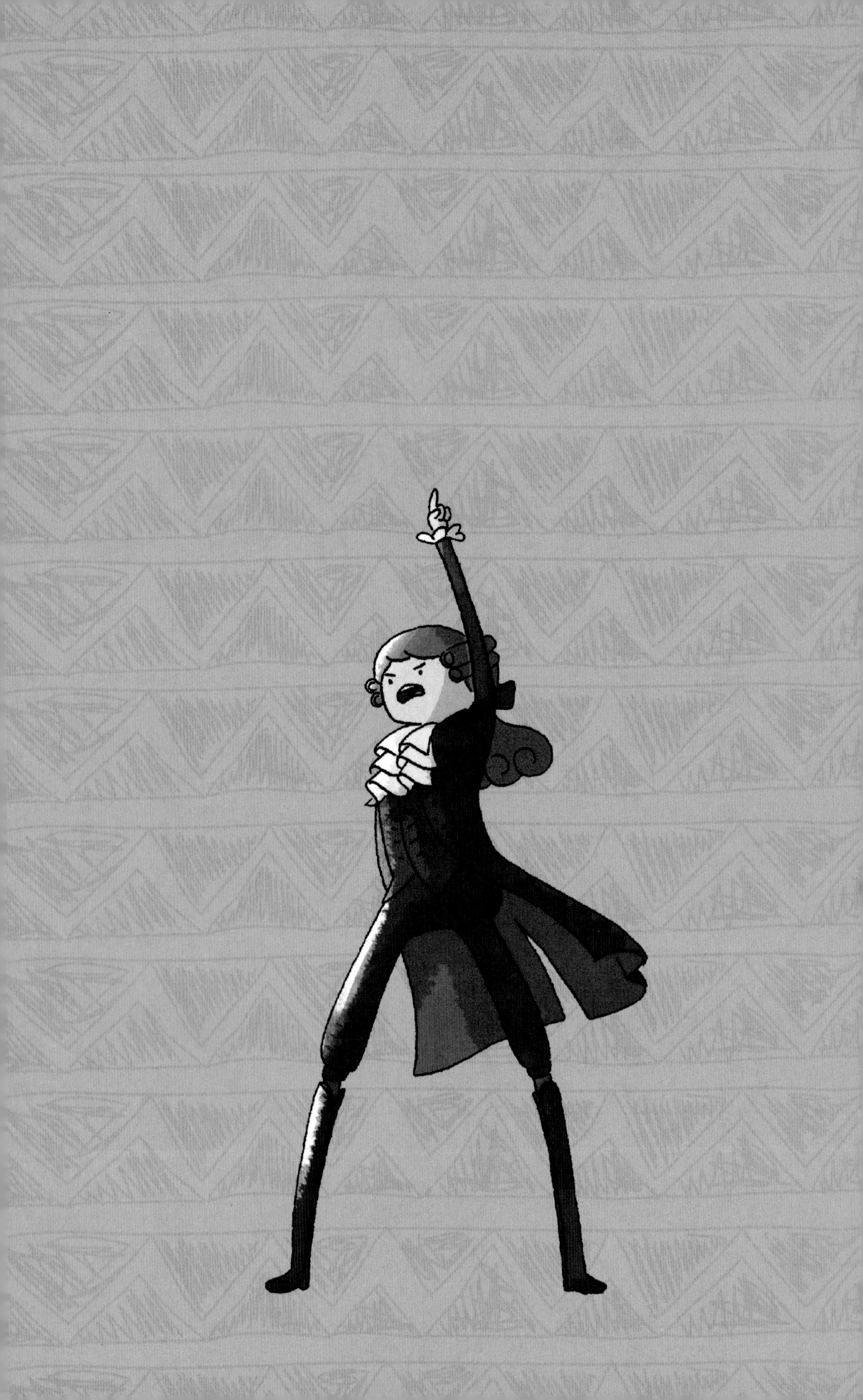

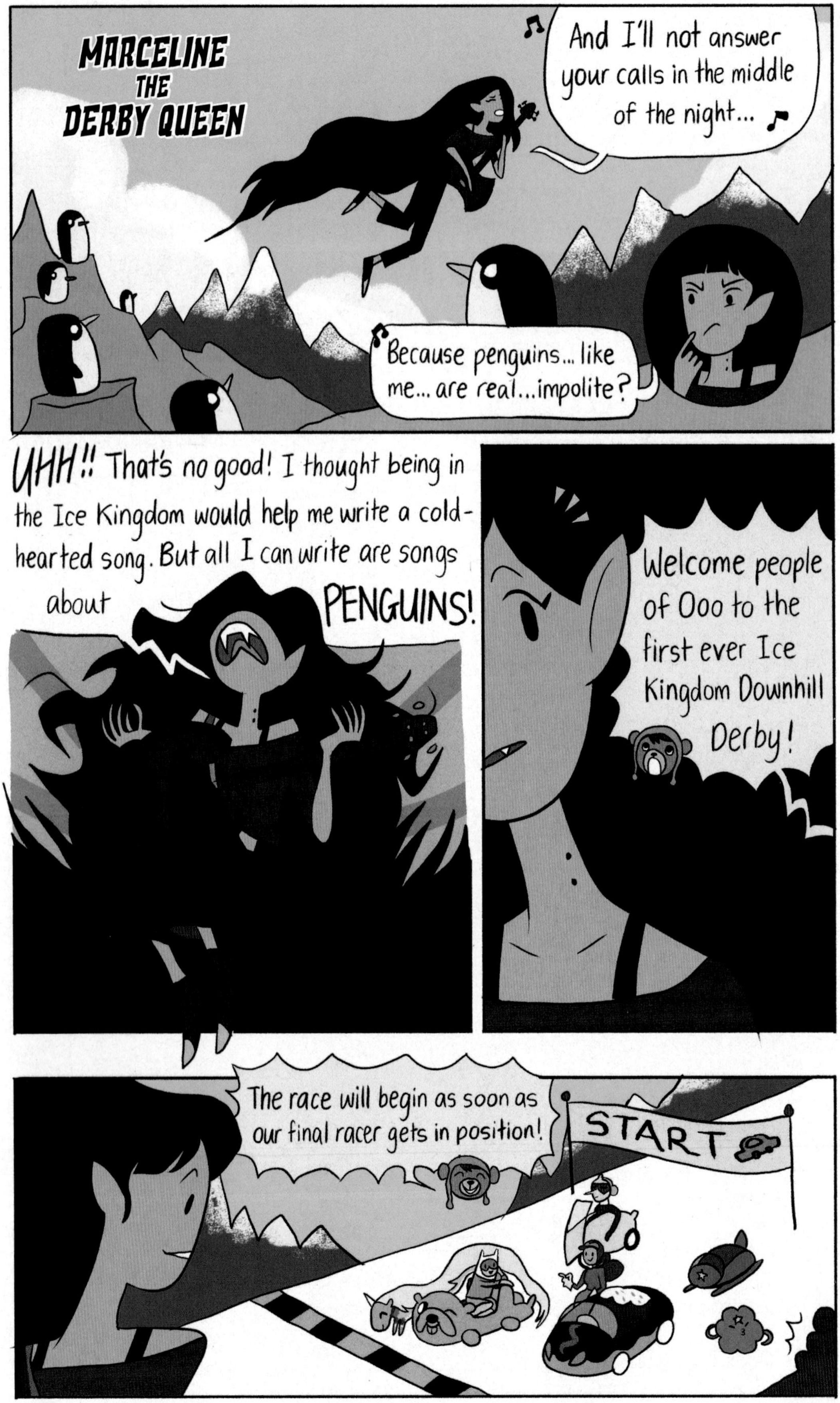
MARCELINE THE DERBY QUEEN
And I'll not answer your calls in the middle of the night...
Because penguins... like me... are real...impolite?
UHH!! That's no good! I thought being in the Ice Kingdom would help me write a cold-hearted song. But all I can write are songs about PENGUINS!
Welcome people of Ooo to the first ever Ice Kingdom Downhill Derby!
The race will begin as soon as our final racer gets in position!
START

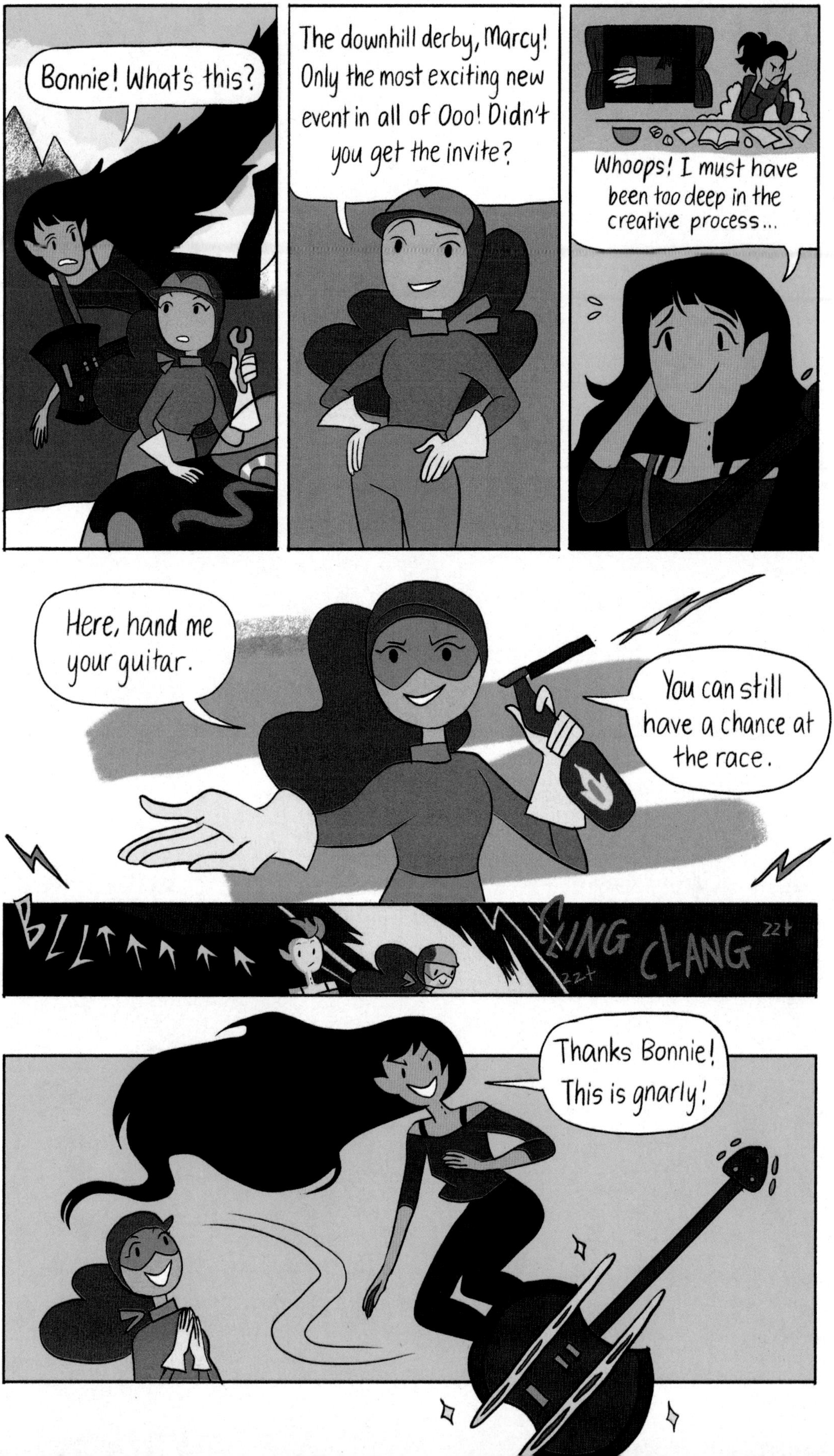
Bonnie! What's this?
The downhill derby, Marcy! Only the most exciting new event in all of Ooo! Didn't you get the invite?
Whoops! I must have been too deep in the creative process...
Here, hand me your guitar.
You can still have a chance at the race.
BLLTTTTTT
CLING CLANG
Thanks Bonnie! This is gnarly!

And with that, the race is on! **3...2...1!!!**

GOOOOO!!!

Hooray!

Go, Finn! Go, Marceline!

Good luck, Princess!

Look at them having fun without old Ice-y! As if this isn't my own kingdom!

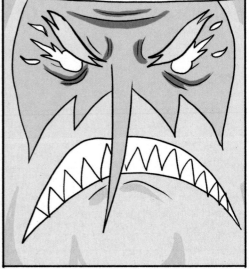

WELL, I'LL SHOW THEM!

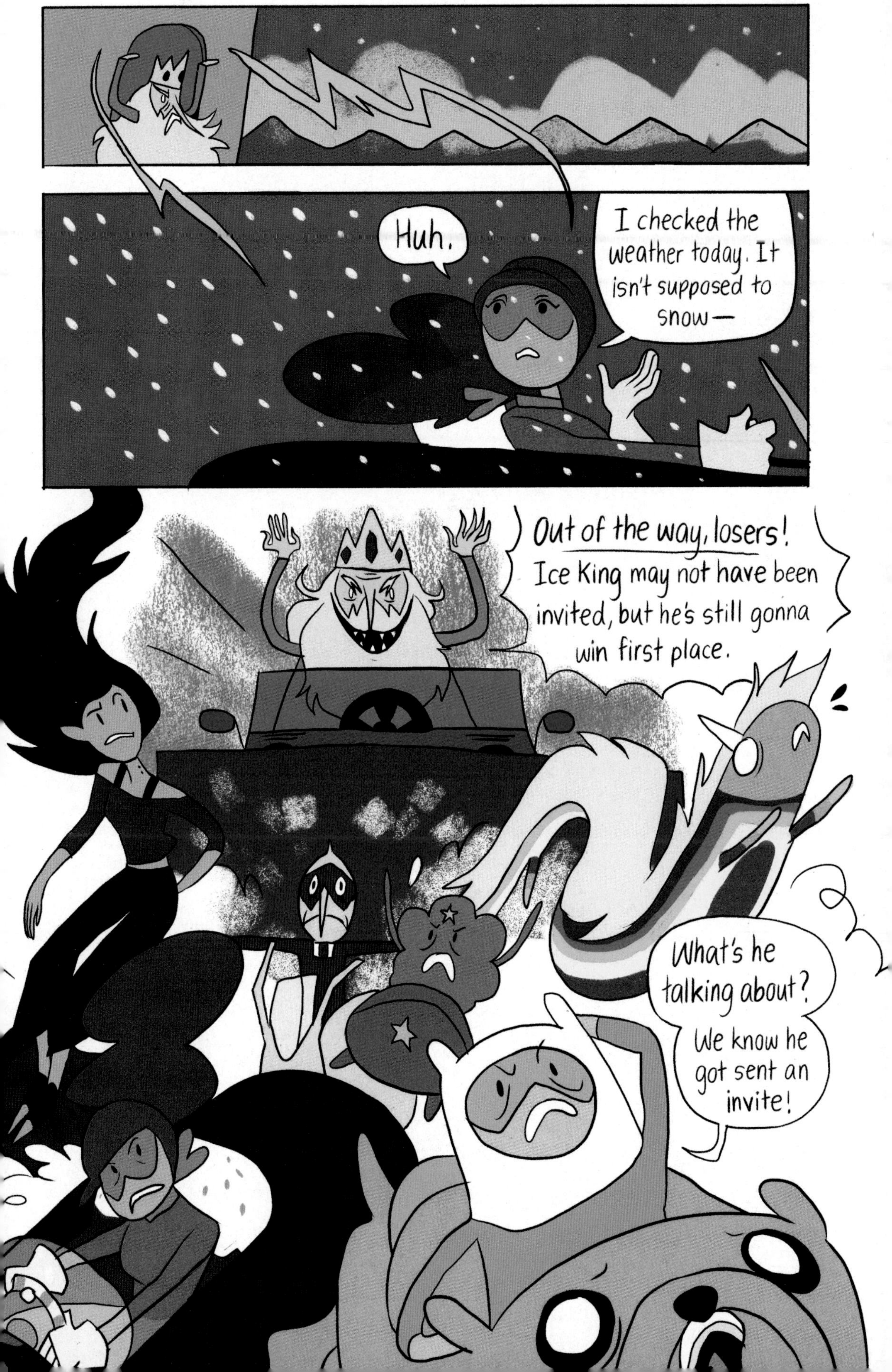
Huh.
I checked the weather today. It isn't supposed to snow—
Out of the way, losers! Ice King may not have been invited, but he's still gonna win first place.
What's he talking about?
We know he got sent an invite!

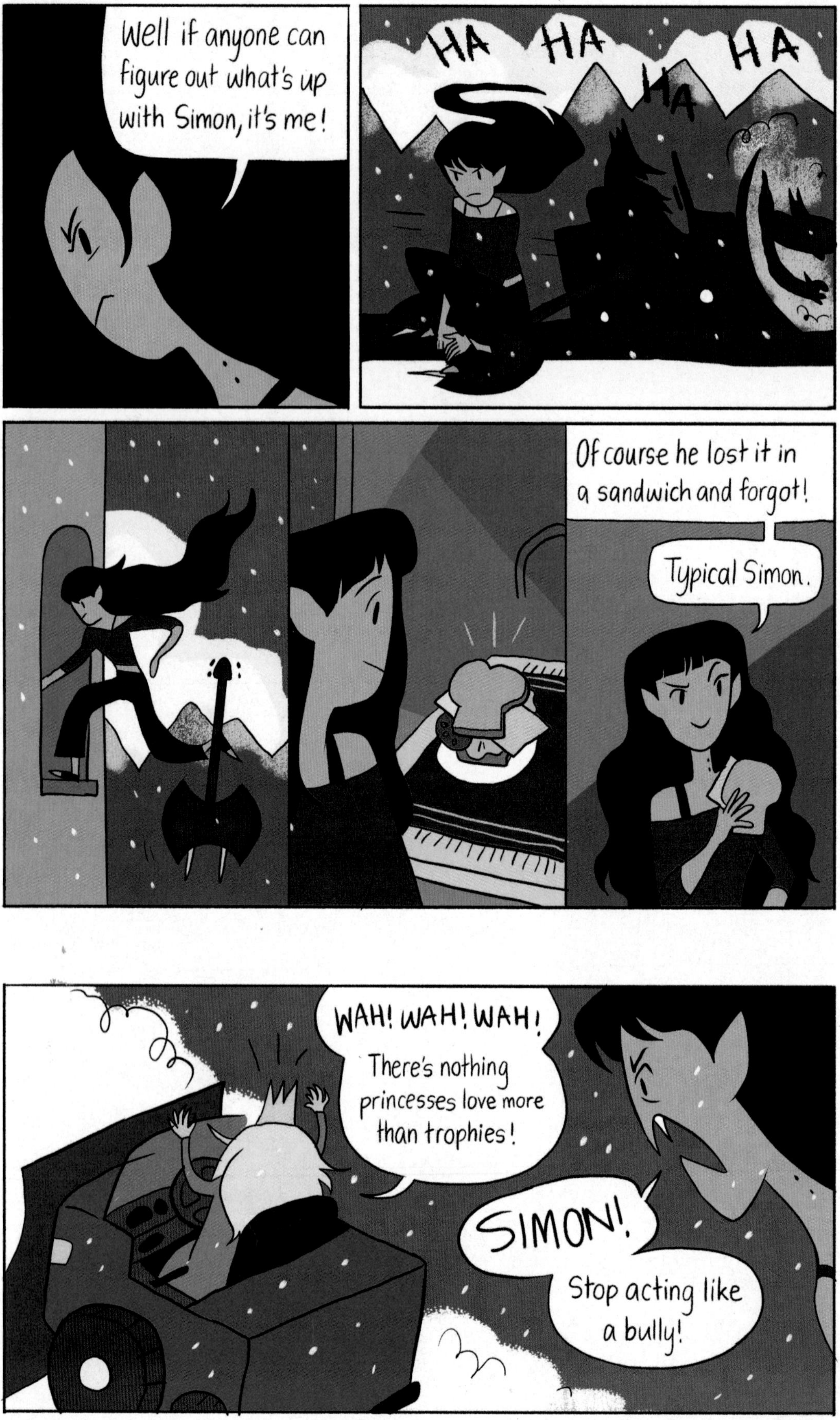
Well if anyone can figure out what's up with Simon, it's me!
HA HA HA HA
Of course he lost it in a sandwich and forgot!
Typical Simon.
WAH! WAH! WAH!
There's nothing princesses love more than trophies!
SIMON!
Stop acting like a bully!

You were sent an invite to the race!

Ice King — please come to the Downhill Derby! ~

Oh no! I goofed! Now everyone must think I'm a big bully!

It's okay to make mistakes, Simon. As long as you work to fix them.

Then I'll make the race even better than it was!

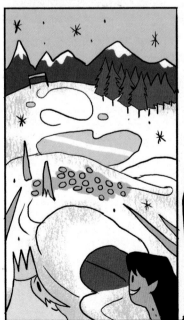

Well, I guess I'll finish my cold-hearted song later because... right now I've a race <u>to win!</u>

I'm coming for you!

Hey!

END!

--and **THIS** is from when my ultra-best-bro **FINN** saved me from that giant **STEAKTOPUS!**

Yeah! I was all like-- k'**CHUNKS!**

What is 'stake-toe-pus'?

Y'know. An old witch cursed a bunch of meats. They **WOMP**'ed together into a tentacle-thing? She might've meant it to be more of a **SQUID**, but we couldn't figure out a good name with that.

Hey, Finn. If you're done with it, I'mma put this baby away--

--with the **REST** of the "Adventure Mementos."

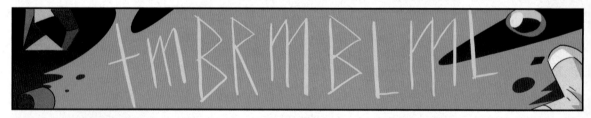

TMBRMBLML

Yowza.

How the hay did we **FIT** all this stuff in that closet to begin with?!

We got one wish from that **CLEANING GENIE**, remember?

Knew we shoulda wished for more wishes...

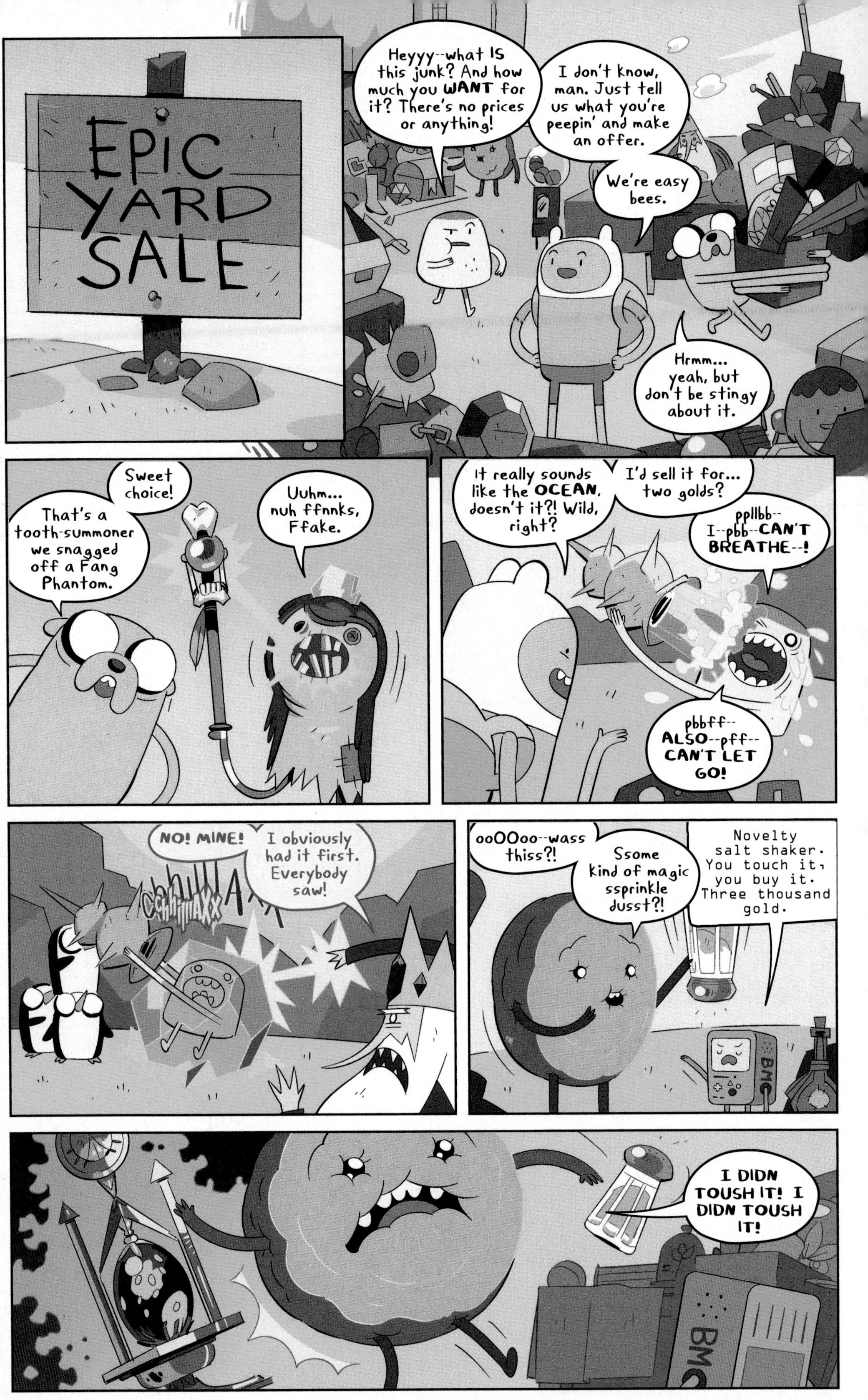
EPIC YARD SALE
Heyyy--what IS this junk? And how much you WANT for it? There's no prices or anything!
I don't know, man. Just tell us what you're peepin' and make an offer.
We're easy bees.
Hrmm... yeah, but don't be stingy about it.
Sweet choice!
That's a tooth-summoner we snagged off a Fang Phantom.
Uuhm... nuh ffnnks, Ffake.
It really sounds like the OCEAN, doesn't it?! Wild, right?
I'd sell it for... two golds?
ppllbb-- I--pbb--CAN'T BREATHE--!
pbbff-- ALSO--pff-- CAN'T LET GO!
NO! MINE!
I obviously had it first. Everybody saw!
ooOOoo--wass thiss?!
Ssome kind of magic ssprinkle dusst?!
Novelty salt shaker. You touch it, you buy it. Three thousand gold.
I DIDN TOUSH IT! I DIDN TOUSH IT!

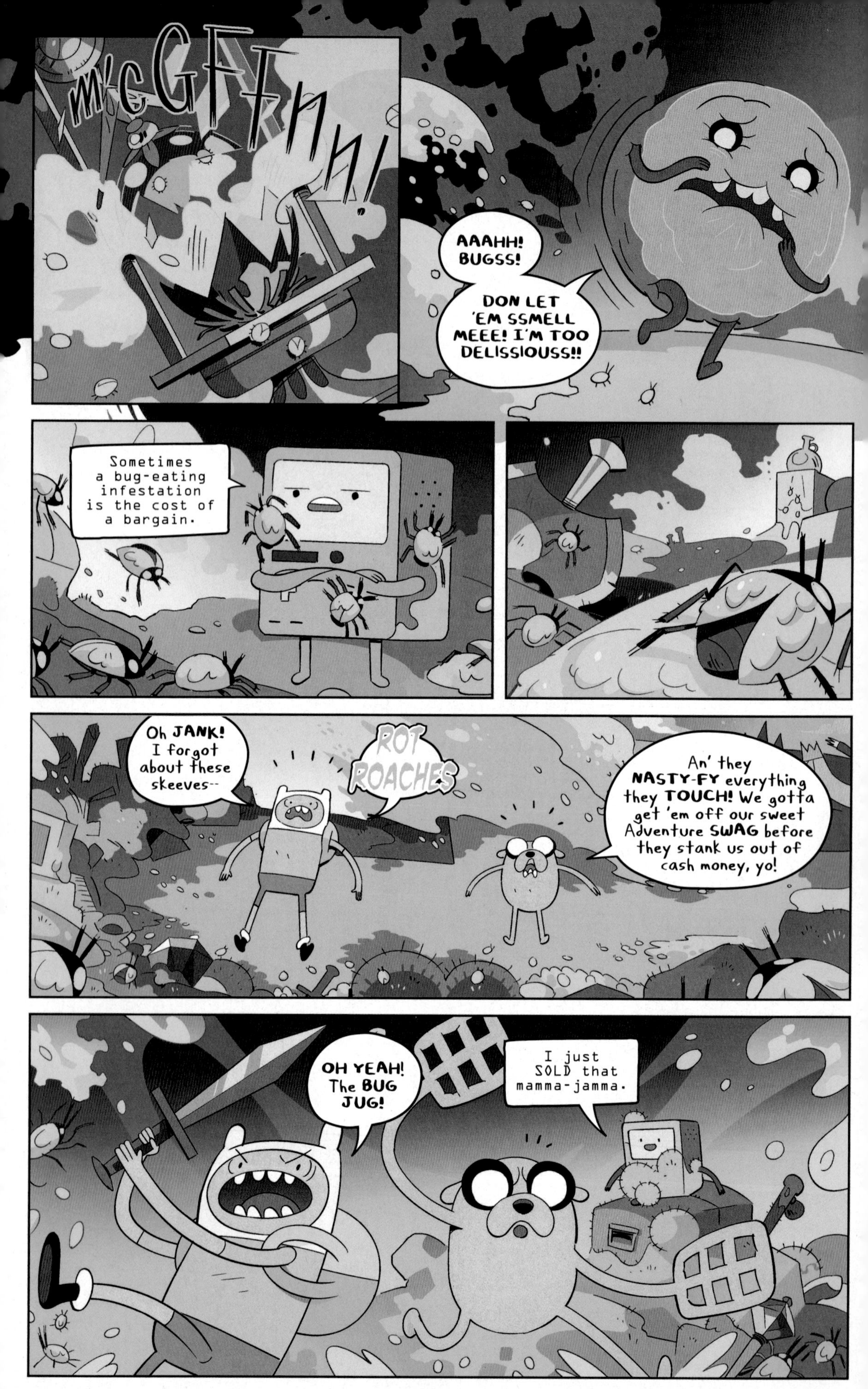

M'GFFFnn!
AAAHH! BUGSS!
DON LET 'EM SSMELL MEEE! I'M TOO DELISSIOUSS!!
Sometimes a bug-eating infestation is the cost of a bargain.
Oh JANK! I forgot about these skeeves--
ROT ROACHES
An' they NASTY-FY everything they TOUCH! We gotta get 'em off our sweet Adventure SWAG before they stank us out of cash money, yo!
OH YEAH! The BUG JUG!
I just SOLD that mamma-jamma.

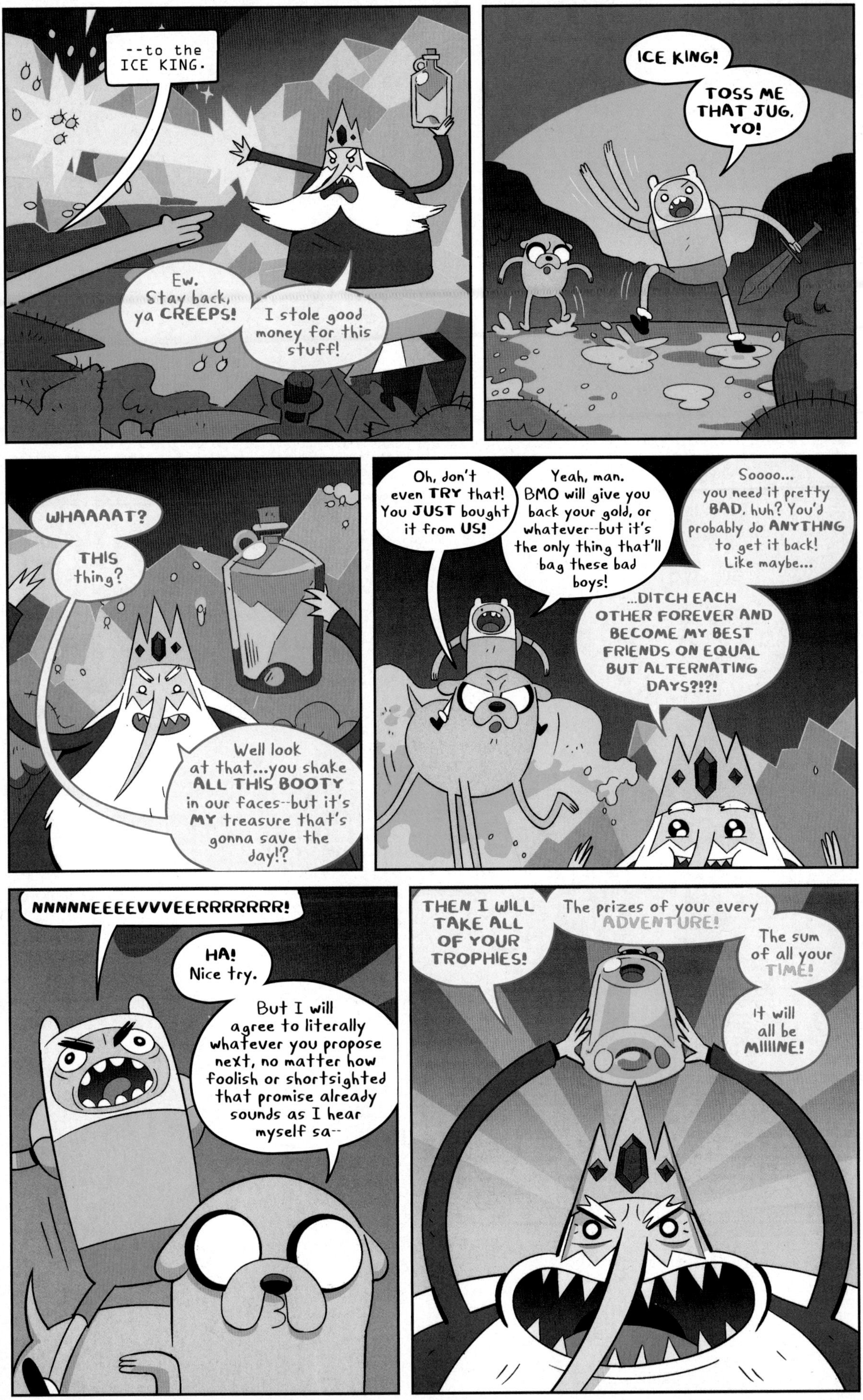
--to the ICE KING.
Ew. Stay back, ya CREEPS!
I stole good money for this stuff!
ICE KING!
TOSS ME THAT JUG, YO!
WHAAAAT?
THIS thing?
Well look at that...you shake ALL THIS BOOTY in our faces--but it's MY treasure that's gonna save the day!?
Oh, don't even TRY that! You JUST bought it from US!
Yeah, man. BMO will give you back your gold, or whatever--but it's the only thing that'll bag these bad boys!
Soooo... you need it pretty BAD, huh? You'd probably do ANYTHNG to get it back! Like maybe...
...DITCH EACH OTHER FOREVER AND BECOME MY BEST FRIENDS ON EQUAL BUT ALTERNATING DAYS?!?!
NNNNNEEEEVVVEERRRRRRR!
HA! Nice try.
But I will agree to literally whatever you propose next, no matter how foolish or shortsighted that promise already sounds as I hear myself sa--
THEN I WILL TAKE ALL OF YOUR TROPHIES!
The prizes of your every ADVENTURE!
The sum of all your TIME!
It will all be MIIIINE!

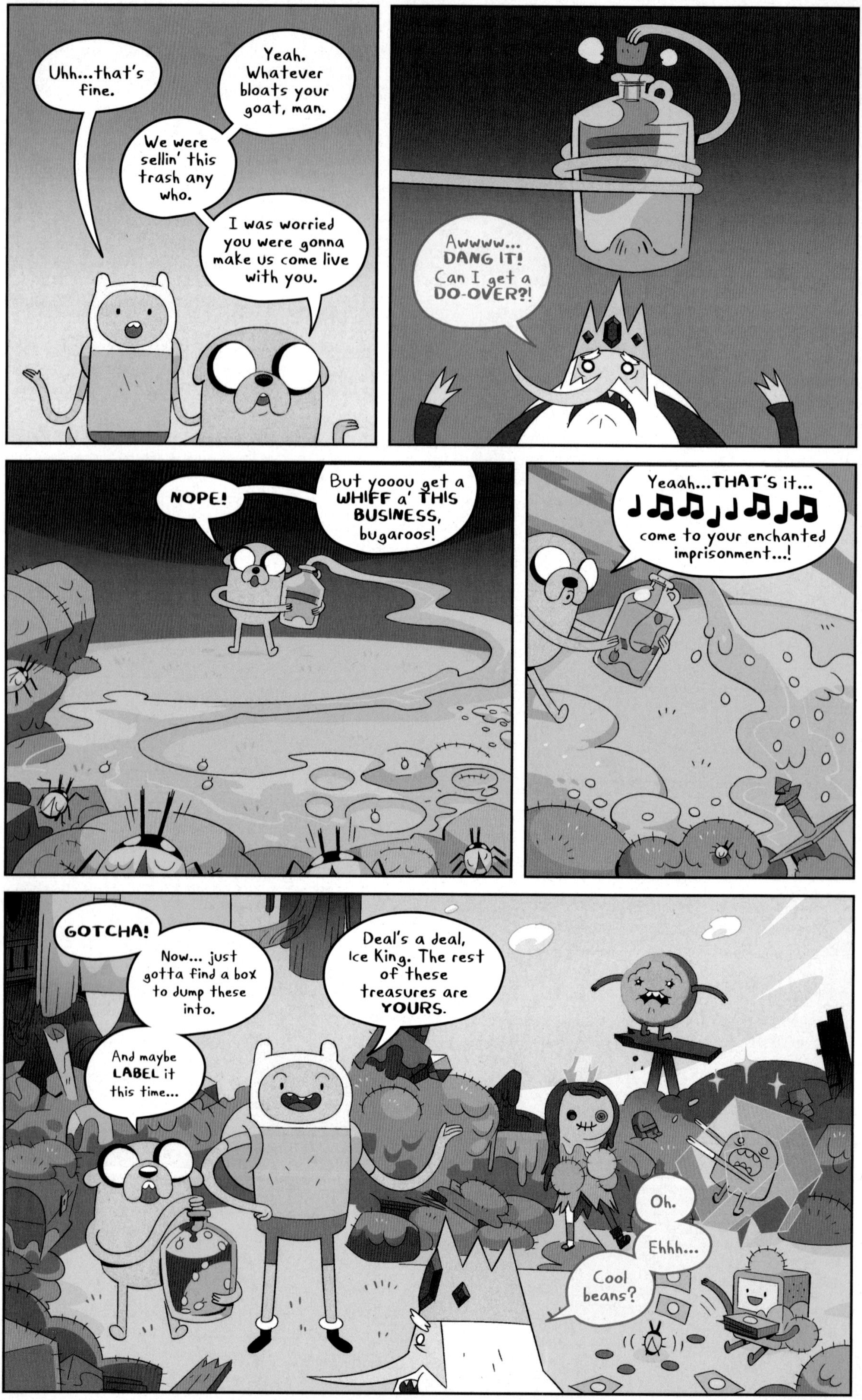
Uhh...that's fine.
Yeah. Whatever bloats your goat, man.
We were sellin' this trash any who.
I was worried you were gonna make us come live with you.
Awwww... DANG IT! Can I get a DO-OVER?!
NOPE!
But yooou get a WHIFF a' THIS BUSINESS, bugaroos!
Yeaah...THAT'S it... ♩♫♫♩♩♫♩♫
come to your enchanted imprisonment...!
GOTCHA!
Now... just gotta find a box to dump these into.
And maybe LABEL it this time...
Deal's a deal, Ice King. The rest of these treasures are YOURS.
Oh.
Ehhh...
Cool beans?

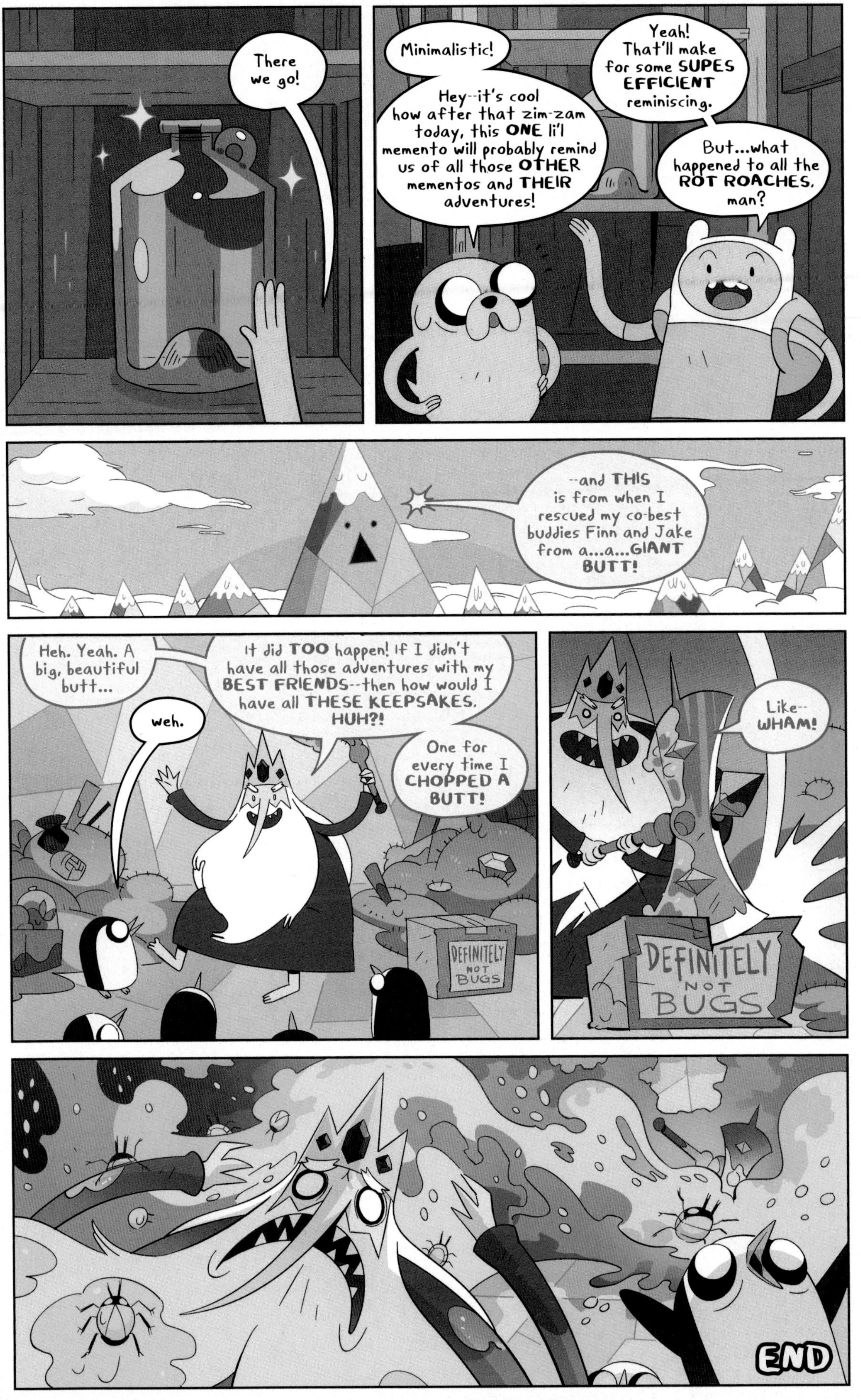

There we go!
Minimalistic!
Hey--it's cool how after that zim-zam today, this ONE li'l memento will probably remind us of all those OTHER mementos and THEIR adventures!
Yeah! That'll make for some SUPES EFFICIENT reminiscing.
But...what happened to all the ROT ROACHES, man?
--and THIS is from when I rescued my co-best buddies Finn and Jake from a...a...GIANT BUTT!
Heh. Yeah. A big, beautiful butt...
weh.
It did TOO happen! If I didn't have all those adventures with my BEST FRIENDS--then how would I have all THESE KEEPSAKES, HUH?!
One for every time I CHOPPED A BUTT!
DEFINITELY NOT BUGS
Like-- WHAM!
DEFINITELY NOT BUGS
END

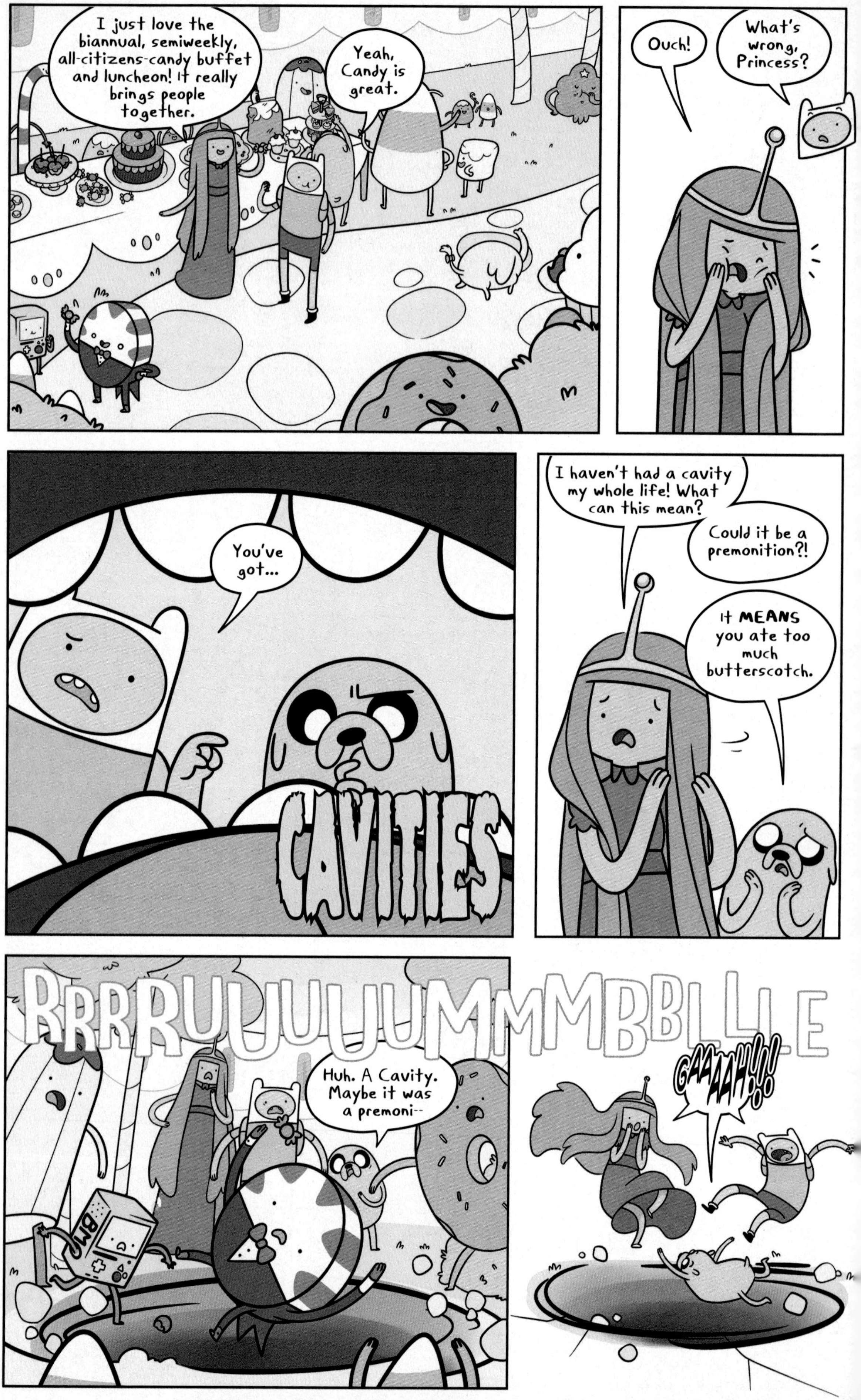
I just love the biannual, semiweekly, all-citizens-candy buffet and luncheon! It really brings people together.
Yeah, Candy is great.
Ouch!
What's wrong, Princess?
You've got...
CAVITIES
I haven't had a cavity my whole life! What can this mean?
Could it be a premonition?!
It MEANS you ate too much butterscotch.
RRRRUUUUUMMMMBBLLLE
Huh. A Cavity. Maybe it was a premoni--
GAAAAH!!!

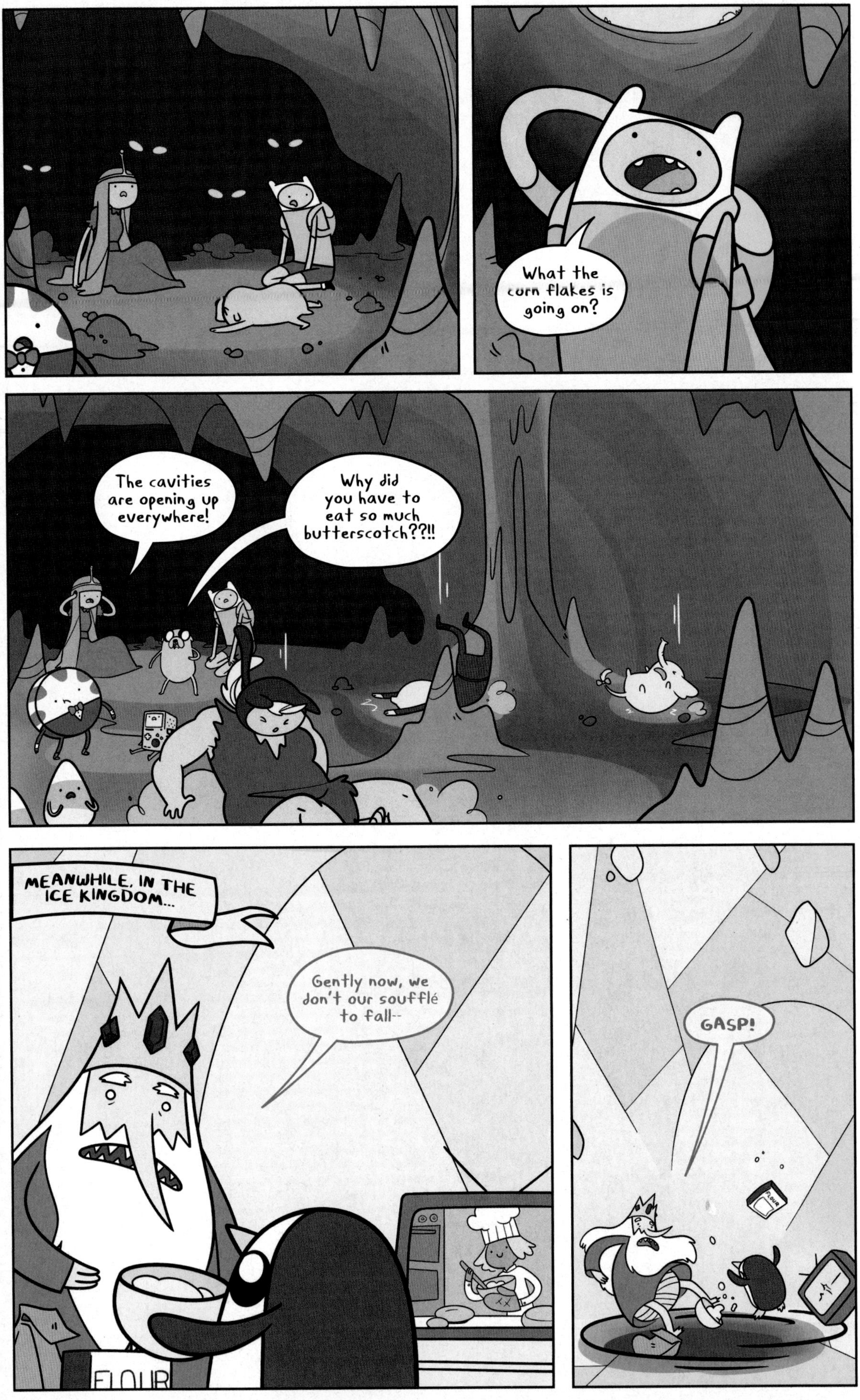
What the corn flakes is going on?
The cavities are opening up everywhere!
Why did you have to eat so much butterscotch??!!
MEANWHILE, IN THE ICE KINGDOM...
Gently now, we don't our soufflé to fall--
FLOUR
GASP!

Unacceptable!! This entire area is filthy! It smells like a dungeon!

Maybe Lady Raincorn could fly us all out of here.

Can she prevent the earth from crumbling beneath us?!

Can you?

SHAKE SHAKE

There's only one way out of this...An EPIC BATTLE!

You want us to beat up a bunch of Stalagmites?!

Are those the hangy-downey ones, or the sticky uppies?

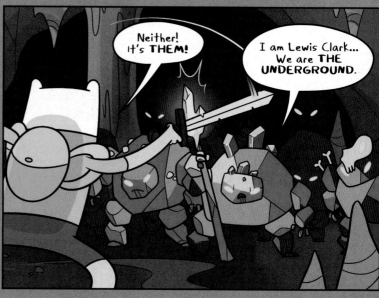

Neither! It's THEM!

I am Lewis Clark... We are THE UNDERGROUND.

That's a great name for a villainous horde, right?

Totally...

Millenia ago, before the Great Mushroom War, prior to the Rhubarb Police Action, we lived on the surface. When the magic faded, people lost patience with those who were...different. We were banished underground--simply because we valued nature above progress, open fields to buildings...

And because you're talking rocks, that's weird.

We waited for eons for the right time to reclaim the surface. That time has come. The Land of Ooo has but two champions...and we can totally beat you, Finn and Jake.

Rude.

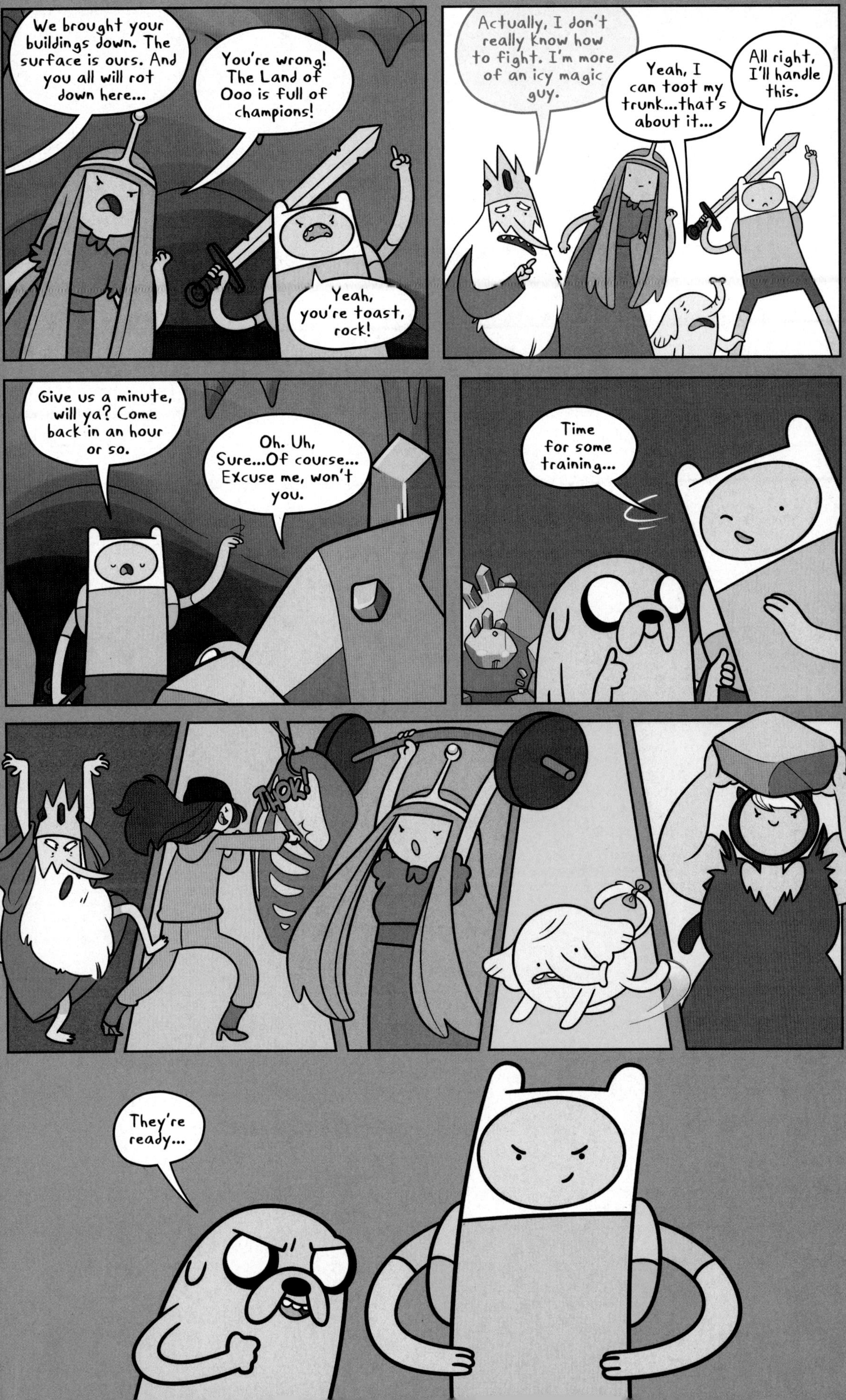
We brought your buildings down. The surface is ours. And you all will rot down here...
You're wrong! The Land of Ooo is full of champions!
Yeah, you're toast, rock!
Actually, I don't really know how to fight. I'm more of an icy magic guy.
Yeah, I can toot my trunk...that's about it...
All right, I'll handle this.
Give us a minute, will ya? Come back in an hour or so.
Oh. Uh, Sure...Of course... Excuse me, won't you.
Time for some training...
THOK!
They're ready...

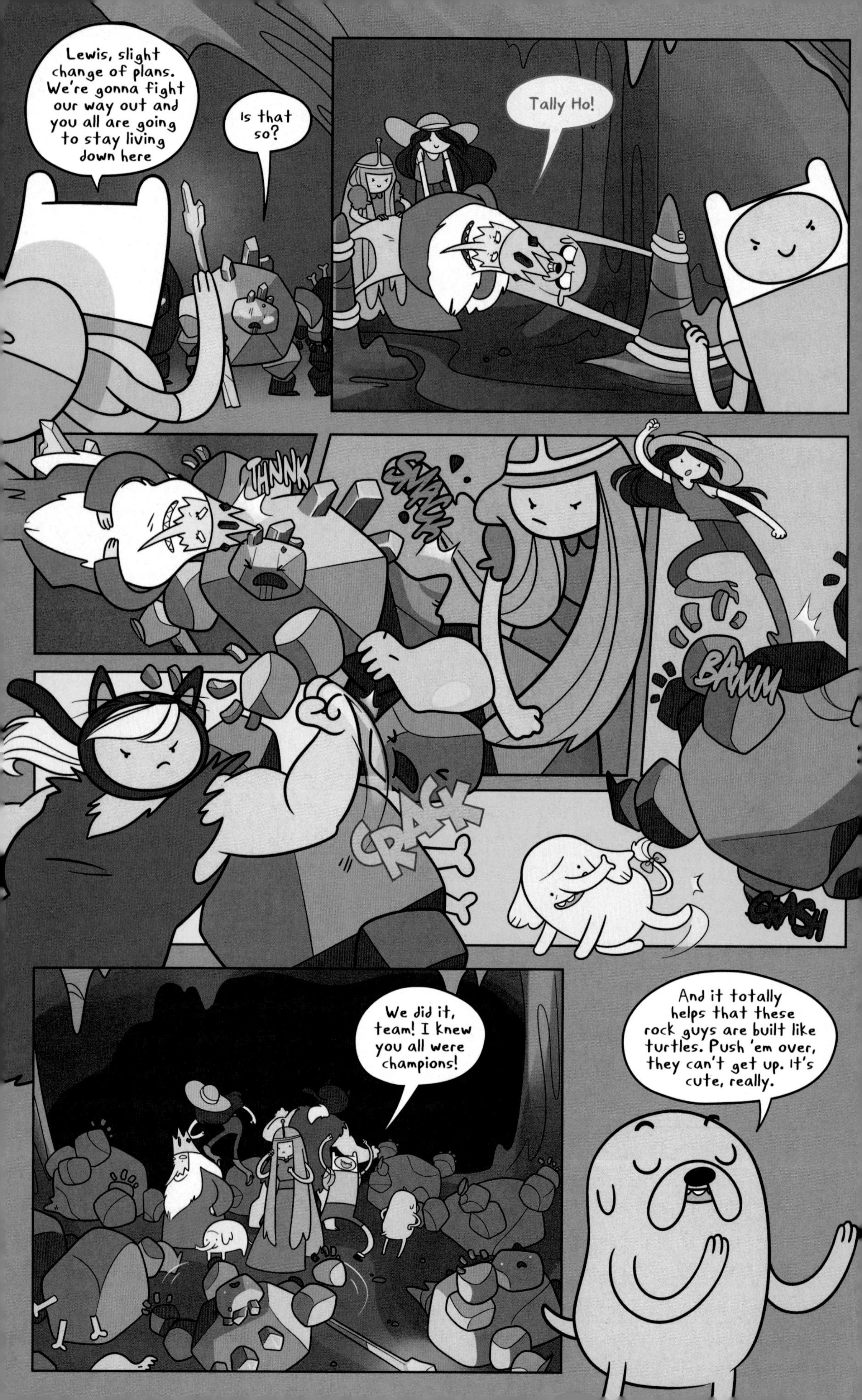

Lewis, slight change of plans. We're gonna fight our way out and you all are going to stay living down here
Is that so?
Tally Ho!
THNNK
SMACK
BAMM
CRACK
CRASH
We did it, team! I knew you all were champions!
And it totally helps that these rock guys are built like turtles. Push 'em over, they can't get up. It's cute, really.

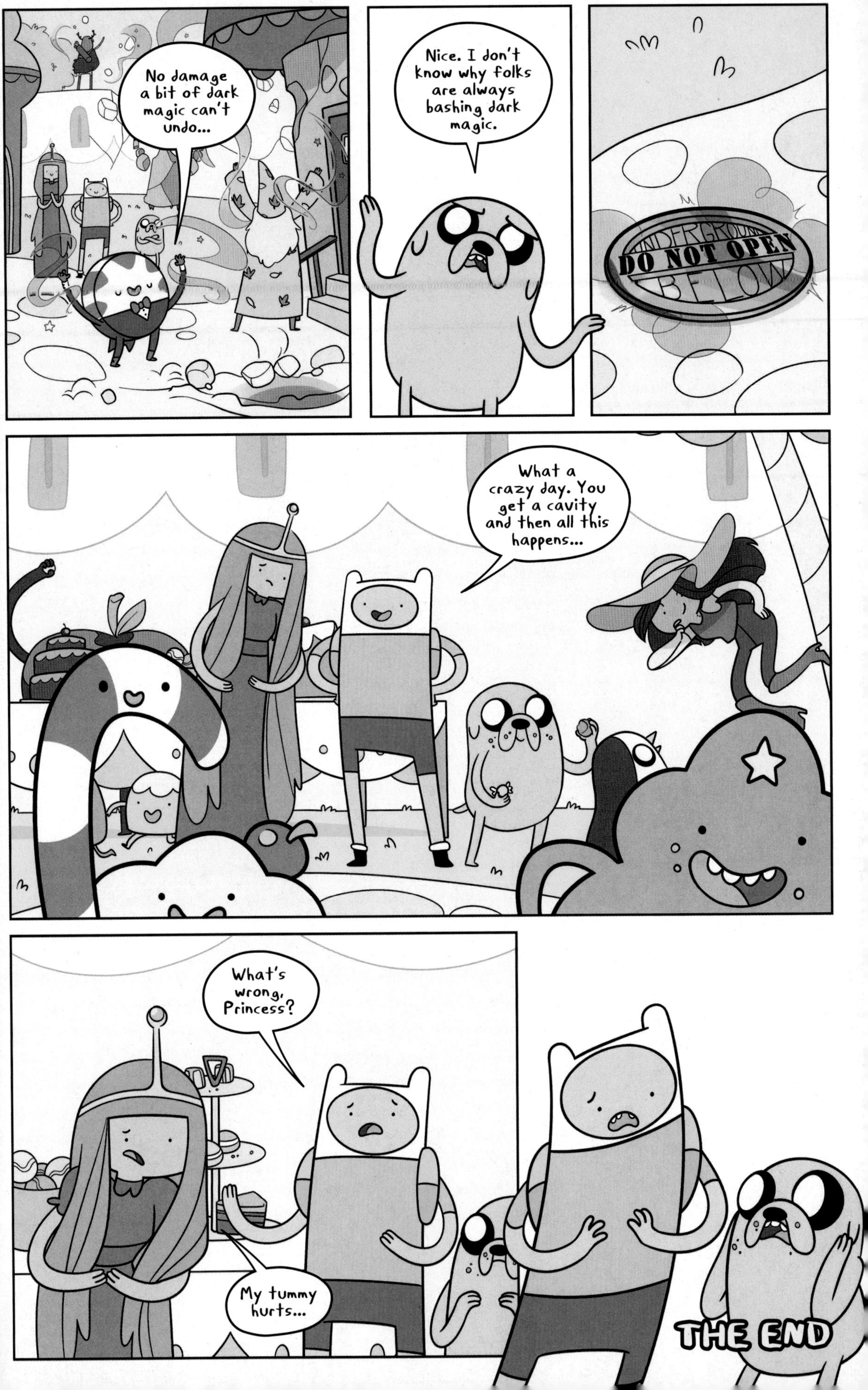
No damage a bit of dark magic can't undo...
Nice. I don't know why folks are always bashing dark magic.
UNDERGROUND DO NOT OPEN BELOW
What a crazy day. You get a cavity and then all this happens...
What's wrong, Princess?
My tummy hurts...
THE END

How does a massive, blob-like,
creature of pink gum from a ceiling,
dropped in the middle of a
post-apocalyptic unappealing city,
through providence, impoverished,
in squalor,
grow up to be a ruler
and a scholar?

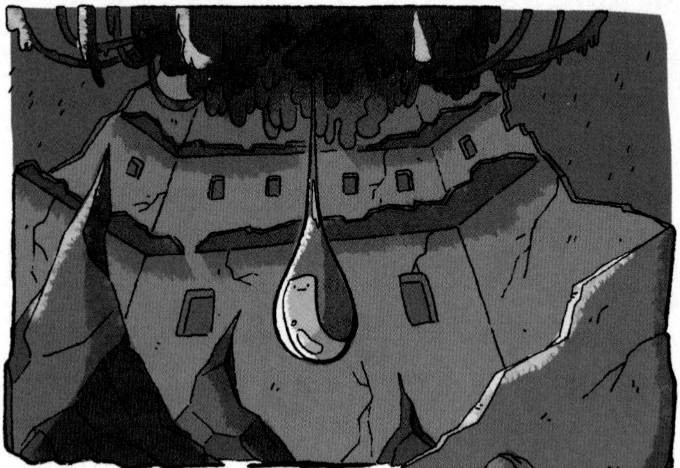

The gum creature, future teacher
without a feature,
got a lot farther
by working
a lot harder-

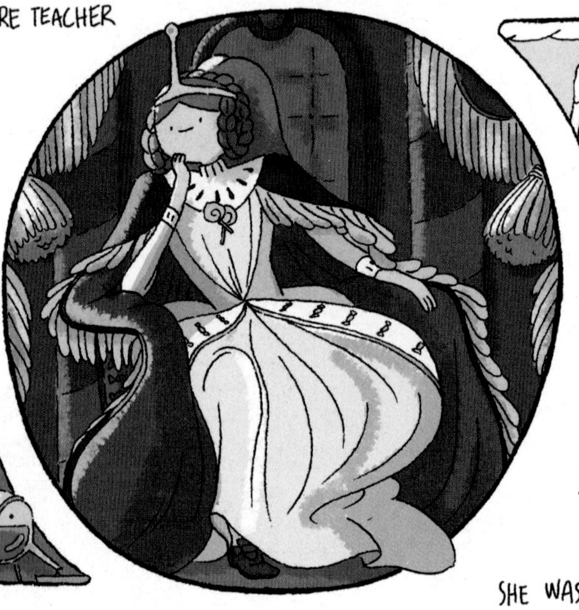

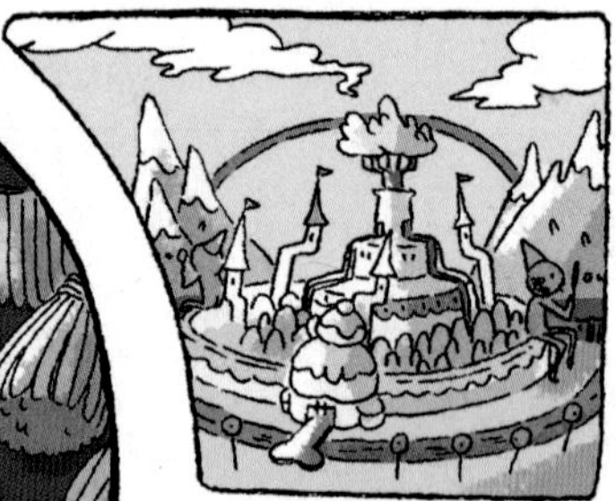

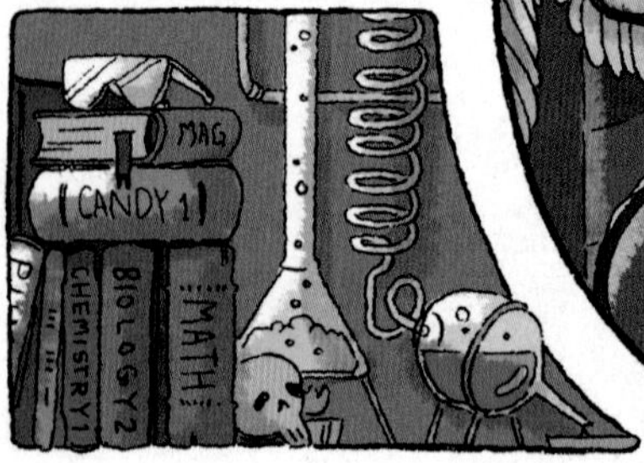
MAG
CANDY 1
CHEMISTRY 1
BIOLOGY 2
MATH

By being
a lot smarter,
by being a self-starter,
by eighteen,
she was the ruling candy queen.

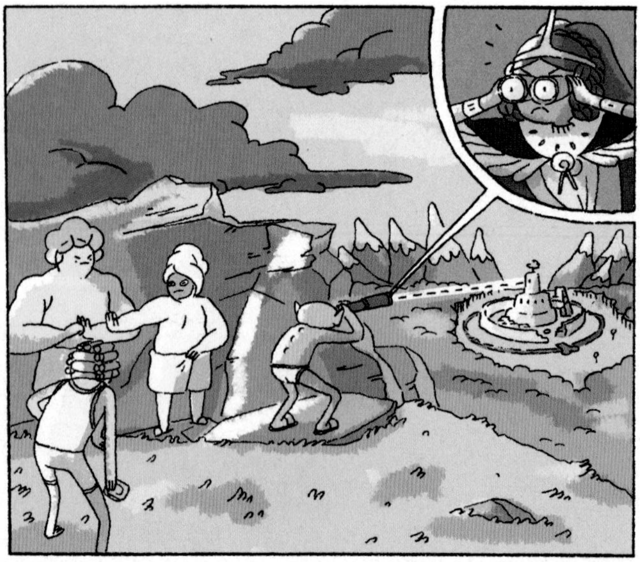

And every day while bath boys
were plotting and being spotted
away beyond the range,
she struggled and kept her guard up.
Inside, she was longing
to build something and to start up,
the sister was ready to
boycott, complot, garrote and barter.

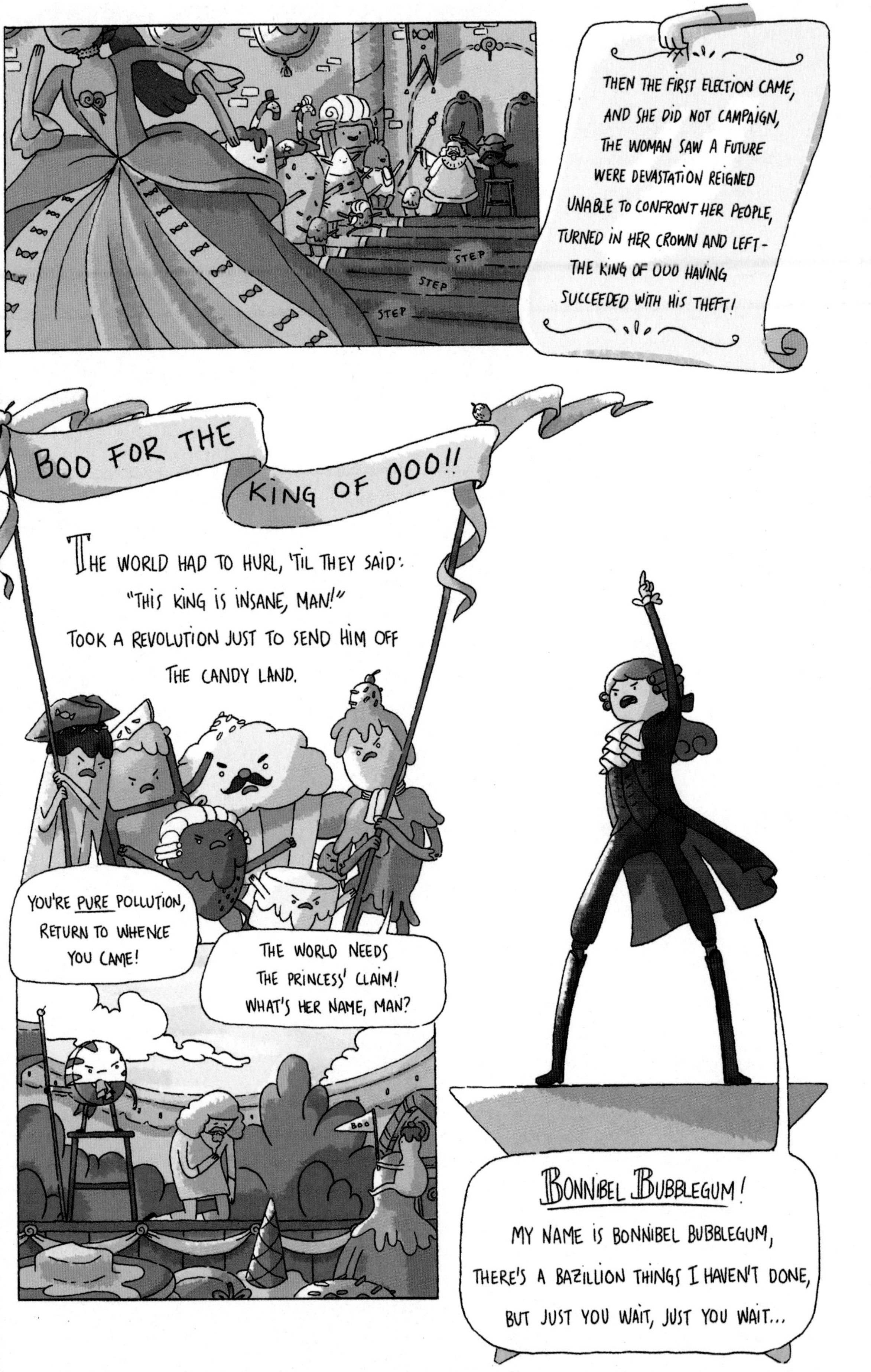
THEN THE FIRST ELECTION CAME, AND SHE DID NOT CAMPAIGN, THE WOMAN SAW A FUTURE WERE DEVASTATION REIGNED UNABLE TO CONFRONT HER PEOPLE, TURNED IN HER CROWN AND LEFT- THE KING OF OOO HAVING SUCCEEDED WITH HIS THEFT!
STEP
STEP
STEP
BOO FOR THE KING OF OOO!!
THE WORLD HAD TO HURL, 'TIL THEY SAID: "THIS KING IS INSANE, MAN!" TOOK A REVOLUTION JUST TO SEND HIM OFF THE CANDY LAND.
YOU'RE PURE POLLUTION, RETURN TO WHENCE YOU CAME!
THE WORLD NEEDS THE PRINCESS' CLAIM! WHAT'S HER NAME, MAN?
BOO
BONNIBEL BUBBLEGUM!
MY NAME IS BONNIBEL BUBBLEGUM, THERE'S A BAZILLION THINGS I HAVEN'T DONE, BUT JUST YOU WAIT, JUST YOU WAIT...

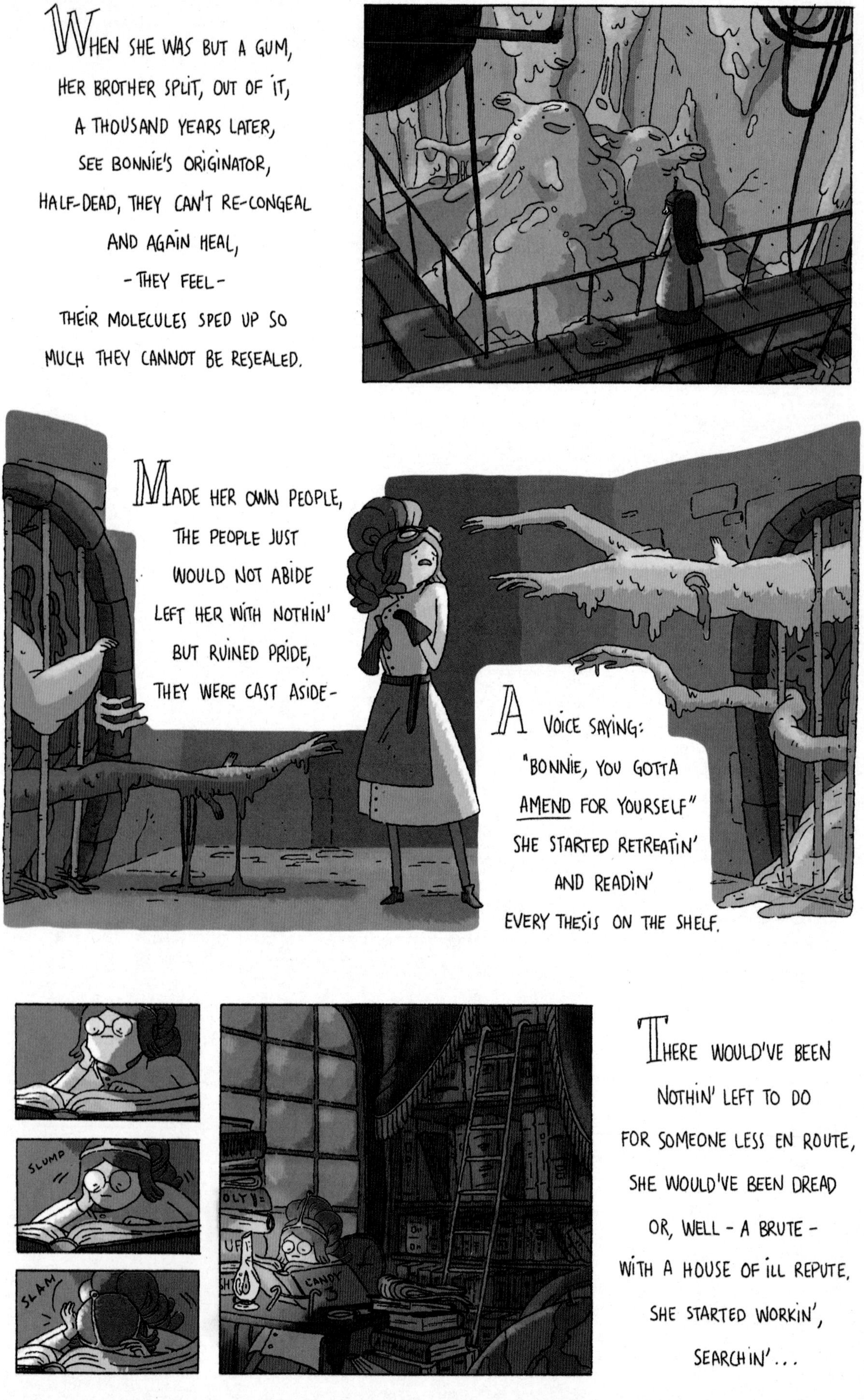
WHEN SHE WAS BUT A GUM,
HER BROTHER SPLIT, OUT OF IT,
A THOUSAND YEARS LATER,
SEE BONNIE'S ORIGINATOR,
HALF-DEAD, THEY CAN'T RE-CONGEAL
AND AGAIN HEAL,
- THEY FEEL -
THEIR MOLECULES SPED UP SO
MUCH THEY CANNOT BE RESEALED.
MADE HER OWN PEOPLE,
THE PEOPLE JUST
WOULD NOT ABIDE
LEFT HER WITH NOTHIN'
BUT RUINED PRIDE,
THEY WERE CAST ASIDE-
A VOICE SAYING:
"BONNIE, YOU GOTTA
AMEND FOR YOURSELF"
SHE STARTED RETREATIN'
AND READIN'
EVERY THESIS ON THE SHELF.
SLUMP
SLAM
THERE WOULD'VE BEEN
NOTHIN' LEFT TO DO
FOR SOMEONE LESS EN ROUTE,
SHE WOULD'VE BEEN DREAD
OR, WELL - A BRUTE -
WITH A HOUSE OF ILL REPUTE,
SHE STARTED WORKIN',
SEARCHIN'...

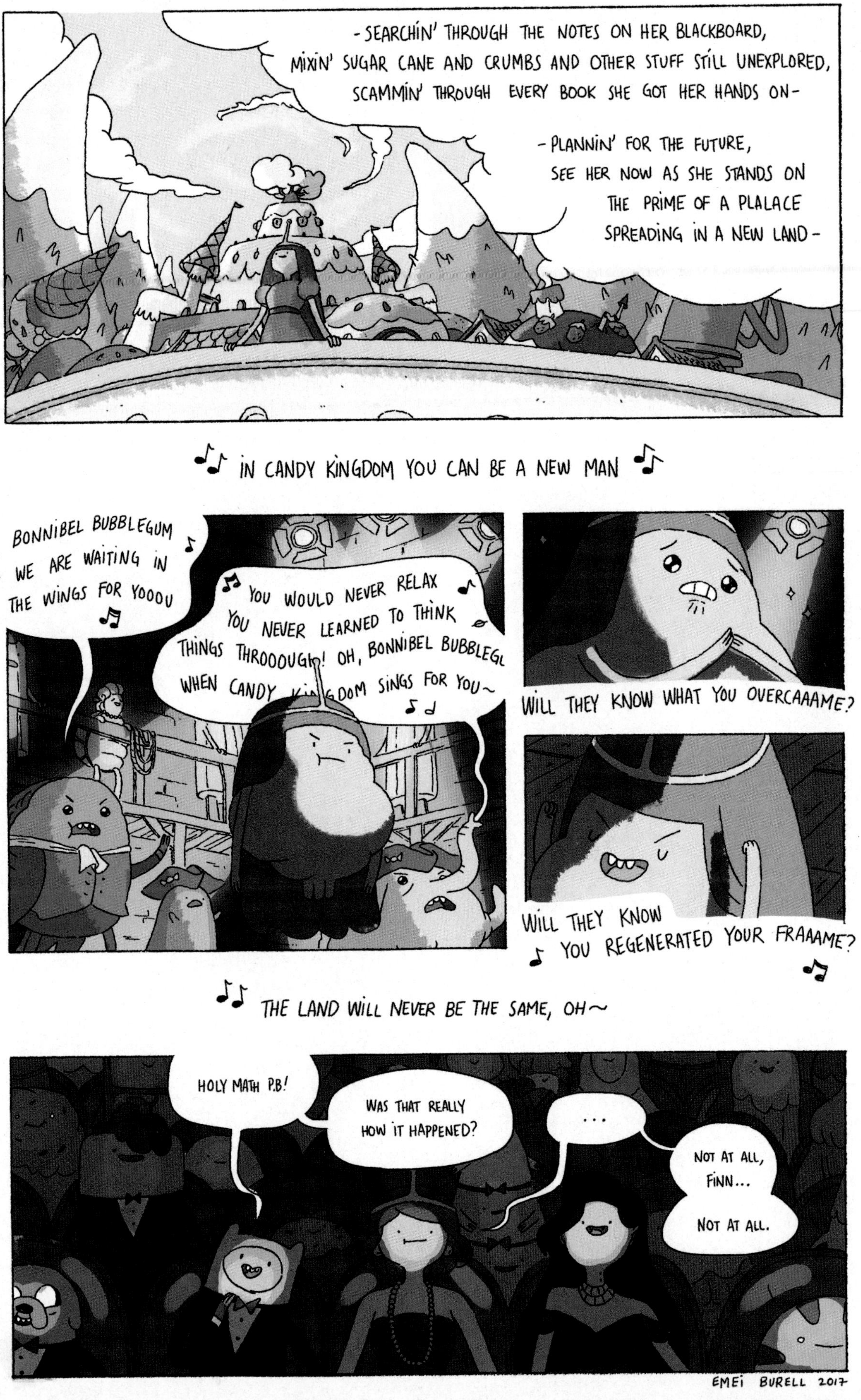

-SEARCHIN' THROUGH THE NOTES ON HER BLACKBOARD, MIXIN' SUGAR CANE AND CRUMBS AND OTHER STUFF STILL UNEXPLORED, SCAMMIN' THROUGH EVERY BOOK SHE GOT HER HANDS ON-
-PLANNIN' FOR THE FUTURE, SEE HER NOW AS SHE STANDS ON THE PRIME OF A PLALACE SPREADING IN A NEW LAND-
IN CANDY KINGDOM YOU CAN BE A NEW MAN
BONNIBEL BUBBLEGUM WE ARE WAITING IN THE WINGS FOR YOOOU
YOU WOULD NEVER RELAX YOU NEVER LEARNED TO THINK THINGS THROOOUGH! OH, BONNIBEL BUBBLEG
WHEN CANDY
GDOM SINGS FOR YOU~
WILL THEY KNOW WHAT YOU OVERCAAAME?
WILL THEY KNOW YOU REGENERATED YOUR FRAAAME?
THE LAND WILL NEVER BE THE SAME, OH~
HOLY MATH P.B!
WAS THAT REALLY HOW IT HAPPENED?
...
NOT AT ALL, FINN...
NOT AT ALL.
EMEI BURELL 2017

COVER
GALLERY

Issue #17 Main Cover

COLE CLOSSER

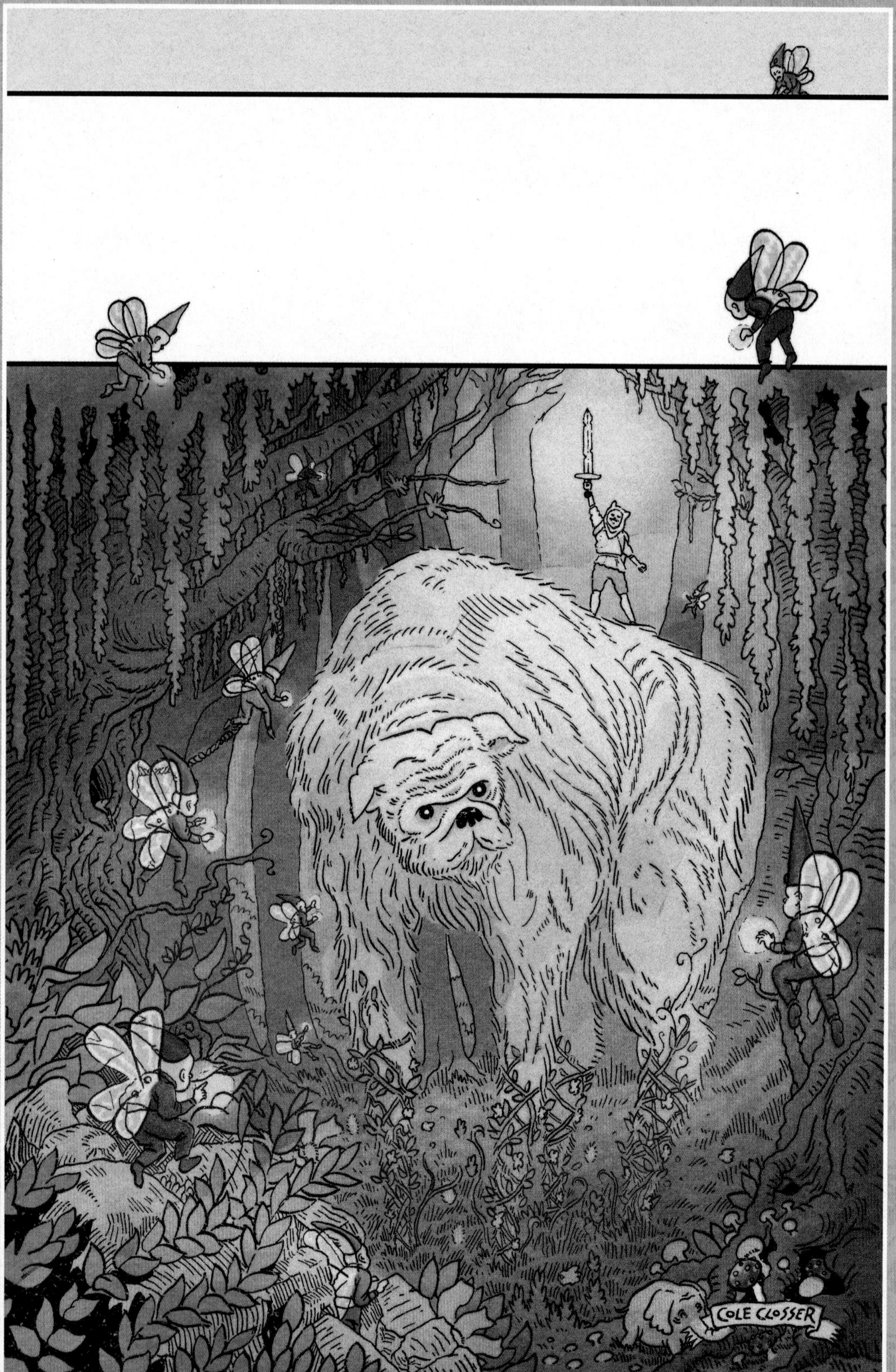
COLE CLOSSER

Issue #17 Subscription Cover

BENJAMIN MARRA

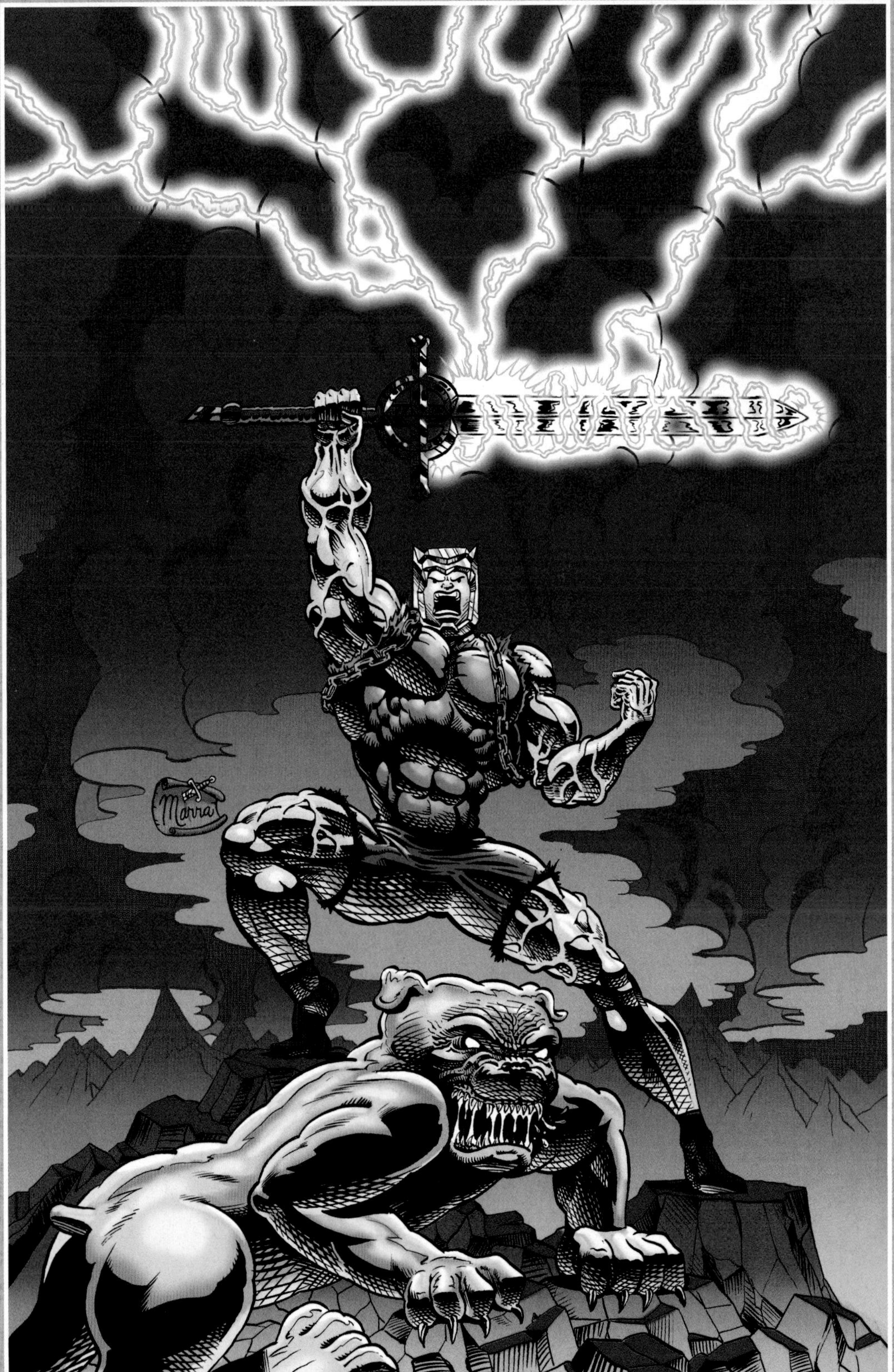
Marra

Issue #17 Variant Cover

CHRISTOPHER MITTEN

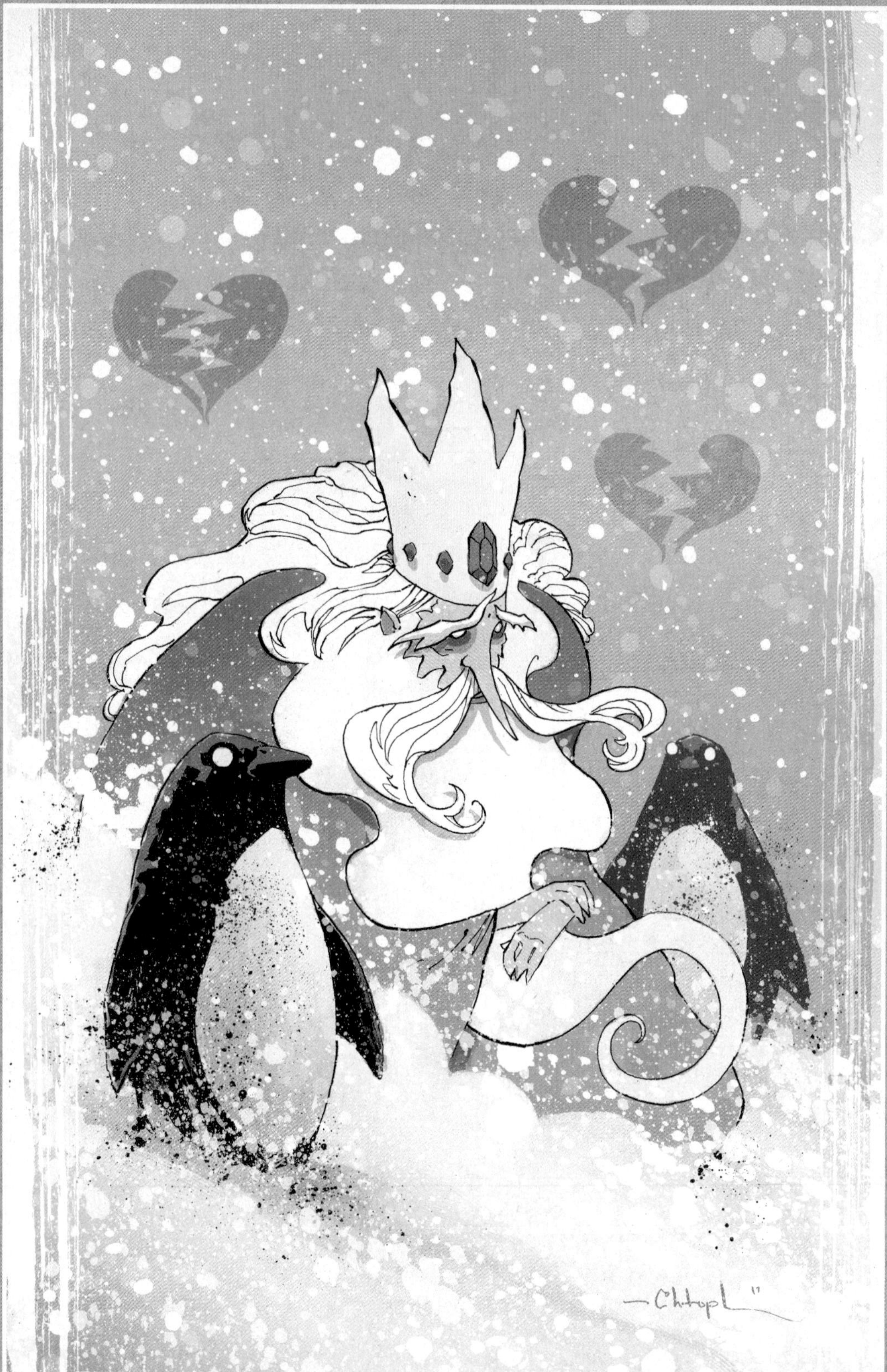

Issue #18 Main Cover

DEREK LAUFMAN

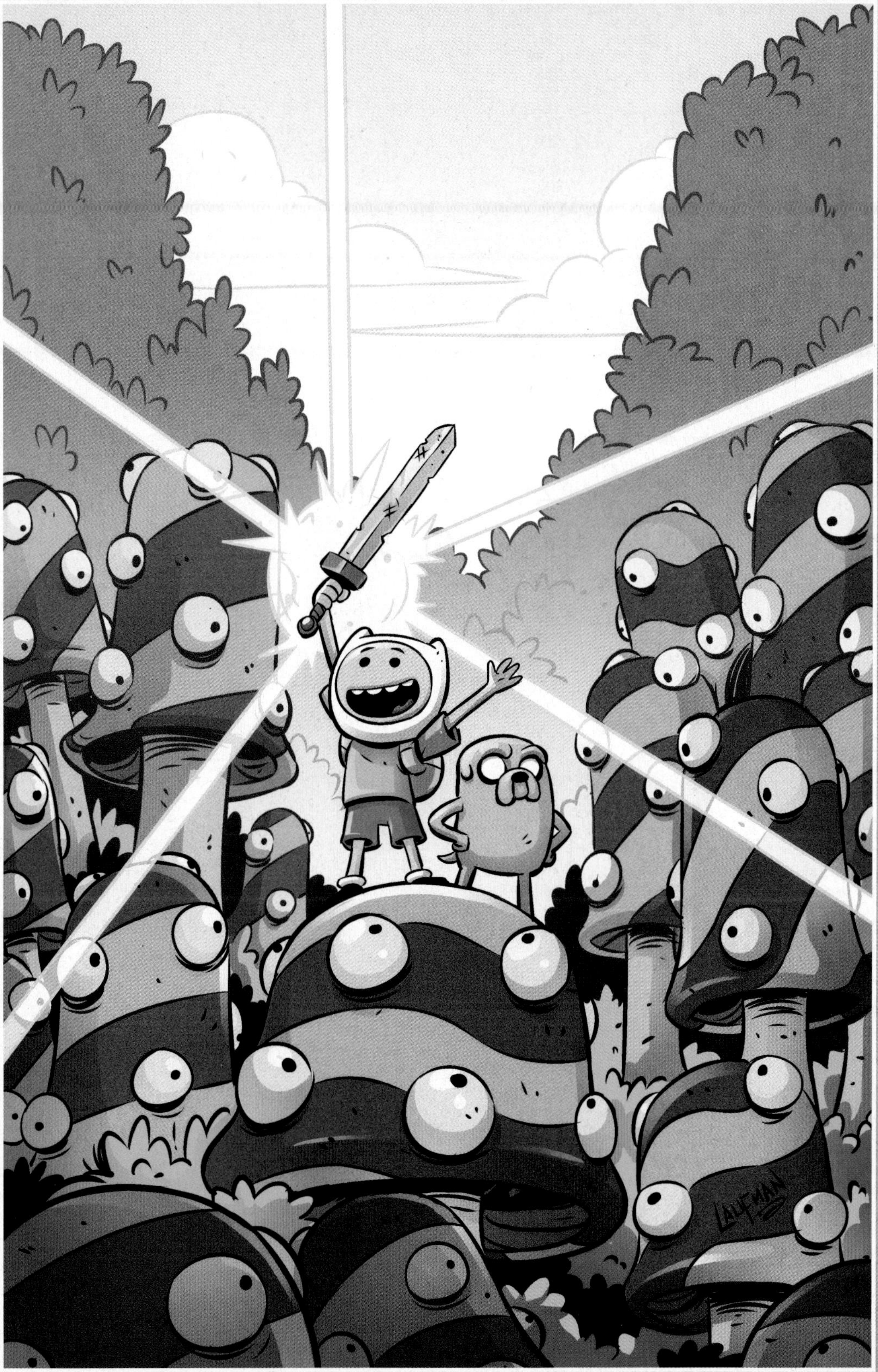
LAUFMAN

Issue #18 Subscription Cover

LUCA PIZZARI

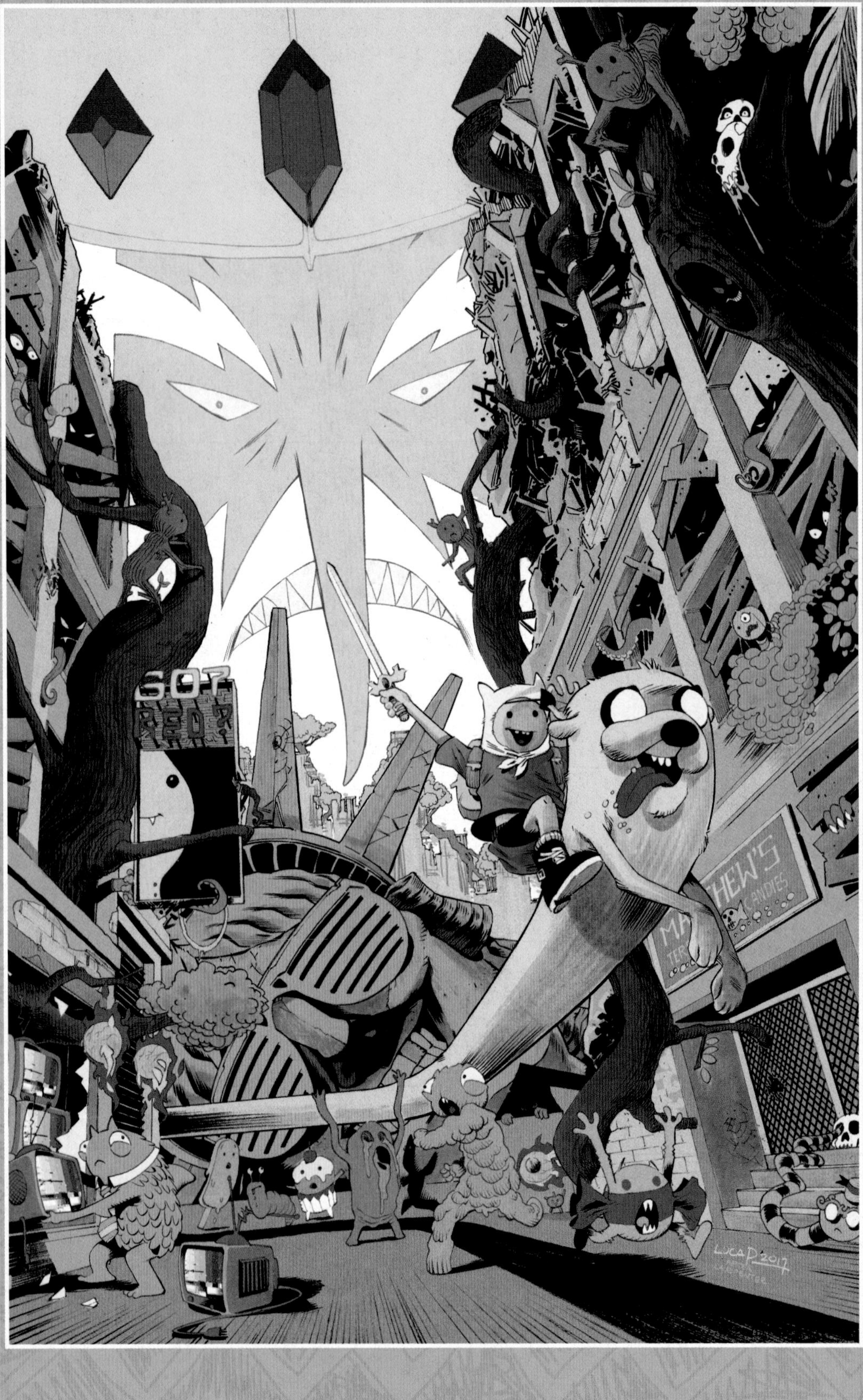
GOT
RED?
...HEW'S
CANDIES
MA
TER
LUCA P 2017

Issue #18 Variant Cover

NATALIE DOMBOIS

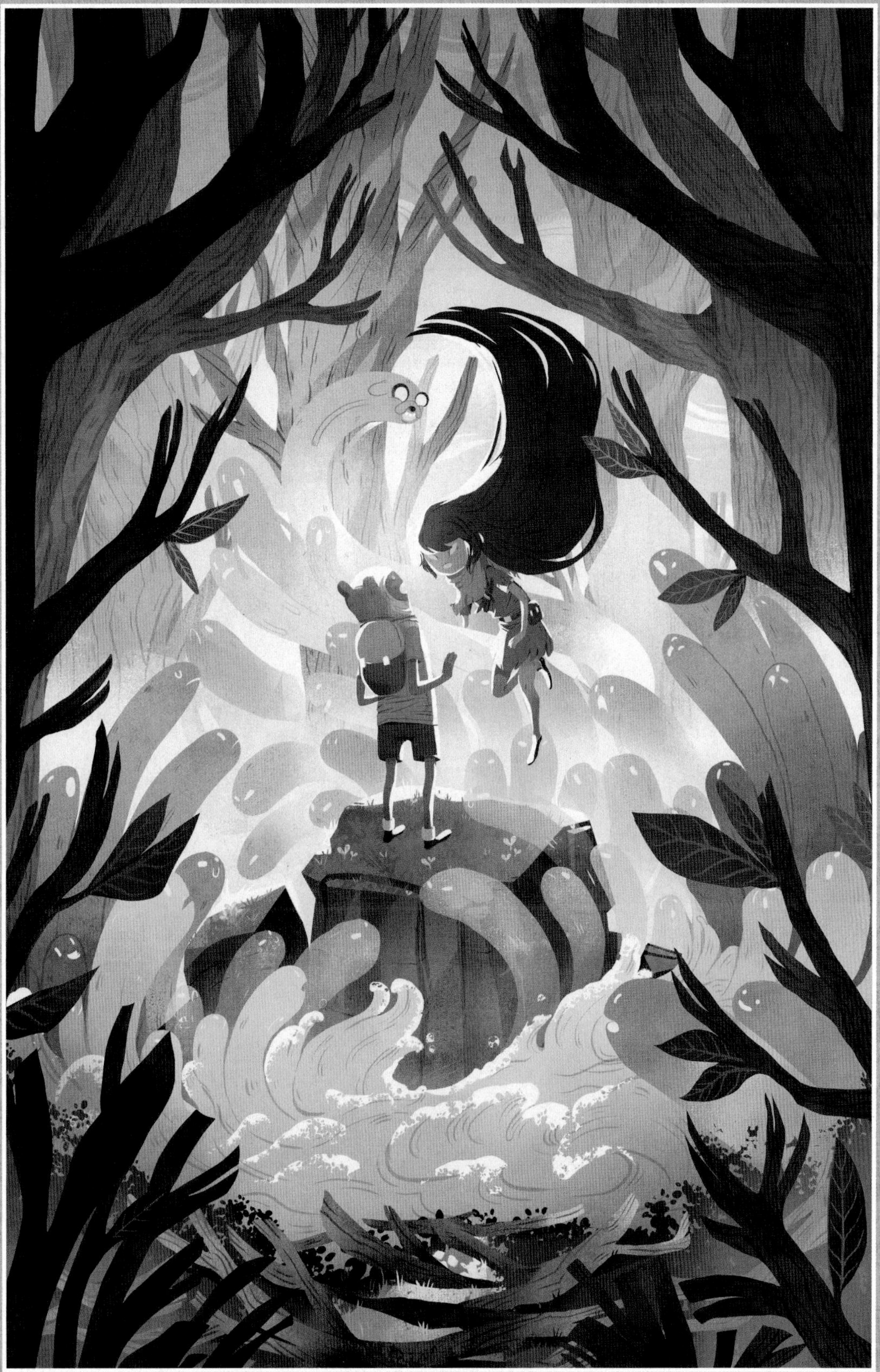

Issue #19 Main Cover

JAMIE COE

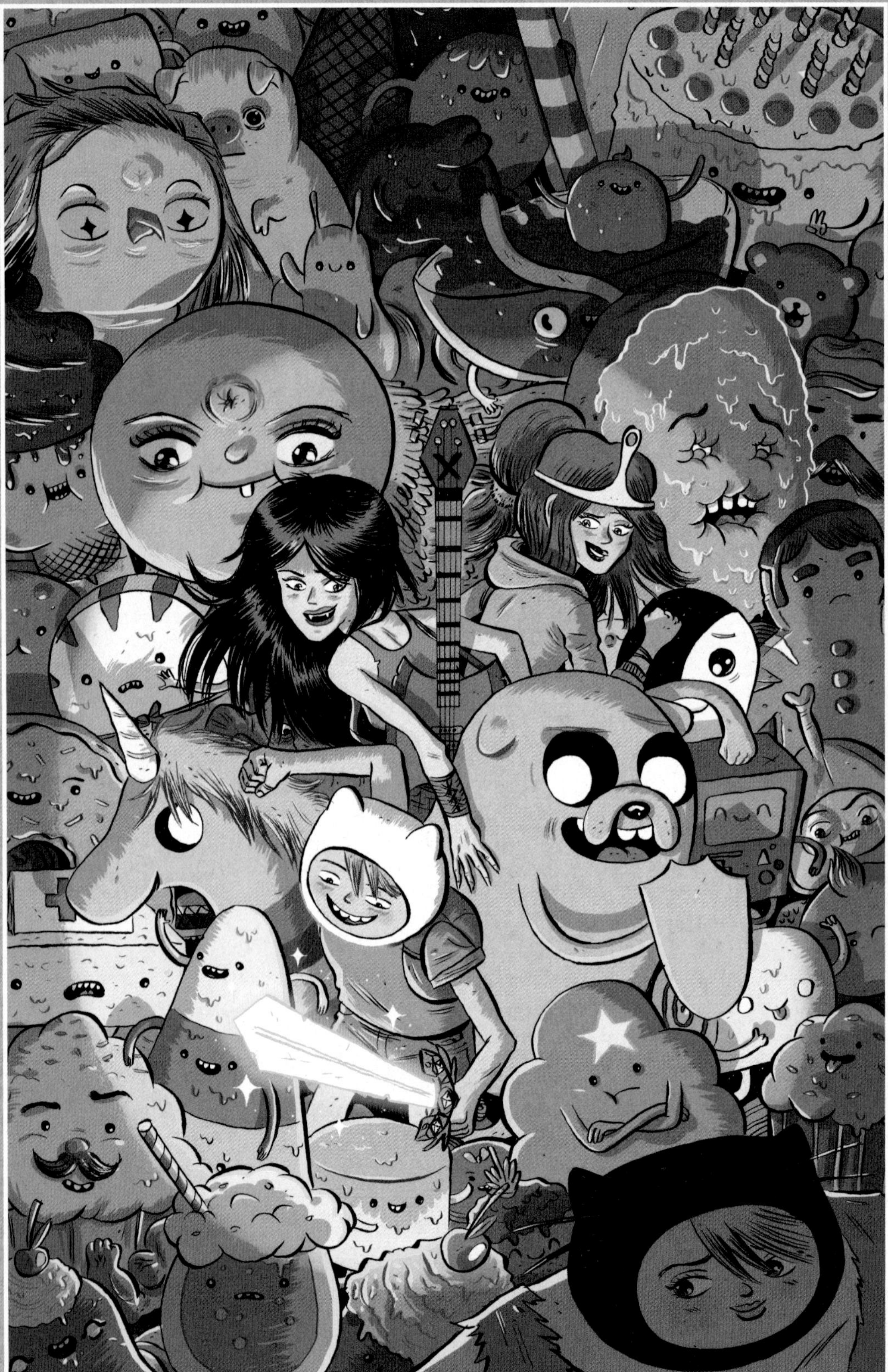

Issue #19 Subscription Cover

JEFFREY VEREGGE

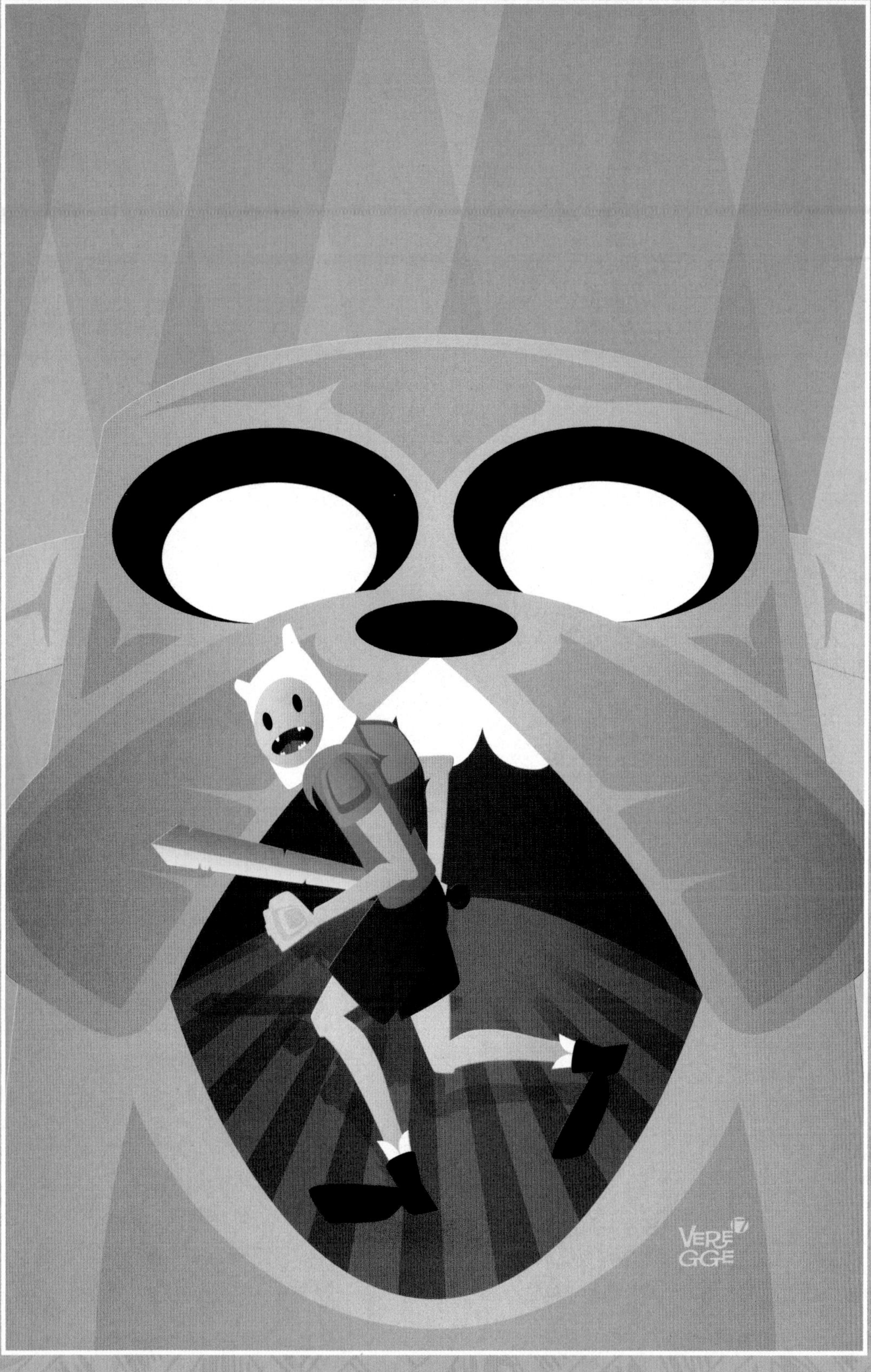
VEREGGE

Issue #19 Variant Cover

BENJAMIN DEWEY

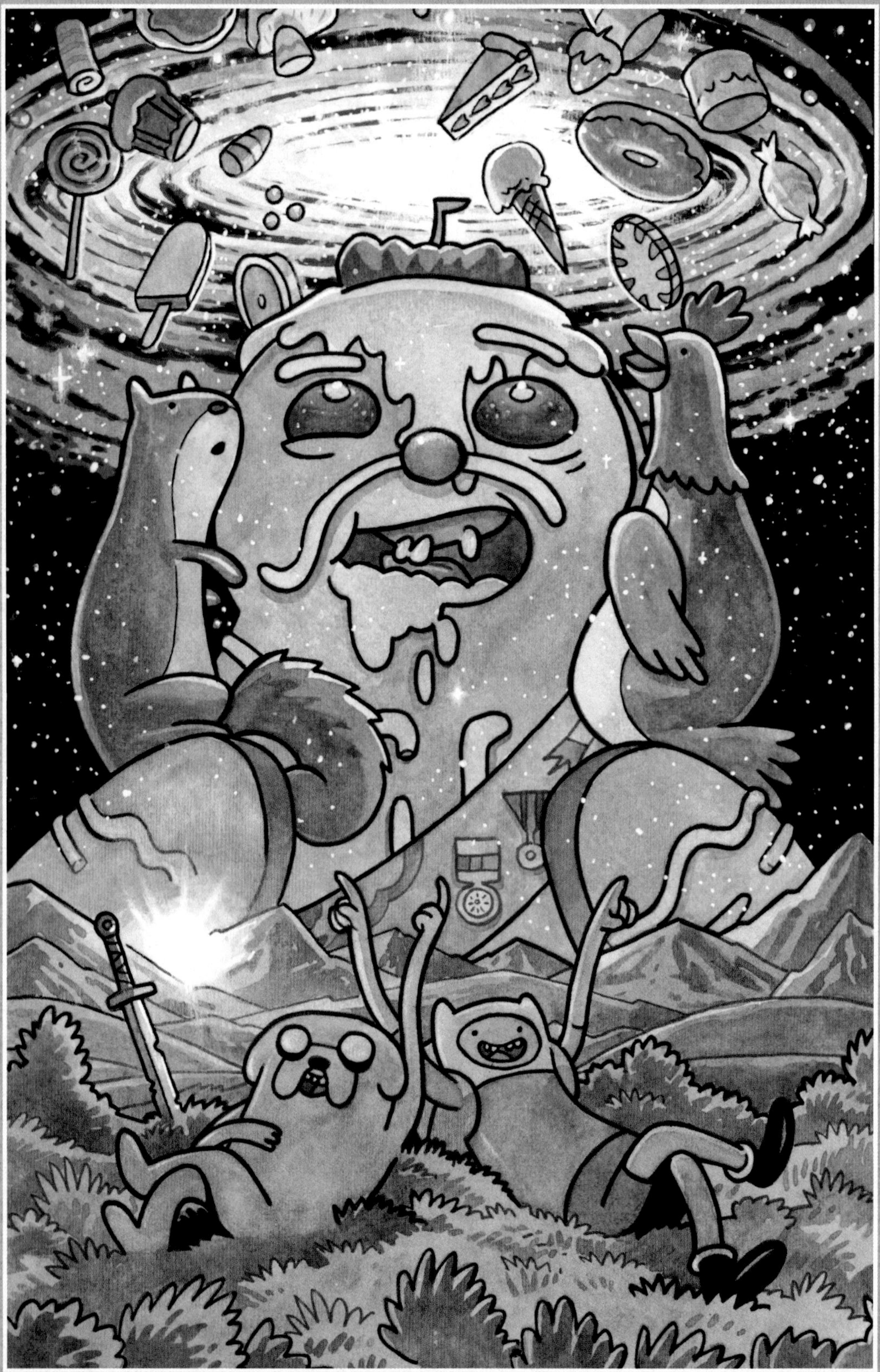

Issue #20 Main Cover
ROD REIS

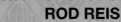

Issue #20 Subscription Cover
MATT FRANK

Issue #20 Variant Cover
DIRK SCHULZ

DISCOVER
EXPLOSIVE NEW WORLDS

Adventure Time

Sam Sykes · Selina Espiritu · Sarah Stern
Brave Chef Brianna

KELLY THOMPSON BRIANNE DROUHARD M. VICTORIA ROBADO
MEGA PRINCESS

THE NOT-SO SECRET SOCIETY
DALEY · CRAFTS · CLARK · BRUNI
KEEP OUT
CAUTION

OVER THE GARDEN WALL

STEVEN UNIVERSE
VOLUME ONE

Adventure Time
Pendleton Ward and Others
Volume 1
ISBN: 978-1-60886-280-1 | $14.99 US
Volume 2
ISBN: 978-1-60886-323-5 | $14.99 US
Adventure Time: Islands
ISBN: 978-1-60886-972-5 | $9.99 US

The Amazing World of Gumball
Ben Bocquelet and Others
Volume 1
ISBN: 978-1-60886-488-1 | $14.99 US
Volume 2
ISBN: 978-1-60886-793-6 | $14.99 US

Brave Chef Brianna
Sam Sykes, Selina Espiritu
ISBN: 978-1-68415-050-2 | $14.99 US

Mega Princess
Kelly Thompson, Brianne Drouhard
ISBN: 978-1-68415-007-6 | $14.99 US

The Not-So Secret Society
Matthew Daley, Arlene Daley, Wook Jin Clark
ISBN: 978-1-60886-997-8 | $9.99 US

Over the Garden Wall
Patrick McHale, Jim Campbell and Others
Volume 1
ISBN: 978-1-60886-940-4 | $14.99 US
Volume 2
ISBN: 978-1-68415-006-9 | $14.99 US

Steven Universe
Rebecca Sugar and Others
Volume 1
ISBN: 978-1-60886-706-6 | $14.99 US
Volume 2
ISBN: 978-1-60886-796-7 | $14.99 US

Steven Universe & The Crystal Gems
ISBN: 978-1-60886-921-3 | $14.99 US

Steven Universe: Too Cool for School
ISBN: 978-1-60886-771-4 | $14.99 US

kaboom!™

AVAILABLE AT YOUR LOCAL COMICS SHOP AND BOOKSTORE
To find a comics shop in your area, call 1-888-266-4226
WWW.**BOOM-STUDIOS**.COM